SLAUGHTER HORSE

Michael Maguire

A STAR BOOK
published by
WYNDHAM PUBLICATIONS

A Star Book
published in 1976 by
Wyndham Publications Ltd
123 King Street, London W6 9JG
First published in Great Britain by
Allan Wingate (Publishers) Ltd, 1975

All the characters, racehorses and events portrayed in
this story are fictitious

Printed in Great Britain by
Richard Clay (The Chaucer Press) Ltd, Bungay, Suffolk

ISBN 0352 39785 3

For Rodney Simpson and Johnny Curant
two of the nicest guys in the racing game.

Chapter One

RACING FEVER sizzled in the crisp mid-October air. A tense mesmerized buzz erupted from the crowd as the loudspeaker commentary crackled across the Newmarket stands. Thirty thousand pairs of eyes narrowed, necks craned, heads bobbed anxiously in an effort to glimpse the advancing medley of shimmering racing silks. The expectant blur of voices gathered in intensity and suddenly the commentary was swallowed up in a nucleus of sound.

Four gruelling furlongs to go, three, two . . . General O'Hara lengthened his stride and burst from the pack. The big chestnut horse was flying. The crowd went delirious, enthralled by the phenomenal acceleration that this high-powered racing machine could produce.

The jockey snatched a glance over his shoulder, then moulded himself into the heaving, sweating mass of blood and muscle. His arms worked furiously, increasing in tempo, beating out a coercive rhythm . . . pushing . . . urging . . .

General O'Hara knew what was being asked, knew all about liaison between horse and jockey. There was no need to pull out all the stops, no need for a final massive effort, for the big lion-hearted horse never gave anything except his all. He piled on the pressure and devoured the last hundred yards of turf in his usual never-give-an-inch way. He passed the post showing his rivals his rump and six lengths of daylight, and left his fans and backers hoarse with excitement.

'What an animal,' Grant's voice was barely audible as we were carried by the tide of people towards the winners' enclosure. 'A supreme British thoroughbred—a world-beater.'

I agreed and who wouldn't. Nobody could argue that

unbeaten General O'Hara, winner of eighteen races and over a quarter of a million pounds in prize money, was anything less than 'supreme'.

The glossy, ruggedly framed chestnut colt was a born showman, and had won the hearts and admiration of the racing public. Today they had turned out in force to see the General notch up his nineteenth and final victory and to give him a champion's ovation before he embarked on his new career as a stud stallion.

I was also about to embark on a new assignment and was now waiting for Grant to fill in the details. I stood silently watching the horse, doing my best to look interested as Grant's interpretation of the race filtered into my ears. The pleasantries began to bore me. I decided to push for information. 'The animal is a super-star of the turf,' I said, 'but I'm damn sure you didn't drag me to Suffolk for a long last look at umpteen hundred-weight of gilt-edged horseflesh.'

'Quite so.' He gave me a tilted smile and absently finger-combed the grey hair that sprouted from beneath his trilby. 'We're not interested in General O'Hara, but there is a tenuous link between the animal and the task I have in mind for you.'

'Such as?'

'The name Falloway,' Grant said.

'Not Alison Falloway?' I put a match to a Chesterfield, swivelled to meet the Security Chief's sober brown eyes. 'I would hardly call the General's owner a tenuous link.'

'Alison Falloway's conduct is beyond reproach,' he put in quickly. 'We're interested in the son and heir, Wesley Falloway.'

The name registered distantly in my mind. I said, 'I've read about him. Bit-part actor, playboy type who owns fast cars, fast women and slow horses.'

'Only the horses aren't so slow any more. They've been doing supernaturally well. So much so, in fact, that we smell sharp practice.'

'Dope?'

'If it is, then we can't trace it.' He rubbed a hand over his

8

ruddy complexion, fingering the somewhat purplish flesh round the jowl. 'Urine and saliva tests have proved negative. It could be a new one on us, of course, but . . .'

'You want me to check it out, uh?'

'Well, it is tailor-made for you, Simon,' he stated, sounding as brisk and assured as always. 'You've worked with horses and you know most of the angles. I'm sure this investigation won't present any problems to a man of your many talents.'

I smiled at the flattery. He'd obviously convinced himself that I was the man for the job and was now doing his best to convince me of the fact.

'You can refuse, of course,' he went on, 'but when I've enlightened you on the various aspects of the Falloway case I feel sure you will lend us your services.'

When Simon Drake worked, which was usually about six months of every year, I worked for the Turf Security Division. I was classified as a freelance operator, which meant I had the option of accepting or rejecting an assignment. This was through choice, my choice. I didn't want to be shackled with an organizational bridle or permanently dangled on the end of Howard Grant's lead-rein. I valued my freedom too highly, and the Security Division offered employment, but only when I felt inclined to make use of it. Two or three successful assignments a year and I could live even better than in the manner to which I'd been accustomed. I just didn't see any point in working your guts out at a job, earning good money, and never having the time to spend it, or at least really enjoy spending it. I'd felt differently before the death of my wife, during those few brief years of togetherness, and perhaps that had taught me to live for the moment. Now I thought and acted like a single guy, and a rebellious one at that. Tomorrow wasn't important any more. Not an original philosophy I know, but it worked for me—so what the hell.

Grant's operators were highly paid and the Division remained healthy because every racecourse in the country subscribed hefty cash payments to keep it that way. They got what they paid for.

The money bought the services of a team of professional investigators who could be called upon to probe anything from itching powder in a jockey's underpants to the nobbling of a Derby favourite. As a Sunday newspaper reporter with a flair for superlatives once put it: 'Feared by opportunists and racketeers, the Turf Security Division is the invaluable custodian and watchdog of the racing world.'

'Wesley Falloway is standing by the far rail, next to the good-looking blonde.' Grant dropped his voice to a conspiratorial whisper and indicated with his chin. 'He must have travelled up especially for the General's last race.'

My eyes panned, focused. 'Does he have a runner?'

Grant shook his head. 'They would be completely out of their depth.'

He had the tall, well-built architecture of a male model, and deeply tanned, clean-cut features, spoilt only by a mouth that was a little too wide. Women would find him handsome, no doubt ignore the wide mouth. He also had a natural elegance which I envied, and judging by the well-stacked blonde who clung to his arm, he had an excellent taste in matters of the opposite sex. I would have put him at around the same age as myself—twenty-eight.

'The girl is worth noting,' Grant was saying. 'It's all in the dossier, of course, but briefly her name is Vicky Annesley, she's a twenty-nine-year-old divorcee and Wesley's latest playmate.'

'She looks interesting.'

'Get to know her, Simon. You could profit by it.'

The assignment suddenly seemed that much more appealing. I said, 'Tell me more—such as how the gorgeous Mrs Annesley got herself attached to our playboy friend.'

'She inherited a small string of horses when her father died. She's recently switched stables and transferred them to Neil McQuillan at Chinhurst Lodge.'

'And Wesley uses McQuillan?'

He nodded.

'Why the switch?'

'We're not positively sure. McQuillan's cheap, that much I do know.'

'So finance was the reason for the move?'

'More than likely. She's not poor, but she's not rich, either. The money she inherited from her father was whittled down considerably by death duties.'

'Perhaps she's a gold-digger,' I mused sourly, watching her giggle as Wesley's wide mouth whispered sweet nothings into her ear. 'Perhaps Mrs Annesley is figuring on buying a marital share in the Falloway mine.'

Grant shook his head expressively, and extended long spatulate fingers to the sleeve of my jacket. Without a word he guided me through the ever-mounting throng of racegoers and took up a rail position near the weighing-room. 'Digging would just be hard labour,' he informed me in between General O'Hara's exit from the winners' enclosure and the cheers that resounded in the animal's wake. 'Alison Falloway keeps Wesley on a very tight halter and her hands firmly on the purse-strings.'

I followed Grant's gaze and contemplated the fleshless woman who sat slightly hunched in a wheelchair by the weighing-room steps. Alison Falloway looked iron-willed yet fragile. Her hard, intolerant face remained fixed and impervious to the noisy enthusiasm which emanated from the spectators. She watched the chestnut wonder horse disappear towards the stable area, then, straightening the monogrammed rug that covered her knees, she snapped departure instructions to the manservant who stood by her side.

Grant said quietly, 'Don't be fooled into thinking she's senile. Her accident may have aged her physically, but mentally she's sharp—very sharp indeed.'

The publicity media had given Alison Falloway pretty full coverage during General O'Hara's rise to fame. I, along with millions of others, had read how a riding accident some eleven years ago had damaged her spine and confined her to life in a wheelchair. No amount of money or expensive surgery could buy back the use of her legs, and this must have come as a very bitter pill to an active horse-loving woman who once rode regularly to hounds. Grant was right, the accident had drastically aged her. This was manifest in her prematurely iron-grey hair, her thinness, and the deep weary lines that scored her face. The once attractive wife of shipping magnate, Clement Falloway, was now a fifty-seven-year-old widow with the physical appearance of a maiden aunt in her seventies.

'Her son is a born waster,' Grant said, teasing out a cigarette from a silver case and lighting it carefully. 'Wesley fritters away money on anything that takes his fancy, usually clothes, cars and women. He drives a red XJ 12 Jaguar, gambles heavily, loses heavily, and at one time used to rely on his mother to bale him out of any financial crisis.'

'The Duchess has closed his account, uh?'

'Duchess?'

'Mrs Falloway. She has the look of a storybook Duchess about her, don't you think?'

He grunted. I was bringing in an irrelevancy and he didn't like it. 'Wesley lives in his mother's house and enjoys all the amenities, but the door to the vault has been bolted.'

'Additional income?'

'His father left him a monthly allowance and this is supplemented by any money he makes as an actor.'

'But it's obviously not enough,' I said. 'He's living beyond his means and has hit on a method of hotting-up his horses to provide the additional income. You've checked his bookmaker's accounts?'

'Mm, along with McQuillan's and Vicky Annesley's. Certainly none of them has made a fortune from backing the suspect horses. Wesley has gained the prize money, of course, but his betting on the animals in question can only be described as moderate.'

I showed him my puzzled expression, made no comment.

Grant indicated the cafeteria, and then striding briskly through the concentration of racegoers relayed his own theory as to Falloway's possible motive.

'Resentment?' I murmured, trying to grasp the gist of his words. 'Wesley resents his mother's success with General O'Hara and is trying to emulate that success with his own horses?'

'Rather a weak juxtaposition, I know,' Grant added, 'but in his own small way Wesley could be trying to capture a little of the prestige, the glory, for himself.'

It was an angle that hadn't come readily to mind. Certainly Grant had a point and if money wasn't the overriding factor, then Wesley Falloway's winning run could be to satisfy his own egoism. Given time, I would be able to formulate my own opinion—right now, I was more concerned with how the horses were being geed-up, and more particularly what course of action Grant wanted taken to prevent it.

'You'll be working with a familiar face,' Grant's voice was wryly apologetic as we stepped into the cafeteria. 'I've brought him up from the West Country for this meeting and I'll be taking him back tonight. I suppose you still remember Len Potter?'

The name stopped me in my tracks, hit me with the jarring impact of a straight jab. I swivelled, found his eyes. 'If you think I'm working with a cocky, contemptuous kid like Potter...'

'Take it easy.' Grant raised placatory hands. 'We needed somebody on the inside, and Len Potter fitted the bill. A necessary evil, I'm afraid.'

'An unscrupulous little bastard, you mean,' I almost shouted.

'But suitable, nevertheless. You see, we arranged for one of McQuillan's stable lads to take an unscheduled holiday, and got Potter to fill the vacancy. Chinhurst Lodge can hardly be described as the pinnacle of racing stables, so someone like Potter gets accepted without a second glance.'

I remembered the adage about setting a thief to catch a thief. It seemed to fit the circumstances, but it didn't make me want to shake Grant by the hand and congratulate him on selecting Potter as my collaborator.

'You'll soon get used to the arrangement,' Grant said politely. 'Having the boy on the inside will be a great asset to you.'

'You're too kind,' I murmured, just as politely.

Grant grunted and guided me towards a corner table. There, molesting steak-and-chips, wearing a donkey jacket and his habitual expression of self-assurance, sat Len Potter. The thin ferrety face with its pale unhealthy features, the sunken eyes accentuated by the overhead neon lighting, stared up at me with jeering amusement.

'Wotcha, Drakey,' he drawled, curling a ketchup-soaked chip round the prongs of his fork and stuffing it into his mouth. 'I 'ear we're gonna be workin' together.'

I smiled sourly. 'Like old times, eh?'

'Sure, like old times.'

'Funny, ain't it.'

'Funny?'

'Yeah, me being asked to 'elp out the Security Division.'

'Ironic,' I said with feeling.

'Yeah, ironic,' he mused, forking the last mouthful of steak. 'You're right, Drakey—it's bleedin' ironic, that's what it is.'

Grant said with an air of authority, 'You'll treat Mr Drake as your superior, Potter. Help him at all times, take instructions from him, and for God's sake act with discretion.'

'Yes, Mr Grant, sir.'

'Follow our orders and you'll be well paid.'

'Yes, Mr Grant, sir!' The boy saluted with his knife and displayed orange-peel teeth in an expansive smile. 'Do I get the bread now?'

Grant hesitated. 'Bread?' he said.

'Yeah, the oof, the 'ackers. Y'know, Charlie Clore's wall-paper.'

Grant sighed. 'You'll get your money on completion.'

'Yer mean at the end?'

'That's exactly what I mean.'

He showed me that demented grin of his. 'Oh-kay, jus' so's I know, like.'

I eyed him menacingly and relaxed weakly in a plastic chair. God help the Division, the assignment, and most of all Simon Drake, I thought, as Grant mumbled something about coffee and retreated to the sanctuary of the lunch counter.

'You ill?' Potter asked, wiping his mouth with a grubby handkerchief.

'Pre-assignment nerves,' I temporized. 'It's an occupational hazard.'

'Not in my case it ain't.'

'Really?' I gave him a slow parody of a smile. 'Perhaps you're a cut above the rest of us, eh?'

'Yeah, p'raps I am. Got fixed up at McQuillans, didn't I?'

'Easy, was it?'

'Piss easy, mate. The ref'rences that Grant give me done the trick, plus me 'onest looks, o'course. All McQuillan did was eye me up and down like I was some friggin' yearling at Tatt's sales, then 'e shakes me right 'and wiv 'is left and says—you've got yerself a job, Mr Potter.'

'With his left?' I queried.

'His right's a dud, ain't it.'

'A dud?'

He clawed at the air with stiff fingers. 'It's a dud sure enough. No question abaht it being T-B-U.'

'Tee bee what?'

'Totally-bloody-useless, Drakey, you know, *Kaput*. 'E's got this shiny metal one now wiv diff'rent attachments fer doin' diff'rent jobs. Creepy fing it is.'

'You're talking a load of cock.'

'No I ain't, it's the truth I tell yer. The lads call it McQuillan's claw.' He raised his eyes heavenwards and made a mumbled request for God to strike him dead if he was lying.

'He's perfectly correct,' Grant affirmed, issuing cups of steaming coffee and crushing any chances of the brash little figure being drawn into a bottomless pit. 'McQuillan lost his right hand about five years ago in a car accident. He manages very well with this stainless-steel one by all accounts.'

'Pokes yer wiv it, 'e does,' Potter complained.

'Hard, I hope,' I said sourly.

'Worse yard I've ever worked in. Fer twenny-five lousy quid a week I dunno 'ow the boys stick it.'

'Perhaps they enjoy their work, Lennie, something you wouldn't know about.'

'Huh, you gotta be jokin'.' He sniffed and proceeded to dig out morsels of steak from his teeth with a matchstick. ' 'Cos no other yard would 'ave 'em, yer mean. 'Ard lotta sods they are. Biggest bunch of villains this side of the East End.'

'All the more reason for you to keep in with them,' Grant interjected. 'Pass on any snatches of gossip you hear in relation to Wesley Falloway's horses to Mr Drake.'

'And I should 'ear plenty. I've been given four of 'is horses to look after.'

'Couldn't be better.' Grant nodded his head with satisfaction and reached for his briefcase. 'With only a few weeks of the flat-racing season left, it's up to both of you to pull together and wrap up this case in double-quick time.'

Potter pulled one of his nothing-could-be-simpler faces, noisily sucked down coffee and lit a worse-for-wear Woodbine from a dog-eared packet of ten. He leaned back precariously and eyed me from across the table with a slow, sly grin. A look of swaggering self-confidence that just begged to be eradicated by having the chair kicked out from under him. Only Grant's authoritarian presence and the knowledge that Potter was supposedly on the side of the 'good guys' temporarily curbed my violent intentions. I swallowed black coffee, thought pleasant thoughts, and simmered.

'All the details are in here.' Grant pushed a spring-back binder into my hands. 'I suggest you study them carefully and make an active start on the case tomorrow morning.'

'Sunday?' I was vaguely surprised.

'Most of McQuillan's owners take advantage of Sunday to visit their horses. Wesley Falloway will be there and so will you.'

The tone of his voice indicated absolute obedience. Relieving him of the binder, I said, 'Any camouflage?'

'That's all been arranged. Your name is Simon Preston and you're a journalist employed by the *Racing Times*. It's a water-tight cover because a lot of backroom boys in the Division have spent the past week sealing up all the holes. If anyone makes enquiries about your journalistic status, you can be sure it will check out.' He delved into his briefcase and handed me a press card and a copy of the magazine. 'I expect you're already familiar with the layout, but browse through the articles on horses in training and pay particular attention to the "Around the Stables" feature.'

'Is McQuillan expecting me?'

'He knows the magazine intends to interview him. Your arrival won't come as any surprise.'

'So the *Racing Times* is going to publicize Chinhurst Lodge as their stable of the month, uh?'

'Sweat-shop of the month, Drakey,' Potter put in.

'Preston!' I growled, banging a sauce bottle down hard on to his nicotined fingers. 'Mr Preston from now on—got it!'

'Ahh, you sod!' He winced and sucked tomato-smudged knuckles.

'Shut up, Potter.' Grant, always lacking in humour, totally absorbed in his role as Security Chief, was stirring the remains of his coffee. 'Get the name right from now on,' he said without looking up, 'or you'll put yourself, us, and the whole assignment in jeopardy.'

'Yes, Mr Grant . . . sir.' It was almost a whimper.

The cafeteria started to fill. The babble of loud, happy voices rose and fell around us. As Len Potter sat hunched and silent, nursing his hand and puffing sulkily at his Woodbine, Grant turned his attention to me.

'To appear authentic, Simon, you're going to need a photo-grapher. The *Racing Times* is full of photographs, and McQuillan will expect to have his picture taken.'

'So you're giving me an assistant.'

'Kelly Meredith.'

The name meant nothing to me, but then why the hell should it. The Division employed at least six full-time investigators and being freelance I'd rarely had much to do with them. I didn't relish the idea of an assistant. Experience had taught me that one man paddled a canoe faster than two.

Grant made a pyramid with his fingers. 'I know you're a bit of a lone wolf, but if you're accompanied by a bona fide photographer—'

'Bona fide? So Meredith doesn't work for the Security Division?'

'No, the *Racing Times*. That's why your cover's so good.'

'But can we trust an outsider?'

'We've gone very carefully into Kelly's background and there's nothing to suggest we can't. You ought to be grateful to the magazine, Simon. Without their cooperation we wouldn't stand a hope in hell's chance of clearing this up before next season.'

I saw the advantages all right. If you're acting out the part of a journalist on a well-known periodical, then its nice to have an employee of that periodical along to answer the awkward questions, perhaps questions contrived to test your authenticity. That's fine, but for me at least it didn't outweigh the responsibility of carrying a passenger. I reckoned I could bluff my way through with the best of them, and the luxury of a photographer was a liability I could well do without.

'Kelly's been fully briefed,' Grant was saying. 'I think the pair of you will strike a good balance—profit from each other's experience.' A faint smile played around his lips as he added, 'Statistically, there isn't very much Kelly Meredith doesn't know about horses.'

'Great,' I murmured, almost sarcastically, resigning myself to the fact that I wouldn't be working alone. 'When and where do we tie up?'

'Monday lunchtime, the Horse and Groom. The pub is close to Chinhurst Lodge and frequented by McQuillan's stable lads.'

'A good place for loose talk, huh?'

'That's where we had hoped to base you, but there wasn't any accommodation available. We've booked you into the Highway Motel. It's only a short drive from McQuillan's and therefore accessible for either day or night visits by our friend here.' He indicated Potter, and added, 'Kelly will be staying at the Eclipse Hotel in Minehead.'

Potter spat out a shred of tobacco and rubbed it into the linoleum with his boot. 'That's the swanky joint Fallerway and 'is bird use, ain't it?'

'And that's the very reason we've put her there,' Grant said.

'*Her?*' I looked at him. 'You mean Kelly Meredith is . . . ?'

His face remained expressionless. 'Didn't I make myself clear?'

'You couldn't have done,' I said, slightly at a loss. 'I just assumed that he, I mean she, was male.'

He shook his head. 'Sorry to disappoint you.'

'Lucky sod,' Potter put in.

I ignored him, said to Grant, 'You'll only disappoint me if you tell me she's the sporty, tweedy type, who twenty-five years ago swopped her Roedean cricket bat for a box Brownie.'

'She's twenty-two, and trendy rather than tweedy.'

'Lucky sod,' Potter said again, and I had to admit that the assignment had suddenly presented an unexpected bonus.

'You look pleased wiv yerself,' Potter leered.

A key, held by its plastic fob was swinging a few inches from my eyes like a hypnotizing pendant. 'Chalet number ten,' Grant advised. 'You'll have to be up early to catch McQuillan, so I suggest you get under way.'

'And I'll be up at six, muckin' out me boxes,' Potter complained.

I looked at him. 'Lucky sod,' I said.

I turned as I reached the door, lifted my hand in a parting gesture. Grant's eyes looked steadily at me over the rim of his coffee-cup. He nodded discreetly. Potter curled his lip and chewed moodily on the match that had previously cleaned his teeth. I smiled and stepped out into the cool afternoon air.

Chapter Two

THAT NIGHT I wallowed in typescript. Eighty-two tightly packed, single-spaced, eye-blurring, sleep-inducing, foolscap pages of it. I'd taken a hot shower to wash the journey out of my pores, and then a cold one to revive my jaded brain-cells. My chalet was more clinical than comfortable. It was new, finished in imitation knotty pine and it smelled strongly of emulsion paint. It wasn't home, but I wasn't complaining. I lay on the bed, propped my head on a couple of pillows and opened Grant's binder.

Midnight found me with a cigarette in my mouth and a cup of hot black coffee in my hand. The yards of information I had just digested made interesting reading but did little in the way of stimulating fresh ideas. I juggled with the facts, hopefully optimistic that some kind of theory might float to the surface like a bloated corpse rising from the watery depths. It didn't. It was a lousy night for corpses.

The typewritten pages contained a mass of well-researched information. I learned, for instance, that Wesley Falloway had been educated at Eton and Cambridge, spent the first two years of his working life in his father's shipping business, and at one time owned a flat in Chelsea Square. I also learned how his career as an actor had brought him small mediocre roles in even smaller mediocre films, the latest of which was being filmed on location in Cornwall.

Thirteen female names followed. A formidable list of girl friends and ex-girl friends with a couple of hundred words devoted to Vicky Annesley, the thirteenth and current Falloway playmate of the month.

The voluptuous Mrs Annesley *née* Tyler, daughter of a

Somerset gentleman farmer and formerly married to racing driver Guy Annesley, was described in the dossier as capable, self-willed and financially independent. She had divorced her high-speed husband twelve months ago after five years of (in her own words) incompatible hell. Apparently even her shapeliness and desirability couldn't compete with the curves of Brands Hatch or the sensual lines of a Formula One car.

I chuckled softly, extinguished my cigarette and pondered on the infinitely memorable Vicky Annesley for about as long as it takes a cup of coffee to go cold, and for reasons that Grant and his organization wouldn't have approved of. This mental exercise helped to provide me with fresh ideas, great ideas, but only the prurient kind. As my fee was payable on results, I decided to put money as my priority, curb my overindulgent hormones, and concentrate instead on Neil McQuillan and the suspect horses.

A former successful National Hunt jockey, McQuillan, thirty-five years old and a bachelor, had turned his talents towards training racehorses after being injured in a motorway collision. He appeared to be having a lean time.

Chinhurst Stables carried a hefty mortgage and McQuillan's financial position was described as 'barely in the black'. He kept his training fees low, his wages bill and running expenses to a minimum and attracted moderate to poor quality horseflesh.

He also attracted second-rate staff. Most had dubious backgrounds and words such as undependable, conscienceless and corruptible were used to describe the McQuillan work-force from the head lad down to the travelling box driver. Len Potter, I figured, was in good company.

I thumbed my way through the forensic laboratory reports on the five controversial horses. All told the same story. According to the experts no known stimulant was present in any of the samples taken, and the words 'analysis negative' appeared on every sheet. Somebody was being clever and it was paying off. Doped or not, the five Falloway horses were winning, and winning consistently.

'Unusual improvement in form' was typed in red alongside Lunar Prince, winner of a £700 handicap in June. 'Outstanding improvement in form' appeared against Double Top, winner of a £650 handicap in July, and so on and so forth until all eight races had been covered.

The total prize money to date was £7,800. The highest value race won was worth £2,000—the lowest £500.

Before this sudden transformation, Falloway's horses were slightly less than middle-of-the-road handicappers. Race fillers, that given a following wind and a prayer, might occasionally squeeze into the frame. But now they were notching up wins like a fruit machine with its circuits in ribbons—and the Security Division was coming up lemons.

Neil McQuillan, the travelling head lad, and stable jockey Roy Biggs had all been cross-questioned by the Stewards, but little or nothing had emerged. Biggs' riding equipment was thoroughly checked for mechanical gadgets, shock devices, etc., but again nothing was found.

A freelance jockey had been engaged to ride one of the suspect horses last month owing to Biggs' being ill. He stated after the race: 'The horse took the bit and ran away with me. He passed the post like a runaway sledge on the Cresta Run.'

With sagging eyelids and wilting enthusiasm, I ploughed through the final segment of Grant's dossier. This concerned itself with those odds jugglers *par excellence* and flying lady mascot collectors—the bookmakers. Wesley Falloway used the services of two such gentlemen and both had supplied detailed accounts of his wagers.

I sorted out the relevant betting slips, cross-checking them against the eight suspect races and totalling the amount won. The figure was pathetic—a few hundred pounds. The stakes in each case were ridiculously small and for a heavy gambler like Falloway, an absurdity. A handwritten footnote informed me that as far as it had been possible to ascertain, no one connected with either Falloway or McQuillan had won big money by backing any of the question-mark horses.

It didn't make any kind of sense. Was I really expected to believe that the only monetary gain was the prize money? That five horses were being successively geed-up and had less than ten thousand pounds to show for it? O.K., so an undetectable booster was being used—but why push your luck? One horse, one certainty, carrying a mammoth wad of stake money and Falloway could afford to buy his own film company. A grand-slam I could understand. But this seemingly senseless five-card-trick left my reasoning processes in a state of collapse.

The dossier had told me everything and yet nothing. I ditched it, snicked off the bedside lamp and lay with my hands behind my head, reflecting on Grant's 'prestige' theory. The son versus mother in the glory stakes idea.

The more I thought about it, the less appealing it became. I was starting to yawn and the jumbled facts were beginning to confuse me. I closed my eyes, pushing the nagging uncertainties far away into my subconscious. The problems floated away. Falloway and his horses melted from my mind as I slipped quietly into the blessed world of sleep.

The following morning I had breakfast in bed. It was an appetizing, traditionally English fry-up, cooked to perfection and spoiled only by the rather bored-looking chalet maid who accompanied it. She busied herself parting curtains and opening windows and complained bitterly about some girl called Maureen who never gave anyone 'a rotten thank you' for helping out. Not knowing what the hell she was talking about, or how I was expected to react, I made a few sympathetic noises as I ate and eventually got rid of the empties and her by announcing I always slept naked and always took a shower after breakfast.

By nine-thirty I was dressed and ready to leave. Armed with my cunning and my press card, I left the motel behind me and despatched my blue M.G.C. towards Chinhurst Lodge.

Driving fast but just within limits I cruised past the Horse and Groom, a quaint ivy-covered little place with baskets of geraniums hanging either side of its doors, and on arrival at the stables I parked on a tiny forecourt that was littered with cars. Red was a popular colour but Falloway's immaculate XJ 12 Jaguar stuck out like a king-size poppy on Armistice Day.

Inside the yard, small scattered groups of owners stood peering into loose-boxes, chatting to skinny stable hands and seeming to take an interest in each other's horses. I marked time, my eyes meandering over the dossier-come-to-life surroundings. A boy emerged from one of the boxes clutching a saddle and bridle. He kicked at the broken hinges, needing all his weight to shut the split door, then made his way across the yard to what I presumed was the tack-room—a dark, ancient-looking place with cracked window-panes held together by the grace of God and several feet of sticky tape.

Everything looked run down and impoverished. The Lodge, large, rambling, neglected, was the kind of property that breeds dry rot in places where other people haven't even got places, and sends borough surveyors away with galloping apoplexy.

Grimy, dejected outbuildings, badly in need of creosote and a little kindness, stood rotting slowly away in the damp morning air. The whole set-up smelled of mordant decay. Shoe-string operating at its worst. It was almost sad.

I crossed to the office. As I reached the open doorway a stocky, long-haired youth with manners to match his appearance lurched out and shouldered me aside. Remembering my passive role as a journalist, I hurled choice but silent invective at his receding shoulder blades and stepped in to meet the Chinhurst trainer.

The office was cold and unwelcoming, its trappings dowdy and inexpensive. Two light leather armchairs, a desk, and a filing cabinet stood on linoleum the colour of old mustard, and the pictures which embellished the walls had warped and discoloured in the damp, musty atmosphere.

My first impression of Neil McQuillan as he unfolded himself from his unkempt desk was that of a rather docile chimpanzee. A cheap, ill-fitting jacket, elbows leather-patched, hung loosely on his slender frame and his small button eyes peering out from underslung pouches viewed me with a kind of clownish interest. He possessed a squat, cavernous nose and his hair, short and well lubricated, completed the ape-like effect by its ineffective hiding of slightly prominent ears.

I gave him a chummy grin and a brief glimpse at my press card. 'Preston,' I said. '*Racing Times*.'

He gave me a wide dental smile back and a left to right handshake as enthusiastically as if I'd just invited him to guest on Desert Island Discs.

'I've been expecting you, Mr Preston,' he said. 'I'm flattered that your magazine should take an interest in our comparatively small yard.' Still smiling, he waved his good hand to indicate a chair facing him. 'I really am extremely honoured, may I tell you that?'

I told him he might.

'I was surprised and delighted when I heard.'

'Our pleasure,' I said.

'Have you fixed yourself up with any local accommodation?'

'I'm at the Highway Motel.'

'A pity. Duncan Stroud's mother keeps a small guest house in the village. The food is excellent, so I'm told.'

'Duncan Stroud?'

'My travelling head lad. You probably met him on the way in.'

'The scrum-half? Yes, I did.'

He looked at me as if searching for a double meaning, but then, finding none, released a quick nod and said, 'He's a good boy. Intelligent and a damned hard worker. A rare combination in these days of do as little as you can for as much as you can.'

Playing along with the preliminaries, I said, 'Do you find staff a problem?'

'Who doesn't. There isn't a trainer in the country who's having it easy as far as labour is concerned. In this day and age, Mr Preston, there are a lot less demanding ways of earning a living.'

'So you can't afford to pick and choose?'

'Not any more. I take whoever I can get and if they have a

25

knowledge of horses I say a silent prayer to Allah and count my blessings.'

He smiled again, showing those large white chimpanzee teeth of his and I couldn't help smiling back. I had come fully prepared to dislike McQuillan and his grubby little set-up. My mind had conjured up its own conception of a pompous, self-assured individual who was doing a first-class job of putting one over on the Security Division. The latter part was probably true, but whatever else McQuillan might be, he certainly wasn't pompous.

I found myself warming to his easy manner. I liked his style, his phrasing, his directness. I wanted an adverse reaction towards him because I worked better and harder with a hate complex. But that big affable grin was knocking my complexes for six.

'How long will you be staying?' He expertly opened a cigarette box with the hook-like attachment on his metal hand and manoeuvred the box towards me. 'I trust this isn't a flying visit?'

'I'll be under your feet for a week, maybe two,' I said. 'I like to get the feel of a place, delve beneath the surface before committing anything to paper. I'm afraid ours is a quality magazine that deals in thoroughness rather than sketchy facts.'

'The publicity will do the stable a power of good.' he enthused. 'Might even help to fill some of our empty loose-boxes with decent animals.'

'Is business bad?'

'It could be better.'

'But you're getting the winners.'

'Less than our share.'

'You won a £2,000 handicap last month with Counterfoil.' He laughed. 'You've been doing your homework.'

'We deal in thoroughness,' I reminded him.

'Of course.' He lowered his eyes, said to the blotter, 'Unfortunately one swallow doesn't make a summer, Mr

Preston. None of our horses are out of the top drawer. Counter-foil's win came as an eye-opener, and the percentage will pay some of the bills. We really need to attract good-class animals to Chinhurst, and I'm hoping your feature might act as the magnet.'

I wasn't quite sure what he meant by an 'eye-opener', or why he'd bothered to use the words at all. He certainly spoke frankly and as I didn't want to raise any suspicions by probing too deeply, I decided to let the statement go unchallenged.

Instead, I rattled out a lot of spiel about various ideas I had for the feature, making most of it up as I went along and trying to sound convincing while I was doing it.

McQuillan was the perfect listener. I was expecting him to throw in a few suggestions, argue a little, but he sat motionless and never interrupted. He was also the perfect host. When I'd finished, he produced a bottle of sherry from the filing cabinet, a cheap blend with a wine supermarket's brand name, and proceeded to toast my health and the success of the *Racing Times*.

I felt a heel. He really believed that my imaginary feature was going to bring in the customers, lift Chinhurst Lodge out of the doldrums. He honestly thought that a few strokes from my pen would encourage the clatter of expensive hooves to seek out his shabby loose-boxes.

Like I said, he struck me as being on the level—a nice guy. I was probably wrong. I reminded myself that the Falloway horses weren't doping themselves. It eased my conscience, but the sherry stuck in my throat just the same.

'I understand you'll be taking some pictures?' He patted his hair gently with his good hand as if to assure himself it was neat and in place.

'My photographer arrives tomorrow.'

'Then that gives us a bit of time to spruce up the yard. You've caught us at the end of the season—I was leaving the odd jobs, repairs and suchlike, for the winter months.'

I offered no comment.

'The problem of staff again, I'm afraid.' He felt he had to justify his previous statement, and added, 'Boys come, boys go. At present we haven't the money or the manpower for perfectionism.'

'So you're reckoning on things getting better.'

'I have plans in here,' he winked, tapped his temple.

'Something I could include in the feature?'

'Very private plans, Mr Preston.' He grinned, glanced at his wristwatch, and levered himself up. 'I must make an appearance. On Sunday morning I'm expected to turn on the charm, mingle with the owners.'

'O.K. if I mingle too?'

'If you're sure you won't be bored by the small talk.'

'On the contrary, I might well find it enlightening.'

'All good background stuff, eh?' He laughed good-naturedly, made a well-practised effort of concealing his metal hand in his jacket pocket, and strode briskly out into the hazy sunshine.

He chatted freely as we walked along the cracked flagstone path that led to the stable area. The conversation yielded no information from the assignment point of view, and ranged from a breakdown of yard routine to the pipe-dream of modernization.

I humoured McQuillan with a couple of feature-type questions and made a few doodles in my pocket book. They didn't mean anything but I figured he expected it of me; if my activities were going to look journalistic, I should put on some kind of show.

We stopped by the tack-room. As a cluster of owners descended on the trainer, I busied myself taking a tour of the loose-boxes.

Surprisingly, the interiors were spotlessly clean. I expected to find grimy mangers, dirty urine-smelling straw, and scrawny horses. Instead, I found clean mangers, fresh sweet-smelling straw beds, and healthy well-nourished animals. Every horse looked contented. I reminded myself they didn't care about flashy accoutrements, only creature comforts. Such things as outdated buildings and flaking paintwork went unnoticed in the equine world.

I'd covered about ten boxes when Wesley Falloway and the long-haired Duncan Stroud arrived on the scene. Falloway, head held high, shoulders squared, appeared to be heading in my direction. I turned my back on him, found the nearest occupied box, and interested myself by looking at the contents—a young bay colt which regarded me with amiable curiosity.

The footsteps closed in. Snippets of conversation filtered towards me. Two totally different accents. One harsh, indistinct, which presumably belonged to Stroud—the other crisp, cultured and in keeping with Falloway's Eton background.

As I listened, a third voice—louder this time, echoed from inside a loose-box only two doors away. Recognizing the cockney vocal chords of Len Potter, I made a half-turn and focused on a barely legible nameplate which proclaimed: *Counterfoil.*

'Walkin' dog fodder,' Potter was saying, 'that's what this lump of 'orse meat is—walkin' bloody dog fodder.'

Another young voice replied, 'You're jus' sour 'cause yer got left on the gallops, ain'tcher?'

'No I ain't. P'raps 'e's busted 'is elastic band or summit, but 'e's 'opeless I tellya.'

I stood immobile, my eyes fixed on Falloway and Stroud. They had heard the voices, stopped short of Counterfoil's box, and were now engaged in the gentle art of eavesdropping. The loose talk flowed and I sweated. I listened, I sweated, and I silently called Len Potter all the goddamn loud-mouthed bastards under the sun.

'Dunno 'ow Counterfoil won two fousand quid,' he was saying. 'Must 'ave bin up against a bunch of pit-ponies wiv their legs tied together.'

As the other lad let out a burst of high-pitched laughter, the short martingale that checked Falloway's rising temper broke free. He lunged forward, threw back the bolt on the box door and said with soft relish, 'That boy there—yes, you—come here!'

I stood looking at the bay colt, marshalling my thoughts. I was stiff with uncertainty. The way I saw it I could do one of two things. Walk away, stay out of the limelight and leave Potter to talk himself out of trouble—pray he wouldn't blow the assignment in the process. Or else, stay and step in if Potter's mouth, or the situation, got out of hand.

If the boy lost his job, we would be out in the cold. Without inside information it was 'goodbye speedy conclusion—the flat racing season's at an end'. And goodbye to my fee.

Squinting into the sun and brandishing a Dandy brush, he made his exit. He slouched towards Falloway, switched on a who-the-hell-are-you grimace and murmured, 'Can I 'elp yer?'

Stroud said, 'This is Mr Falloway, Potter. He owns four of the horses in your care—Counterfoil being one of them.'

As Potter flushed guiltily, the other lad emerged from the loose-box, mumbled something unintelligible and beat a hasty retreat.

Falloway said softly, 'Who was that boy?'

'A mate,' Potter said.

'Name?' Falloway snapped his thin fingers.

'My name or 'is?'

'Yours will suffice.'

'Leonard Maximillian Potter.'

'Don't try to be clever, little man.'

'I ain't. Me name is Leonard Maximillian Potter and you're right—I 'ave 'ad a busy day.'

A vein began pulsing in Falloways's neck as he swung to Stroud. 'I don't remember seeing this boy before,' he said heavily. 'Who the devil put him in charge of my horses? Where's my usual stable lad?'

'Sid Doyle has left us,' the travelling head lad began. Potter's taken over the job while . . .'

'I don't like him,' Falloway cut in. 'I don't like his type or his manner. And what's more to the point, Duncan, we both

30

heard him make some very derogatory remarks about my horse. I want you to keep him here while I fetch Mr McQuillan.'

As Falloway stamped angrily away, Stroud said, 'What the hell are you playing at, Potter? Don't you know that today is Sunday and on Sunday owners come to visit their horses? Isn't it bloody obvious, even to someone as thick as you, that that big mouth of yours can easily be overheard?'

Potter shrugged cockily.

'And what's with this Leonard Maximillian bit? Owners like Mr Falloway are our bread-and-butter. The last thing they want or expect from a little schmuck like you is cheek—savvy?'

'Yeah, I savvy— but wot I said was true,' Potter murmured defensively. 'In my opinion that nag of 'is ain't worf two penn'orth of cold shit.'

'*Your* opinion! Who the hell do you think values *your* opinion!'

'People.'

'What *people*.'

'Important people,' Potter mused smugly, causing my stomach muscles to tighten. 'You'd be surprised.'

'Like who?'

'Like none of yer business.'

'O.K., give.' Stroud's lips retracted as, gripping the polo-neck of Potter's sweater, he yanked the boy towards him. 'Are you selling information to punters? If you're bloody tipping, Potter, McQuillan will have you out on your arse so fast ...'

'Ferchrissake ...' Potter croaked, breathing like a cart-horse, his cheeks tinged with violet, 'you're bleedin' chokin' me ...'

'Who are these important people? I want the truth!'

I decided to wait no longer. Stroud had obviously read something sinister into Potter's words and seemed determined to press for information. Whether or not the boy would open the wrong side of his mouth was in the lap of the Gods. I hoped my presence would relieve them of their decision and put the odds in my favour.

'Is this a private mugging?' I asked, 'or are the general

31

public admitted?' It was the world's worst witticism, but I wasn't at my inventive best.

'Who are you?' Stroud, somewhat startled, drew back his lips as though undecided whether to smile or sink his teeth into my windpipe.

'Preston. Simon Preston.' I made some effort at politeness.

Stroud said, 'Are you an owner, Mr Preston?'

'No. A visitor.'

'You've seen Mr McQuillan?'

'If by that you mean was I invited, or did I just stroll in—I was invited, Mr Stroud.'

'You know me?'

'We collided briefly at the office if you remember. McQuillan mentioned your name.'

'Of course.' He smiled unpleasantly.

Duncan Stroud's face was the naturally pale, anaemic-looking kind, with sunken cheeks like a scooped-out avocado pear. He was stocky but short. By the side of Falloway he'd looked a pigmy, and as with many of his physical build, he concealed this feeling of smallness in a belligerent air of high-mightiness.

I said, 'Are you performing some kind of initiation ceremony —an obscure stable custom? Or is this just a straightforward roughing-up?'

'It's nothing for you to concern yourself with,' Stroud contended, releasing his grip on Potter as though he was something obscene. 'This is a personal matter between me and the boy.'

'With a little violence thrown in, eh?'

'Violence?' Falloway's breath fanned the nape of my neck. 'Did you say violence, Mr . . . er . . . ? I don't think I've had the pleasure . . .'

'Preston,' I said without offering him my hand. 'And yes, I did say violence.'

He let his eyes ripple over my face—those strange, unblinking eyes that somehow made you feel uncomfortable. 'You're mistaken, surely?'

'Not from where I was standing.' I indicated the loose-box.

'I see.' He turned to Stroud. 'Can you explain, Duncan?'

Duncan Stroud could and he did. He took Falloway neatly over Potter's 'important people' dialogue and blamed the boy's attitude for the ensuing loss of temper.

'Who are these important people?' Falloway asked grimly.

'He wouldn't say, sir.'

'Obviously a figment of the boy's imagination,' I covered quickly. 'You don't think he's serious, surely?'

'You appear to be making excuses for him, Mr Preston, and I find myself asking, why?'

'Not through choice. I just happened to be in the right place at the wrong time.'

'And that's the only reason?'

'No.'

'Well?'

'In fox-hunting my sympathies lie with the fox.'

'Very commendable. But this isn't a fox—merely an uncouth boy with a rather truculent manner.'

'Then he's hardly worth making a fuss over, is he?'

Falloway said nothing.

Potter, who had been regarding me with a vague grin of liberation, muttered, 'I meant no 'arm, I jus' got carried away a bit, that's all.'

Stroud gave a derisive grunt. 'He could be tipping—I'm not sure.'

'I ain't no tipster. I know the rules.'

'Then just what exactly are you?' Falloway's eyes were watching him shrewdly.

'Stable lad, ain't I.'

'And these important people?'

'There ain't none. I only said it 'cos Stroudy was chuckin' 'is weight around.'

'Why couldn't you have said so before?' Falloway snapped.

'Couldn't, Mr Fallerway, sir. 'E was chokin' me, sir.'

'Who was choking you?' The dulcet tones of Neil McQuillan

interrupted any further conversation. He eyed Potter speculatively as he crossed towards Counterfoil's box and snapped on the outside bolts. Vicky Annesley came with him.

I watched the bounce of blonde hair on her narrow shoulders as she homed on Wesley Falloway and linked an arm through his. She looked even more appetizing than I remembered. The compelling blue eyes, enhanced by large artificial eyelashes, smiled at whoever they happened to fall upon and triggered off that old chemical reaction that can get a guy in trouble. By any standard, she was a difficult girl to ignore. The tight white trouser suit housed impressive statistics—the kind that weren't easily forgotten.

'Stroudy tried t'frottle me,' Potter was saying, giving a practical demonstration by clutching his own throat with both hands. 'Nearly a gonner I was—'urt somethin' chronic it did.'

Stroud gave an embarrassed little laugh. 'That's absolute rubbish, sir. The boy is exaggerating the facts.'

'The facts will keep until later.' McQuillan spoke softly, unemotionally, 'the last thing I want is for this to be blown up into an international incident, just because tempers are running high.'

Falloway said, 'Potter made some very humiliating comments about one of my horses—erroneous, of course—and then had the effrontery to suggest that certain people in high places would be more than interested to hear his views.'

'I can only apologize, Wesley, and assure you the boy will be reprimanded.'

Falloway and Stroud exchanged glances.

McQuillan turned to me, switching his chimpanzee smile to maximal wattage. 'You appear to have been caught up in all this, Mr Preston.'

'Misunderstandings happen in the best run stables,' I said.

'Potter hasn't been with us long, but he'll soon learn our ways.'

'He should be sacked,' Falloway interjected. 'The boy is a downright little trouble-maker.'

34

This comment sparked off a garbled explanation from Potter, but McQuillan, in an authoritative voice, meant to silence any further outbursts, told him he had already caused enough trouble and ordered him to wait in the office. I watched his sluggish, oath-murmuring departure with grateful relief and offered a silent prayer of thanks to whoever might be listening.

Falloway grunted impatiently, 'I don't like being made to look a fool, Neil. I don't like it one iota.'

'Well, for my part I've already apologized,' McQuillan told him. 'I'll also make quite sure you get an apology from Potter.'

'I don't want a damned apology!'

'Then what do you want, Wesley?' McQuillan contrived a smile and kept his voice calm, but his tone indicated that Falloway wasn't top of any Chinhurst popularity polls.

'It's my horses I'm concerned about! With an asinine stable lad like that in charge of my animals—God knows what could happen.'

'Potter knows his job. His references were perfectly adequate.'

'So you don't intend moving him?'

'Be reasonable, Wesley. With the flat season nearing its end, it would be unfair at this stage to switch lads.'

Falloway looked unconvinced. Any moment now, I figured, he might produce his big guns and threaten to remove his horses. *Might*? Sure. Perhaps there were nearly ten thousand good reasons why he *wouldn't*. But either way, I couldn't risk it. I said, trying to save Potter's job and the situation, 'We know the boy's got a mouth like a torn pocket, but I've never heard of an animal's performance being impaired by hot air from a pair of cockney lungs.'

Stroud's tight face cracked a little and Vicky Annesley broke the tension by laughing uninhibitedly. She extended long silver-pink fingernails to Falloway's cheek and pouted, 'They're right, darling. You really are worrying yourself over nothing.'

The girl had shown her colours. If Falloway persisted in sticking to his present mood of thinking, he was going to look even more of a fool, and he knew it. A flash of annoyance rippled over his face which changed almost instantly into a slow crooked smile as phoney as a wreath of plastic flowers. 'Perhaps I am,' he murmured with effort. 'I can't say I'm happy with the arrangement, but if it will please you, darling, I'll let the matter rest.'

With Falloway swallowing his pride and showing everyone the benevolent side of his nature, the air had been cleared for introductions.

McQuillan announced that I would be a regular visitor for the next couple of weeks, then looking at Stroud he added, 'I shall expect you to give Mr Preston your full cooperation, Duncan. Answer his questions and offer him any help you can.'

Stroud looked puzzled, but nodded.

Falloway, his curiosity aroused, said amusedly, 'A regular visitor? Are you cultivating a prospective client, Neil?'

'No, Wesley,' McQuillan replied. 'The *Racing Times* is cultivating *me*. Mr Preston is one of their writers.'

It was a beautifully timed track-stopper. I wouldn't have missed the stunned look that fell over Falloway's face for an athletic weekend with a dozen Vicky Annesleys. But then I'm a realist—a dozen Vicky Annesleys? Who's kidding who?

Chapter Three

On Monday I slept late. It was one of those crisp, cold, clear-sky sort of autumn mornings which promote enthusiastic comments from people wearing only the barest essentials, who stamp their feet and blow on their hands as they talk about the 'good healthy weather'.

Midday found me behind the wheel of the M.G. With a few puffs of cloud in the powder-blue sky, and only the occasional farm punctuating my progress, I drove across country for my appointment with Kelly Meredith at the Horse and Groom.

The public bar held no more than a handful of customers. I ordered a vodka-and-orange from the landlord, a cheerful guy with a Dickensian face, and made small-talk as I looked past the display of hanging copperware and into the saloon. I'd parked next to a two-tone Bentley, and the distinguished-looking vehicle made me curious as to the owner.

There were just two people in the adjacent bar, a man and a woman. I could see the man clearly. Late thirties, bull-like physique and bloodhound eyes. He was making sympathetic noises to a dark, smartly dressed woman who was sitting with her back towards me.

The features of the man were unmistakable. I remembered him guiding the fragile, wheelchair-bound Mrs Falloway through the Newmarket crowds with the ease that one guides an empty shopping trolley through a deserted supermarket. His voice matched his build. Although speaking in undertones, it was powerful and deep—as if providing the commentary for some once-in-a-lifetime television spectacular.

I paid for another drink and decided to act ignorant. 'Nice Bentley outside,' I said to the landlord. 'Yours?'

He laughed. 'Couldn't afford the petrol, sir.'

'A thirsty animal, all right.'

'Twelve to the gallon.'

'Less in town.'

'You have to be wealthy to run a machine like that.'

'Somebody local?' I enquired.

'Not really local, sir.' He lowered his voice. 'Have you heard of Alison Falloway?'

'She's here?'

'Her chauffeur and housekeeper are.' He polished a glass and tilted his head towards the saloon bar. 'Once a month, always a Monday, and regular as clockwork. Did you know the old lady was crippled?'

I told him I did.

'That's the reason, you see.'

'Reason?'

'They take her for physiotherapy treatment at Dulverton. Once a month, and always in the Bentley.' He leaned forward, adding disgustedly, 'They kill the time between dropping and picking her up in my pub. He always has half of lager and she has a tomato juice. The last of the big spenders, those two are.'

'What about the son?' He seemed talkative, so I probed.

'Wesley? Keeps his horses over the road but never sets foot in this establishment. Beneath his dignity from what I've heard of him. No sir, yours truly will never make a profit out of the Falloways.' He laughed heartily, excused himself and went to serve a waiting customer.

I finished my drink and scanned the assortment of faces for Kelly Meredith. There was no one remotely young and female in either bar. I lit a cigarette and went to the Gents'. The walls displayed the usual obscene scrawl, faded in places where it had been attacked by a caustic cleanser, but still perfectly readable. Judging from the comments it was obvious that the McQuillan work-force were the culprits. Libellous statements about various jockeys and trainers were intermingled with the type of skilful etchings you'd only find in sex educational books—the kind

38

that offer a hundred and one love positions, two-thirds of which only apply to Bendy Toys.

I washed my hands and began drying them in the warm-air machine. Above the noise of the motor I could hear the throaty sound of a tuned exhaust system, the revving of an engine, and the shrill of tyres as a vehicle skidded to a halt on the tarmac outside. One of the frosted-glass windows was partially open, so I pushed it all the way and peered out on the car park.

My eyes connected instantly with a mustard-coloured Lotus and a pair of firm brown thighs emerging from long shiny boots. The boots matched the patent material of a skirt, which from my viewing angle was shorter than decency should allow. The girl, her pert little behind tilted skywards, was lugging an equipment bag from the boot and unconsciously treating me to a rear view of black bikini briefs.

The thought that this was Kelly Meredith flashed through my mind, but I didn't really believe my luck until I spotted a *Racing Times* sticker on the bag handle.

I decided to be bold. 'Hello—Miss Meredith?' I called across pleasantly.

She turned and looked at me, surprised, perhaps a little intrigued. Her hair was red. Fiery flame red, and cut in a short boyish-looking style which suited her fine-boned features. As did the enormous tortoiseshell sunglasses that decorated her nose.

'Simon Preston?'

'None other.'

'Well, hello.' She returned my smile with an infectious grin that revealed dimples. 'Are you in the saloon or public bar?'

'At the moment I'm in the Gents'.'

She laughed, honestly amused.

'Stay where you are,' I said. 'I'll come and give you a hand.'

I carried the equipment bag into the bar, found a vacant corner table and purchased some drinks.

'Hungry?' I asked.

'Starved,' she said.

'Smoked-salmon sandwiches?'

She nodded enthusiastically.

The landlord brought us two rounds each and we talked as we ate. In actual fact I let Kelly do most of the talking. I didn't want to appear pontifical, and besides I was still trying to cope with the effect that her neat little figure was having on me.

'You're nice,' she said, as if she meant it, 'but you're not at all what I expected.'

'And what exactly did you expect?'

'Somebody older—you know, fortyish, tallish and heavyish. But you're really quite . . .'

'Weedyish?' I suggested.

'Lean, solid, young,' she said.

I grinned. 'And I take it you've never owned a cricket bat or a box Brownie?'

'I've never what . . . ?'

'Forget it,' I chuckled. 'It just shows how wrong mental pictures can be.'

The bar began to fill. I sipped at my drink, pausing between sips to take her swiftly over the assignment preliminaries and lob back answers to the numerous questioning balls she threw at me.

We spoke softly, ours heads huddled together like a couple of lovesick teenagers. Nothing new emerged from this confabulation but it gave us both a chance to get to know one another, to assess each other's characters, and to form a basis for a working relationship.

'I've been with the *Racing Times* eighteen months,' she was saying. 'Before that I worked on an athletic magazine.'

'Always sport, huh?'

'It seems to have happened that way. What about you, have you always worked for the T.S.D. ?'

'Not so long ago I was manager of a private stud farm.'

'From domestication to investigation, that's quite a step. Captain Grant spoke very highly of you. He said that Simon

Drake, or rather Simon Preston, was the one person who could crack the Falloway case.'

'He said that to me as well,' I grunted, downing the remains of the smoked salmon. 'I only wish I had the old boy's faith.'

'Any leads yet?'

'Nope.'

'Theories?'

'None.'

'Vague ideas?'

'Nothing that makes any sense.' I looked at her. 'Try me with a bit of female logic.'

'Well . . .'

'Yes?'

'An excessive dose of anabolic steroids might do the trick.'

I smiled broadly. 'How come Miss Meredith knows about such things as anabolic steroids?'

'We did an article on the drug a few months ago. If I remember correctly it promotes the build-up of body tissue by enabling the body to retain nitrogen and to push up its protein content.'

I wouldn't have dared to argue with facts like that. I stuck to what I knew. I said, 'But steroids are detectable and we're looking for something that isn't.'

She pulled a cute face and shrugged.

'Have you cast anyone as the villain of the piece?'

'Only the obvious choice of Neil McQuillan. He is in financial difficulties and the Falloway horses have certainly been pushing him up in the trainers' ratings.'

'But why only the Falloway five? What about the other thirty-odd horses in his care?'

'Perhaps Wesley holds the patent on the stimulant, or whatever. McQuillan merely administers it and collects a backhander and a praiseworthy reputation for his pains.'

For a photographer she wasn't doing at all badly. 'It's feasible,' I conceded, 'but when I visited Chinhurst Lodge I got the distinct impression they were anything but partners in crime.'

I grinned and added, 'You're beginning to sound too much like Grant.'

She smiled ruefully.

'Only Grant reckoned it was Wesley who was attempting to build up the reputation. A sort of mother and son rivalry with Wesley trying his best to produce a rather poor string of pseudo General O'Haras.'

'Now there's a racing paragon,' she said, her eyes widening. 'This year alone he's won the Eclipse Stakes, the King George VI and the Benson & Hedges Gold Cup.'

'Plus the Champion Stakes,' I put in. 'Grant and I watched that incredible performance on Saturday.'

'And he thinks it could be a sort of kindred jealousy?'

'They don't get on.'

'Maybe not,' she pulled a face. 'But to compare Wesley's feeble successes with those of a classic horse like the General is ludicrous. O'Hara stands alongside the all-time greats—Man o' War, Hyperion, Ribot, Kelso, Mill . . .' She stopped suddenly, realizing she was beginning to sound like a racing-history book.

I grinned. 'Lady, you certainly know your horseflesh.'

'Before I joined the *Racing Times* I didn't know a forelock from a fetlock. That's what comes of working with horse-crazy reporters.'

'Have you ever met Wesley or his mother?'

She shook her head but made a conscious effort to be helpful. The magazine had produced a souvenir centre-fold feature on General O'Hara, and she had been assigned to take pictures at Gaylawn Stables of trainer Julian Ratcliffe and Mrs Falloway. Under pressure, the Duchess agreed to be interviewed, but refused point-blank when asked to attend the photographic session.

'I'm glad she did in a way,' Kelly continued. 'She's a trifle eccentric—influenced by the planets—that sort of thing. Her horoscope had predicted a day of interruptions from people who were only out for what they could get. She thought our reporter

42

slotted very nicely into that category, and apparently gave him hell.'

She smiled at me and I found myself smiling back, liking her a lot. I said, 'She sounds quite a character.'

'Have you seen the house at Fransham?'

'Not yet.'

'That's unbelievable too. Tudor, I think—all whitewash, black timbers and leaded windows. There's a gate-keeper's cottage complete with gate-keeper and one of those boom-type pole things blocking the entrance. The milkman probably needs a visa to get in there.'

There was a scuffle by the door. Raucous laughter suddenly cut through the rattle of glasses, the babble of thirsty voices. I turned, looked through the indistinguishable blur of bodies and saw three young grinning faces pushing their way to the bar.

'McQuillan's boys?' Kelly asked, following my gaze.

I nodded briefly.

They never reached the bar. The tallest one, a sharp-featured lad with a face full of freckles, stopped suddenly as he spotted Kelly. It wasn't surprising. She was the best-looking thing in the pub, and more than enough to throw any unsuspecting country boy off his stroke. Freckles saw me, nodded a smile, and said something to the other two which resulted in all three dissolving into gasps of laughter. Eventually the joke fizzled out and they came over to meet us.

'Mr Preston, isn't it?' Freckles extended a hard, rough hand. 'Lennie's mate?'

His question caused my blood temperature to rise several degrees. I didn't know quite how to reply, and the smile I was attempting seemed locked on my lips.

'Lennie Potter,' he went on. 'We heard how you stood up to Stroudy—took him down a peg or two. You knocked some of the bigheadedness out of him. Thanks.'

'Ain't bin the same since,' said a thin sallow boy with prominent cheek-bones. 'Got pissed as a newt last night.

Sozzled 'e was, 'ad a right skinful. If the guv'nor sees 'im he'll gerra boot up 'is arse.'

'He's half-tanked this morning,' the third boy added, almost delighted. 'Had nearly a full bottle of Scotch in the hay-loft when I left.'

My initial fears subsided. The fact that I'd stood my ground in order to stop Potter from flapping his mouth had put me on the right side of the fence. Stroud was now drinking himself stupid, much to the pleasure of all his grievance bearers.

Freckles smiled. He dragged his lips back from teeth that were clenched on a cigarette and made the introductions. I suggested refreshment and squeezed my way to the bar. I reckoned on buying the lads a few rounds of drinks and exploiting my present well-favoured position by slipping some carefully phrased questions into the conversation.

I saw the chauffeur again as I collected my change. I found myself facing him over the counter. The housekeeper, very prim, attractive in a homely sort of way, looked anxiously over his shoulder. There was a din of voices all around but his baritone enunciation, purpose-built for eavesdroppers, came swimming across the bar. He asked the landlord for some cigarettes, then turning to the woman, he said, 'I understand your feelings, Emily, but it's vital we unite on this one and agree to say nothing.'

The chat sounded interesting so I stalled for time. With an ear cocked in their direction I decided to distrust the landlord and carefully check my change.

'But if the old girl should find out . . .' the woman began.

'She won't. If anything goes wrong, we'll just have to face up to it, if and when that time comes.'

'I don't like it,' the woman's voice rose a decibel or two. 'She has a sixth sense about these things. You're talking about thousands . . .' The sentence skidded to a halt.

I ventured a quick glance in their direction. The woman was looking at the floor, but the chauffeur was looking at me. Whether he was aware of my interest, I wasn't sure. I didn't

44

hang around to find out. As the landlord gave him his cigarettes, I pocketed my change and returned to Kelly.

'It's hard graft all right,' Freckles was saying. 'We get up at six and don't finish till around seven at night. Course, if the old man's in a bad mood—if his hand's been giving him a bit of aggro—then we'll miss supper and work until nine.'

'It must be a terrible handicap.'

'Working till nine? Puts paid to your love-life I can tell—'

'No, the metal hand. For a trainer to be afflicted in that way, I mean.'

'Not really,' he shrugged. 'Plays him up at times I suppose, but he uses it to his advantage.' He turned to his mates for support. 'Ask Riddle or Sparks, they'll tell you.'

Sparks, the smallest of the three with an ugly but good-natured face, nodded his agreement. 'He belts you with it if he catches you fannying around.'

'Jabbed me in the cobbs,' Riddle added bitterly. 'I ain't bin the same since.'

'If it's that bad you could always leave,' I pointed out.

'No other yard would have him,' Freckles grinned. 'He's all gob and no brains.'

Riddle grinned back, taking the remark as it was intended.

'Certainly sounds a hard life,' Kelly agreed.

'Even harder since you arrived,' Sparks contended. 'The guv'nor's had us scrubbing and painting, sweeping and mending, clean this, fix that. Yesterday we slogged for sixteen bleedin' hours.'

'Is that legal?'

'Legalities belong to the ouside world,' I said, trying to tranquillize their grievances by distributing drinks. 'Racing stables are a law unto themselves. We both know it's a lot better than it was, but some still operate an almost primeval system of working.'

'Like Chinhurst,' Riddle commented. 'Beats me why yer want t'write about it. Daft I call it.'

'Finest yard in the country,' Sparks replied, smirking.

'Ah, gerron wiv yer.'

'Remember the plaque in the old man's office?'

'Wot plaque?'

'It'll pass the post first, if it's trained at Chin-hurst.'

'Bloodyell . . .' Riddle convulsed with laughter. 'Trade Descripshuns oughta 'ear about that . . .'

Freckles ignored them, sipped thoughtfully at his beer. 'I suppose the *Racing Times* pays well for articles and suchlike?'

'As well as most,' I said.

'How much would they pay to know about the shady side?'

I left that one to Kelly. 'Nothing,' she told him. 'In the short term it would probably push up sales, but in the long term it would undoubtedly harm us. We don't want to disillusion our readers. We'd be indirectly killing the very sport we're trying to promote.'

'I see.'

'You know a lot about the shady side?'

'Don't matter.' He smiled crookedly.

'You could try a Sunday paper,' I advised, not wishing to lose the conversational trend. 'They pay the best rates of all.'

'Like?'

'Depends on the content, the originality.'

'You'd get carved up if you did,' Sparks warned him.

'Not if I did it anonymous.'

'They'd break your arms and legs.'

'It needs cleaning up.'

'Are you generalizing or talking about the Chinhurst yard?' Kelly asked.

'I'm talking about racing as a whole. It isn't straight and it never will be.'

'Example?' I prodded him on.

'Off the record, mind.'

'Naturally.'

'O.K., let's start with jockeys—those who work in rings to fix races. A ring is a sort of club for bent jocks. They plan out the race and know the result before they even reach the course.

Others are in collusion with bookmakers. They're told to strangle a particular horse and they get well paid for doing it. The bookies know who's corruptible and who isn't. Once a jock takes a bribe and strangles a horse, then he's in that bookie's pocket for life.'

Kelly lifted her brow in mock surprise and gave a little gasp. She'd obviously heard all this before, but she was doing a good job of egging him on.

'Jockeys aren't the only ones,' he went on bitterly. 'The crooked element creeps in when you're young and trying to gain experience. My brother jacked it in soon after he finished his apprenticeship. Sick of owners and trainers pushing him around, he was. They won't tell you outright to stop a horse. They'll drop a few hints, make it friggin' obvious you're expected to lose—pass you the message all wrapped up in fancy lingo—but you know what they're after all right.'

He was giving an all-embracing picture of British racing. He was telling me how a sport that involved big money had its share of people who were prepared to pervert, defraud or exploit that sport for their own personal gain. Unfortunately he wasn't telling me anything I didn't already know. The words Chinhurst, McQuillan or Falloway weren't creeping into the conversation.

'I could go on and on,' Freckles cracked his knuckles, and did. 'I could tell you all about the small fiddles such as cheating kits—specially made ultra-light boots, breeches and so on. How easy it is to weigh-out without any irons or girths attached to the saddle. I could take you right along the line. Right back to the stable lad who's threatened with a good "doing over" unless he gives a certain horse a dollop of stopper.'

'And what does a dollop of stopper consist of?' Kelly feigned ignorance.

'It can take various forms, but a massive dose of physic powder is as good as anything.'

'Y'damn right it is,' Riddle broke in. 'Dun arf make 'em—'

'Shut up, Riddle,' Freckles censored his words. 'It loosens

47

them up, miss. They don't feel well for a couple of days after that.'

'Worm powders in their night feed would have a similar effect,' Sparks added. 'But you'd need a lot of them and they wouldn't be so quick acting.'

'I was gonna say that,' Riddle complained.

'Tough titty,' Freckles said.

Collecting up the empty glasses I asked him if any of the Chinhurst horses had been stopped in this way.

'Here?' He gave a derisive grunt. 'We haven't got anything worth stopping.'

'That's not strictly true,' Kelly pointed out, naming a few Wesley Falloway winners.

'Flukes.' He shrugged them off.

'But winning flukes nevertheless.'

'A lucky run— it happens.'

'Are you sure it's nothing more?' I probed.

'Doped to win?' He looked horrified.

'Well you haven't exactly conjured up an undefiled, hypodermic-free picture of the Sport of Kings.'

'No, no.' He shook his head emphatically. 'With modern dope testing methods it's nigh on impossible to make a horse win.'

'Falloway's horses have been doing well though . . .' Sparks scratched at the bristles on his chin. 'You're not hinting that—'

'I'm not hinting at anything. You were saying how crooked it all was and I was merely pointing out—'

'Stroudy and Fallerway,' Riddle said suddenly. 'I wouldn't put it past 'em.'

'No, no,' Freckles insisted.

'Oh, I dunno. Dead close those two.'

'How close?' I asked.

'Closer than Gloria's knockers.'

'Gloria's . . . ?'

'She helps out on Saturday mornings,' Sparks said.

48

'What a pair,' Riddle chuckled. 'Couldn't get a fag paper between her bra and the contents. Like Stroudy and Fallerway. Close, dead close.'

I was about to push him a little harder, but Freckles pointed to the empty glasses. 'How about a refill,' he enquired, 'Thirsty work all this talking.'

It seemed to be my day for buying other people drinks. I fought my way to the bar and brooded over the last thirty minutes of chit-chat as I waited to be served. I concluded that I hadn't learned very much, except perhaps that Freckles was just another kid with a vivid imagination who liked hearing the sound of his own voice. Racing stables were full of them. They would carry their tales of corruption to the ears of anyone willing to listen. And the listeners always paid for the drinks.

I lit a cigarette and surveyed the cumulus of beer-sipping humanity which crowded in around me. As my eyes found Kelly and the boys, they also found Duncan Stroud. He'd joined our little gathering and was doing a lot of talking. Whatever he was saying was far too indistinct to decipher, but I could tell by the look on Kelly's face that it wasn't the kind of talk a lady likes hearing.

I made my way back to the table. Stroud was swaying slightly, his feet planted wide, his hands resting arrogantly on his hips. He was higher than a dolly-bird's platform shoes and his words were slipping from his lips in a disdainful slur.

'Y'don't look married t'me,' he was saying. 'Nice-looking chicks play the field, follow the money . . .'

'And ignore travelling head lads who think they're lady-killers.' Kelly retaliated.

'Huh!' He threw back his head and laughed. 'Well, stuck-up little madams are known to be as cold as bloody ice . . . And I bet you're a bloody dead loss in bed anyway.'

The crudeness of the remark had me balling my fist, ready to push it into his grinning unshaven face. If it had been anybody else or anywhere else I wouldn't have hesitated. Reluctantly I

49

uncurled my fingers, reminding myself that this was Duncan Stroud—McQuillan's right arm and Falloway's friend. If I threw the first punch I'd be branded a trouble-maker and I'd be off the assignment for sure.

'Hello, Preston.' He turned to face me, folding his arms in a way that enhanced the width of his chest. 'Lady Cecil Beaton here has jus' given me the bloody brush-off. Y'know I feel sorry for you, Preston . . . don't know why I should but I bloody do . . .'

'Duncan's bin drinking,' Riddle began hesitantly, ' 'E's not usually like—'

'Shuddup you bandy little bed-wetter!' Stroud abruptly cut him off. 'I don't need a kid who piddles his sheets to make excuses for me.' He shuttled towards Kelly, adding, 'That's why we call him Riddle, see . . . follow, do you?'

'Aw, bloodyell, don't tell'er that,' Riddle whimpered.

'Don't pick on him,' Freckles murmured. 'It's a weakness—he can't help it.'

'Pick on him? I don't have to pick on him! He's as thick as an Irish genius and good for bloody nothin' . . . except maybe . . .' He pulled a pound note from the pocket of his jeans and pushed it into Riddle's hand. 'Get me a scotch—a double—and don't tell that fat-gutted old landlord it's for me or I'll lop your bloody balls off!'

Riddle blushed as he glanced at Kelly. He snatched the pound from Stroud and departed. A group of people at the next table looked disapprovingly across at us. My early-warning system predicted trouble if we stayed. I told Kelly we were leaving.

'Now don't be bloody unsociable.' Stroud put a restraining hand on Kelly's shoulder. 'I wanna be friends . . . let's kiss and make up, huh?'

'I trust you're speaking metaphorically, Mr Stroud,' Kelly dug her nails into the soft flesh of his wrist, causing a hasty withdrawal of the hand. 'Because stuck-up little madams never kiss in public.'

Freckles grinned and Sparks smothered a laugh. Stroud didn't look happy. He unleashed a glare in my direction and for a moment I thought he was going to hit me.

'You oughta keep this bird of yours in a cage,' he said, the glare switching suddenly from me to the nail marks on his wrist. 'She nearly drew blood with those claws of hers.'

'Then keep your hands to yourself,' I growled. 'We came in here for a drink, not trouble.'

'So did I.' He wobbled unsteadily as he turned towards the bar. 'If Riddle's frigged off with my quid—'

'He's coming now,' Freckles told him.

' 'Bout bloody time.'

'Haven't you had enough,' Kelly said.

'I can never get enough,' he gave an erotic leer. 'Women and drink are my weaknesses—not gambling—I mustn't gamble . . .'

'All stable hands gamble,' I murmured.

'Not Duncan . . .' He swayed towards me, expelling high-octane breath as he chuckled, 'I mustn't you see—but you can —everybody can . . . shall I tell them?'

'You're smashed,' I said.

'Shall I tell them,' he repeated.

'Tell who?'

'*Them.*'

I turned away.

He cupped his hands to his mouth and yelled, '*Duncan's telling you all to back Paradise Kid tomorrow!*'

'For Chrissake,' Freckles looked worriedly at me as a stunned silence fell over the customers. 'Help me get him out of here, Mr Preston.'

'Let's go, Stroud,' I said.

'Go where . . . ?'

'Home.'

'I wan' my drink.'

'No chance.'

'I wan' my bloody drink!'

'Come on now, Stroudy,' Freckles coaxed, as the landlord

lifted the barflap and made his way towards us. 'We'll all get barred if you keep this up.'

I grabbed a handful of his shirt and began dragging him towards the exit. He didn't want to go. He dug in his heels and swung with a punch that threatened to take away half my jaw—only my jaw wasn't there. Like most drunks his timing was haywire. I'd already ducked and the force behind his swinging arm only served to carry him nearer the door.

He cursed viciously and called me a bastard. My temper snapped. It sent my fist soaring towards his face and it connected with a meaty thud.

I didn't hit him very hard, but then I didn't exactly pull my punch either. He raised his arms like stabilizer fins, taking a couple of slewed steps backward in an effort to keep his balance. It didn't do him much good. Slowly, bit by bit, inch by inch, his knees buckled and he keeled gently over, like a waxwork figure caught in the heat of a blast-furnace.

I was vaguely aware of the landlord standing at my side. 'I saw what happened, sir,' I heard him saying. 'In the circumstances he left you very little choice.'

Sparks and Freckles lifted Stroud's groaning body from the floor and taking an arm each prepared to hoist him outside. A chuckle filtered through the subdued murmur of voices and a cockneyfied accent announced, 'Luverly drop of Scotty, ber-utiful stuff this *Teacher's*.'

I figured the voice belonged to Riddle. I was damn sure it didn't belong to Stroud.

Chapter Four

RAIN, RAIN go away, come again another day. The sentiments seemed particularly appropriate at 8 a.m. on the following morning. Overnight the weather had taken a turn for the worse. Fine misty drizzle had invaded the western half of the country and this had gradually developed into heavy rain. The kind that soaks a three-quarter-length Burberry in two minutes flat and then insidiously drips anklewards and grafts trousers to legs. It was a hell of a way to start a new day.

Kelly and I had met at Chinhurst Lodge. I'd introduced her to a somewhat bemused Neil McQuillan and then offered my verbal support and a few lighthearted laughs as she tried to convince the trainer that weather conditions would improve and that some scheduled interior shots would fill the gap between that time and now. He'd seemed satisfied with the proposal especially when told that a portrait of himself was included in the schedule.

I hung around the yard waiting for the first string of horses to arrive back from the gallops. The stables had been transformed. Broken hinges had been mended, wooden structures creosoted, and grimy stone walls whitewashed. Sparks' sixteen-hour slog was certainly in evidence. With or without a *Racing Times* feature the overnight face-lift went part of the way to providing the visual encouragement needed to entice the right kind of clientele.

Roy Biggs, McQuillan's stable jockey, was riding the much publicized Paradise Kid in this afternoon's three-thirty at Penbury races. When I say much publicized, I'm referring to Stroud's drunken outburst in the Horse and Groom. Certainly the morning papers rated the Falloway nag's chances at zero.

I collared the jockey when he returned with the string. He'd heard of me, so he said, and yes, he'd be delighted if I interviewed him. We didn't use the office. It was clogged up with photographic equipment and McQuillan, looking preened and personable, was trying to adopt a casual pose at his desk, so we bypassed it and made for the tack-room. We sat opposite each other, using racing hampers as chairs, Biggs with a permanent rather unnerving smile on his chubby little sweat-soaked face, and me with a damp uncomfortable look on mine. We talked for the best part of two hours—or rather he did. Whatever the little guy lacked in stature he more than made up for with large unflagging vocal chords, and like most of the racing fraternity, he lived and breathed horses.

This was fine—I gave him the rostrum and listened. I learned very little. The meal was filling but badly lacking in sustenance. I threw in a few loaded questions, such as, 'Don't you think Double Top has improved immeasurably?' and 'Of course you as a jockey must take a lot of the credit for Counterfoil's out-of-the-blue win'. But Biggs, still with a smile on his cherubic little face, said that Double Top was the kind of horse which improves with every race and he couldn't have restrained him even if he'd wanted to. He shrugged off Counterfoil's £2,000 success as 'An easy ride—I merely piloted him home', and then rattled out a lot of garbage about Chinhurst horses being happy horses. Happy horses, he said, indicating that I should write this down, were horses without hang-ups and they responded in kind. They did their job. They won races.

'Is Paradise Kid a happy horse?' I asked him.

'Sure.'

'How do you define "happy"?'

'It's a state of mind.'

I tactfully pointed out that the Falloway horses appeared happier when on a race track than when off one, and rumour had it that none had shown much potential on the gallops at home. 'A happy state of mind can always be artificially induced,' I added.

'Huh?' He looked confused.

'A drunk is happy when he drinks,' I went on, 'a hippy is happy when he's numbing his brain with cannabis.'

This announcement tripped the spring that controlled his composure. It caused him to leap to his feet, ready to defend his honour as a jockey and the honour of Chinhurst. A hostile scowl replaced the smile and he looked decidedly angry.

I stood up too, and this served to remind him I was at least four inches taller and considerably heavier. Jockeys are hard, plucky little guys, strong as high-tensile steel, and they never back away from trouble, but I wasn't looking for any. I passed off my last remark as journalistic licence. I told him that if I was to do my job thoroughly, then I had to ask every type of question. I also told him I had no desire to discredit either his or the stables' good name. I always was a good liar. He calmed and the smile returned. I wound up the interview.

Outside, nothing had changed. Heavy rain spattered the travelling box as Len Potter, Duncan Stroud, and a couple of sodden stable lads coaxed a reluctant Paradise Kid up the ramp. It hadn't had a win in six races as a two-year-old, and in three outings this season it had only been placed once—and that in far minor company than it was meeting today. Whichever way you looked at it—and I hoped Potter would do plenty of looking —the Falloway horse could hardly be classed as a fistful of dynamite.

As Stroud fastened the ramp I could see a slight bluish swelling under his left eye. I doubted whether he remembered my punch, or indeed anything that happened that particular morning. McQuillan had made no mention of the incident and if there was going to be any retaliation on Stroud's behalf, then I reckoned it would have come by now. That was before he turned to look at me. It was a hard, penetrating look, the kind that broadcasted violence. I read it as nothing more than a telepathic warning, but I made a mental note to avoid dark alleyways just the same.

I watched the box trundle out of the yard. I thought about

Grant and his team of veterinary experts waiting at Penbury, ready to pounce with their equinal breathalysers if Paradise Kid decided to play the tipsters for suckers and tramp on the gas pedal.

Kelly was still busy taking snapshots when I eloped from McQuillan's and headed for Fransham. She had been rigged out in oilskins and was now doing a photographic tour of the loose-boxes. I wished her luck and arranged to meet her for dinner at the Eclipse Hotel.

I reached Fransham around a quarter after one. I grabbed a salami sandwich and coffee at a snack bar and then bent my steps in the direction of the public library. Dripping little pools of water on to the ratepayers' polished floor I foraged through the electoral register. I found 'The Cedars' and ran my finger down the list of names . . . BEXSON Gilbert, BYFORD Emily, FALLOWAY Alison, FALLOWAY Wesley. *Emily* struck a sharp chord in my memory. She, I figured, was the housekeeper with the tomato juice and Gilbert Bexson was the lager-drinking chauffeur. I remembered them well. Their highly suspicious repartee of yesterday was still uppermost in my mind. I jotted both names down in my pocket book, asked the librarian for directions to the nearest betting shop, then legged half a mile of pavement to find it. I stood with a dozen or so form-studying, pencil-chewing punters, and listened to Penbury's three-thirty over the blower system. Surprise, surprise, Paradise Kid ran its usual impotent sort of race and finished at the back of the field. Stroud wasn't going to be the most popular guy in the Horse and Groom. Had something gone badly wrong? With scrambled thoughts crowding in, I took a slow drive back to the motel, changed wet clothes for dry and tried to relax.

Biggs had unsettled me. I suppose listening to a person talk, the way Biggs could talk, was enough to unsettle anybody, but I had the feeling he knew a hell of a lot more about the suspect horses than he was letting on. He was confident, almost too confident. I reminded myself he had every reason to be. The guy had been talking to Preston, not Drake, he could afford to feel pleased—smug even. After all, he was reckoning on a well-written feature with his name spelled right, not the possible abolition of his jockey's licence.

I gathered my scattered impressions and temporarily shelved them. Remembering I had a dinner date, I grabbed my still wet Burberry and made tracks for Minehead.

Seven o'clock the lady had said, but six-thirty found me early and nursing the M.G.'s snout into the spacious hotel car park. With rain dimpling the puddles, I fought my way through the revolving door, entered the foyer and headed for the bar. The only thing that felt dry was my throat. I reckoned on equalling things up and getting a little wet on the inside for a change.

I lit a cigarette, ordered a Screwdriver, and blended smoke with alcohol as I took in the surroundings. The place was symbolic of today's with-it society and crammed with commercialized-tinselized trappings. A mixture of chrome fitments, garish murals, and multi-coloured neon. All standard equipment in the King's Road, but downright sacrilege in the reserved county of Somerset.

Gesticulating people sat in little groups around tinted glass tables. Middle-aged business men with diners cards, end-of-season tourists with more money than sense, wives, mistresses, mums, dads, even the odd drifter was thrown in to give the place a truly classless atmosphere.

'Hi!' The monosyllable cut through the circulation of muffled voices like a harpoon with my name etched on the blade.

I turned and located the sender. I saw Vicky Annesley picking her way towards me, her mane of blonde hair tumbling over slim shoulders. She was sheathed in a simple chiffon gown cut so low you almost had to bend down to pick it up and it housed what I judged to be a thirty-six bust undulating deliciously en route.

'Hi!' she said again, resting her shapely buttocks on a stool next to mine and leaning forward, 'Mr Prestwick, isn't it?'

'Preston,' I corrected, doing my best not to contemplate her highly noticeable cleavage. 'Twenty-eight years of age, unattached, all my own teeth, and no visible scars, except . . .' I indicated my broken nose. 'I was born beautiful but tragedies happen.'

She laughed. 'Preston, of course—how silly of me. And you work for the *Racing Times*—right?'

'That's the impression I try to give my editor.'

'Are you good?'

'I'm brilliant.'

'And modest too, I see.'

'I try.'

She laughed, tinkling the ice in her glass. 'Wesley tells me it's quite an accolade for Chinhurst Lodge to be featured in the *Racing Times*. Would you say that it was an accolade, Mr Preston?'

'I'd say Wesley was magnifying the importance of my magazine and I'd also say that he's an optimist. I haven't decided yet on any specific slant to adopt for the Chinhurst feature, let alone how to present it.'

'But you're not going to say nasty things, are you?'

'I never say nasty things, Mrs Annesley. I write the truth, state the facts as accurately as I can—editorial policy and all that, you know.'

Editorial policy? The words emerged under their own power and rolled off my tongue with such professional fluency that I surprised myself. I wasn't too sure what I meant, but it sounded pretty good and, anyway, Vicky Annesley had accepted the statement without so much as a bat from her long spiky lashes. She was now draining her glass and eyeing me over the rim. The eyeing tantamount to 'I don't know quite what to make of you, Mr Preston'.

'Tell me about yourself.' I fished around for something to say.

'There isn't much to tell.'

'You keep horses—that's a start.'

'My horses keep me poor. I do a little modelling and that pays some of the bills.'

'And what do you model?'

'Clothes.'

I grinned. 'I didn't think you modelled plasticine. Do you specialize in any particular mode, if that's the right word?'

'Swimwear mostly. I have the legs for it, so I'm told.'

'You have everything for it,' I said, more to myself than to her.

She lowered her lashes.

'So I write the kind of form men like to study, and you model the kind of form men like to study. We have something in common.'

'I suppose so,' she laughed again. 'You have a sweet way of putting things, Mr Preston.'

'Simon,' I told her. 'Every time you say Mr Preston I keep checking to see if my father's come into the bar.'

At first she looked a little uncertain. I smiled at her while she thought about it though, and eventually she smiled back and said, 'And you can call me Vicky.'

I did. I relieved her of her glass, and asked, 'What does Vicky drink with her ice?'

'Oh I couldn't,' she replied righteously. 'I'm waiting for Wesley, we're having dinner together.'

'Snap! I'm waiting for Kelly, we're having dinner together too. Kelly is my photographer by the way—now let me get you that drink.'

'No really,' she intercepted the glass. 'Wesley can be very funny. I'd rather not if you don't mind.'

Undeterred, I pointed out that Wesley wasn't here.

'By rights I shouldn't even be talking to you,' she said. 'He's very possessive. Not that I mind, you understand. It's rather nice to have a man's undivided attention, even the jealous kind. My ex-husband was so preoccupied with racing cars that consideration for people, and this goes double for me, was virtually non-existent.'

I countered with a question. 'Just to put my mind at rest— just so I don't do something drastic like changing my brand of

toothpaste, would you mind telling me who bought you that?'
I pinged the rim of her glass with my fingernail. 'Or do
unescorted ladies buy their own these days?'

'My brother, Eddie,' she pointed a silver-pink talon towards
a young fresh-faced, fair-haired guy who was necking with a
skinny looking dolly-bird in a cosy corner of the bar. 'He's a
second year student at Wroxford College. Eddie's girl friend
lives in Minehead, so Wesley suggested we made up a foursome
and all dined at the Eclipse.'

'Nice gesture,' I grunted.

'Mm, Eddie's playing truant today—say, why don't you and
your photographer join us and make it a sixsome. I know Wesley
wouldn't mind.'

'Thanks, I'll put the suggestion to Kelly.' I raised my glass
briefly to the brother who nodded in return. His girl friend
smiled sweetly.

'I'm sure you can talk her into it,' she said.

'I'll try,' I said.

She adjusted a sagging shoulder strap and turned towards
the door as Falloway made his on-cue entrance. I shook out a
cigarette and fished for a light, eyeing with faint rivalry the
actor's flawlessly white dress shirt and expensive black velvet
livery. He was certainly dressed for the part and looked to the
manner born. There was strut in all his movements, his carriage
was grandiose, almost arrogant, and he made my off-the-peg
mohair suit feel decidedly type-cast for Oxfam week.

'Darling!' Vicky Annesley threw her bare arms round his
neck and pressed sensuous lips to his. Feeling like the outsider
in a three-horse race, I dragged down a lungful of smoke and
idly perused the décor. 'Darling, this is Simon Preston,' she said
breathlessly, breaking the clinch. 'You remember we met him
on Sunday, he's from the *Racing Times*.'

Falloway manoeuvred his wide mouth into the semblance of
a smile and we crushed hands. 'Of course I remember Mr
Preston,' he said with a hint of cynicism. 'What a pleasant,
unanticipated surprise.'

I didn't like the guy and I was damned sure he didn't like me. The case aside, we were natural opposites. I didn't need a long association to find this out, I felt it every time he looked at me. The human race fell into various subdivisions with Falloway at one end of the personality make-up scale and me at the other. Either you gel or you don't. We didn't.

'Are you staying at the Eclipse?' He carefully selected a cigarette and fitted it into a short ebony holder.

'No such luxury,' I told him, watching his pupils dilate as he produced a flame from nine carats of gold Dunhill. 'I'm based at the Highway Motel.'

'Sounds cosy,' Vicky said.

'It'll do, at least until I've gathered enough material for the feature.'

'Ah yes, the feature—' Falloway blew twin wisps of smoke through slightly flared nostrils and eyed me with interest. 'I've been browsing through some past issues of the *Racing Times*, and to be perfectly frank, Mr Preston, I'm somewhat bewildered to find your magazine's apparent interest in the Chinhurst training establishment.'

'Really?'

'Let me put it this way. In the past you have always selected a high-ranking stable for your feature, perhaps the optimum that racing has to offer, but now you're nominating Neil McQuillan's as your stable of the month, and I find this a trifle inconsistent, to say the least.'

'So in your opinion, Chinhurst Lodge isn't worthy of the *Racing Times* spotlight?'

His thin lips tightened over the ebony holder. 'I'm simply pointing out that your magazine appears to be deviating from its traditional procedure of only featuring the best.'

'And Chinhurst Lodge doesn't fall into that category?'

'Hardly.'

'Then why keep your horses there, Mr Falloway?'

I expected some kind of hesitation on his part, a momentary gathering of thoughts, but his keen mind, trained in the

61

nuances of shrewdness, provided an instantaneous answer. 'Because my horses are winning,' he said, smiling tolerantly. 'Reason enough, wouldn't you say?'

I couldn't argue with logic like that, so I took a slow deliberate swallow of my drink and engaged another gear. 'My magazine isn't prejudiced against any racing stable,' I assured him. 'McQuillan's set-up may be small and commonplace, but we think he's a man who's definitely going places.' Probably the Nick, I thought, but added for Falloway's benefit, 'In the trainers' ratings, that is.'

Vicky Annesley watched me with quiet amusement. She sipped at some lemon-coloured potion with bits of vegetation dancing around in it and said between sips, 'Paradise Kid is the first disappointment Wesley's had. His horses really have been doing wonderfully well this season. I only wish some of their spirit would rub off on mine.'

There was something in the way she looked at me, something between the lines I couldn't quite figure. I felt the vibrations, the kind every man would feel when seated alongside a girl with her almost classical beauty, but there was also something more. Something in those violet blue eyes. Those big beautiful intoxicating eyes. The kind that can tear out a man's heart and then leave him to bleed all over his wallet. They would look at you, give every impression they were flirting with you, but at the same time leave you unsure. Leave you doubting your right to take anything for granted.

It was a game she had obviously played many times before. She represented the original blue-eyed blonde—but without the 'dumb' tie-label. I figured she also represented trouble, for me that is, in the shape of Wesley Falloway, but then nobody wins a prize without first buying a ticket and taking a little risk. And whether I liked it or not, and my common sense didn't, my heart had bought Vicky Annesley's ticket—hook, line and proverbial sinker.

'It was a much fancied horse,' I said matter-of-factly, looking at Falloway.

'Sorry?'

'Paradise Kid. It was strongly tipped to win.'

'You're mistaken, Preston. Neither the sporting press nor the National dailies gave it a mention.'

'True, but Duncan Stroud rated its chances very highly.'

He arched an eyebrow. 'Duncan told you that?'

'He made an announcement of the fact in the Horse and Groom.'

'Duncan made an . . .' He faltered, his eyes grappling with mine.

'He was pretty tanked-up, mind,' I pressed on, watching his every reaction. 'But he seemed so certain. It was probably the drink. He said some things that didn't make much sense.'

'What sort of things?' The words spilled out anxiously.

'Just things. Nothing of any consequence.' I shrugged it off.

He took a final pull on his cigarette and ejected the stub from its holder. 'If it concerns my horse, Mr Preston, then I've a right to know.'

I smiled, sipped slowly at my drink.

Vicky waited for the smoke to dissipate, then said, 'I've never liked Stroud. He drinks excessively and Wesley encourages this by being far too generous with his money.'

'Be quiet, darling,' Falloway snapped. 'I'm waiting for an answer from Mr Preston.'

'Stroud was adamant that Paradise Kid would win,' I said. 'He told everyone in the pub to back it. The funny thing was he had no intention of putting his money were his mouth was, if you'll excuse the expression.'

'Is that all?' Falloway smiled, a little relieved. 'In other words he didn't trust his own judgement. He was drunk and he thought he'd become everybody's friend by tipping a winner. He still had enough sense left to know he wasn't going to risk his own money on the horse. And of course, he was right.'

'A plausible explanation,' I agreed, 'only he didn't say he wasn't going to back the horse—he said he *mustn't* back it.'

'You obviously heard incorrectly.' His tone was sharp, dismissive.

'I never misquote. I can't afford to in my line of work—and anyway, he said it several times.'

'Have they changed the rules?' Vicky asked.

'The no-gambling rule only applies to jockeys and apprentices,' I told her. 'It doesn't include travelling head lads and suchlike.'

Falloway offered no further comment, merely looked into his glass as though its contents would give him divine guidance. I didn't pursue the subject. It was obvious that Stroud was under orders not to bet because a big win would throw suspicion in his direction. The horse had been set up to win all right, but something unforeseen had stopped this from happening.

'Duncan Stroud is drinking your money away,' Vicky pointed out. 'You're far too generous and it's got to stop.'

'Don't start that again,' Falloway countered, 'you know it's customary to give presents.'

'Presents, yes, darling; an open cheque, no.'

I said, 'The lads receive two and a half per cent of the prize money as a matter of procedure, don't they?' I knew damn well that they did, but I liked the conversational drift, so I stoked up the fire.

Vicky threw an appraising glance at the floor. 'Two and a half per cent didn't buy Duncan Stroud a new Hillman Imp.'

'Hillman Imp?' The chat was beginning to bear fruit. I turned to Falloway, laying it on. 'You bought Stroud . . . ? That was very charitable of you.'

He didn't reply so I kicked him on. 'That might be just what my feature needs—a bit of human-interest stuff, some light relief from the horsy statistics.' I snapped inspirational fingers under his nose, and added, 'How about—"Owner buys travelling head lad new car for services rendered".'

It was a headline loaded with innuendo and it caused the spurs to bite deep, very near to the heart. Falloway stiffened like an apprehensive yearling and spilled a little Bacardi on his velvet lapel. 'What the hell are you insinuating?' he growled, reaching frantically for a handkerchief. 'Just how the hell am I supposed to interpret a remark like that?'

Exactly the way you already have, Wesley baby, I thought, but I said, 'Hey, take it easy. You've obviously read something into my words which wasn't intended.'

'You're damn right I have.'

'I apologize,' I said humbly. 'I appear to have unwittingly touched an exposed nerve. Stupid of me, I'm sorry . . .'

'I don't think you're stupid, Preston, in fact I'm damn sure you're not.'

'Is that a compliment, Mr Falloway?'

'I'll let your imagination decide that. I'm not sure what your motives are, only that you're doing your best to provoke me.'

'I deny that categorically,' I said.

'And for your information,' he went on, 'I didn't buy Stroud the car. The money was given in the form of an interest-free loan. I expect to get it back—all of it.'

'Stop this at once!' Vicky Annesley shook her pretty little head, the movement causing her breasts to quiver tantalizingly against the thin chiffon gown. 'You're both behaving like adolescents, and I don't want this silly bickering to drag on over dinner.'

'Over dinner?' Falloway raised a questioning eyebrow.

Vicky explained and he didn't like it. His tan lost some of its lustre, and he said quickly, 'I'm afraid that's out of the question, darling. I've only reserved a table for four.'

'But surely a little word in the manager's ear—'

'The place is crowded, Vicky darling,' he offered her a travesty of a grin. 'I doubt if a big word or an even bigger bribe could secure us a table for six tonight.'

I acknowledged the forced, artificial humour with a subtle smile. 'Please don't resort to bribery on my account,' I said. 'You'll find I'm not the appreciative type.'

He glared at me, threw Vicky Annesley a critical look and growled something about cancelling his subscription to the *Racing Times*. I avoided looking at his riveting eyes or making any comment. Instead I wrapped a hand round his near-empty glass and offered to open my wallet as a peace offering.

'Some other time,' he said acidly, consulting his wristwatch. 'I've a heavy day's filming tomorrow—if you'll excuse me, I think we had better eat.'

'Well hello!' Kelly's voice found my ear. I turned to find her at my elbow. 'Sorry I'm a little late.' She smiled at Falloway. 'Well, aren't you going to introduce me, Simon?'

Falloway smiled back with strained politeness as I made the brief introductions. Vicky offered Kelly her stool and commented that brother Eddie and the dolly-bird were nowhere to be seen. This prompted Falloway to repeat his 'heavy day's filming' routine and it put a few feet of broadloom between them and us before Vicky pouted, 'Nice to have met you again, Mr Preston. We're bound to see more of each other, I'm sure.'

I was sure too. I said, 'Don't forget I want to ask you some searching questions sometime?'

'I think not,' Falloway put in. 'I think we've both had enough of your questions.'

'Now don't be rude, Wesley,' Vicky said. 'Mr Preston is only trying to do his job.'

'Then I suggest he does it in an ethical manner.' He looked at me shrewdly. 'Tell me, does Dexter Stone still work on your journal?'

'Dexter Stone . . . ?' The name caught me off guard. 'Er . . . yes, he does—in a manner of speaking.'

'In a manner of speaking?' he said scathingly. 'What kind of answer is that? Does he or doesn't he?'

'What Simon means is he's now freelance,' Kelly came to my rescue. 'Dexter retired a few months ago but he still contributes the occasional piece of copy.'

'I see.' Falloway's eyes never left my face, but he seemed satisfied. 'It's a pity he isn't doing the write-up on Chinhurst. The old hands are always the best.'

'But a new broom sweeps clean,' I countered, 'and my bristles are very sharp. Sharp enough to do their job thoroughly.'

Falloway bridled at me like a fighting cock. 'Mr Preston, may I say with the greatest respect to your lady photographer, go to bloody hell!'

With that final thrust he turned on his heel and whisked Vicky Annesley out of the bar. I found myself smiling, I couldn't help it.

'You asked for that,' Kelly said.

I shifted on my stool, looked at those big brown eyes under the fringe of red hair. 'I know,' I said. 'I must take a home-study course in sociability.'

'Clash of personalities?'

'Something like that. Thanks for helping me out with that Dexter Stone business. Falloway very nearly tripped me up.'

'I have a habit of materializing when needed.'

'If you'd been any later, well . . .'

'Was he trying to catch you out?'

I shrugged. 'Who knows. What I can tell you is he's right up to his velvet bow-tie in the manipulation of racehorses.'

'Significant evidence, or Simon Drake intuition?'

I bought her a dry Martini and told her about Duncan Stroud and the new Hillman Imp. She didn't seem surprised. She said, 'Perhaps he's traded his special knowledge for the car.'

'Stroud? Special knowledge?'

'Uh-huh. After leaving school he worked for a couple of years as a veterinary assistant and then gave it up and went into racing.'

'That wasn't in the dossier?'

'I had to move a lot of rubble to find it out myself. Stable lads are very talkative about sex and gambling, and who won what and where, but when it comes to boring, immaterial conversation such as Duncan Stroud's veterinary ability, they aren't exactly overflowing with information.'

'So who?' I quirked an eyebrow at her.

'Quilly,' she said.

'McQuillan?'

'Mm, sorry—only the lads call him things like Quilly the

claw and Mac the knife. After listening to it all day long, you tend to become addicted.' She rounded up a droplet of Martini that had escaped down the stem of her glass, and went on, 'Quilly mentioned it in passing. He said that Duncan often saves him money in vet's fees, and then he clarified the point by telling me about the boy's past experience.' She smiled, and added, wistfully, 'Quilly's not a bit like I expected—he's really quite a sweetie.'

'So by all accounts was Bluebeard,' I pointed out. 'Now what else did you manage to uncover?'

She pulled a face, shrugged, and gazed at me despondently over the rim of her glass. 'Only that Quilly talks an awful lot about the future. He's a bit of a dreamer. He gives the impression he's only an arm's length away from that mythical crock of gold at the end of the rainbow.'

'Perhaps it isn't so mythical. Somewhere there's big coinage involved—there has to be—and I'm not talking about a paltry few thousand in prize money.'

She beckoned me closer, breathed in my ear, 'Howard Grant telephoned the stables just after you'd left. He passed himself off as the picture editor. He wanted to speak to you and he sounded worried.'

'Any message?'

'He said something had come up to change the situation, that's all.'

'As if we haven't enough mysteries on our hands,' I murmured. 'Did you manage to tackle Potter about Paradise Kid?'

'Oops!' She flushed guiltily and finished her drink in a gulp.

I looked at her. The brown eyes blinked rapidly.

'I'd forgotten all about Potter,' she said.

'Don't worry, I'll see him tomorrow.'

'No, you don't understand, Simon. I'd forgotten about him because he never came back.'

'He what?'

'The travelling box came back, Duncan Stroud came back, but Len Potter didn't.'

I cursed audibly. 'I bet the little rat's bunked off.'

'Well he can't have bunked very far, his scooter is still there.'

I told her we'd better check to see if he was at the motel. She grabbed her coat and together we weaved our way through the gusty alcoholic laughter. I gave the restaurant a wide berth and tried desperately to ignore the succulent aroma of duckling nambucca, chicken diable, and pork Tahiti—all of which were on the menu outside, and none of which helped to restrain my hunger pangs or dampen my ill-feelings towards Potter. The frivolous names didn't bother me; in my present famished condition I would have willingly settled for a Wimpy and chips.

Rain leaked mournfully from the sombre sky. Neon-lit rivulets of water coursed their way gutterwards as we left the anonymous blur of voices behind us and headed for the car. Kelly, swathed in an orange anorak and a twenties newsboy-style cap looked a hell of a lot prettier than the dilemma in which I now found myself. I tried to smile, it wasn't easy. I manoeuvred the M.G. out of the car park and pushed four rather wet alloy wheels towards the Highway Motel.

'Wesley Falloway's very dishy.' Kelly switched on the map-light, took a compact from her shoulder bag and started doing things to her face. 'He's a real smoothie, quite definitely a ladies' man.'

I grunted. 'With a flattering line in chat to knock vulnerable females right on their pretty little ears.'

She dimpled at me. 'You like her a lot, don't you?'

'Her?'

'Vicky Annesley.'

'Do I?'

'Mm, I think you do. I also think you like her more than you care to admit, and this increases your animosity towards Wesley Falloway.'

'Personal feelings don't enter into it,' I hedged.

'Oh no?' She eyed me via the mirror of her compact.

'No.' I flicked her a penetrating glance. 'Are you trying to psychoanalyse me or something?'

'I can see the beginnings of a witch-hunt, that's all.'

'Falloway's on the fiddle,' I stated emphatically. 'Don't ask me why he's doing it or how he's doing it—I only know that he is. I know because every time he looks at me a fundamental instinct tells me he's a villain.'

I wanted to add that it was going to be a pleasure for me to be instrumental in bringing him down at the last hurdle, but I figured that Kelly would interpret this as some kind of vindictive mania, so I switched the subject to McQuillan and Stroud.

We talked. The wipers slapped rhythmically across the windscreen and the M.G. ate up the mileage. I told her I didn't need to consult my detective manual in order to work out that Stroud was in Falloway's pocket and I also mentioned for the record that McQuillan wouldn't be the first trainer to get into financial difficulties, or to take 'fixing' measures to get out of them.

'Early days, Simon.' Kelly remained noncommital.

'It's the motive that worries me,' I said. 'The fact that the cash gained doesn't warrant the risk taken. It's crazy.'

'Then it has to be prestige.'

'That's crazy too. No amount of clever editing can turn a penny dreadful into a *chef-d'œuvre*.'

'Give it time, Simon. Something will emerge—you'll see.'

I hardly heard her. I was trying to cope with the inky blackness outside, the deluge of rain doing its goddamn best to obscure my vision, and more particularly, I was attempting to organize my thoughts. Something was worrying me, chewing around the edges of my subconscious, something I should have latched on to but hadn't. The unsettling thought finally hit me as we turned into the motel entrance. As the yellow arc from my headlights illuminated chalet number ten, I remembered.

I killed the motor, said to Kelly, 'Had you met or seen Vicky Annesley before tonight?'

'Huh?' She frowned, blinked twice.

I repeated the question and added, 'What about at McQuillan's was she there?'

'No. Why this sudden interest? . . .'

'Or Falloway—did he drop in?'

'I met them both for the first time tonight in the Eclipse bar . . . Hey, what gives?'

'Vicky Annesley knew you were a woman, that's what gives. With a name like Kelly, and photography being a predominantly male profession, she should have assumed you were a man, or at least questioned the point. But she didn't. We were talking about dinner she said something about making it a sixsome and I said I'd have to check it out with you—Kelly that is. Her very words were, "I'm sure you can talk her into it". She knew don't you see?'

'She could have spoken to McQuillan on the telephone and he could have mentioned it in passing.'

'She could have spoken to Falloway and he could have mentioned it in passing, that's more likely.'

'Meaning Stroud told him?'

'Well I doubt if he fraternizes with Riddle and Co.' I looked at her, 'Kelly, sweetheart, they're keeping tabs on our activities. Our presence is shaking them up and they're beginning to make mistakes—like Falloway telling Vicky about you—now that was careless.'

'Perhaps . . .' She leaned forward clasping her knees, eyeing me perceptibly. 'Perhaps it was Vicky Annesley who was careless. Perhaps Falloway didn't mention me at all. Perhaps Mrs Annesley knows more about this business than meets the eye.'

Perhaps her perhapses were right and she had a point. I didn't labour on it. I lit a cigarette, breathed smoke and scanned the surrounding murk for any sign of Potter. The cold grey light of a television screen flickered in a distant window. The tinny refrains of a pop-record percolated through the inky wetness. Somewhere a baby was crying.

I just sat smoking and thinking. Thinking about Vicky,

trying to discount any notions that she was involved, and yet all the time wondering if she was something more than just Falloway's playmate. I was suddenly asking myself questions I hadn't bothered to ask before. Probing questions, such as, why had she transferred her horses to McQuillan's? And was it just coincidence that shortly after meeting her, Falloway had started his winning run? The questions were easy, the problem was getting the right kind of answers and I was getting the worst kind. The ambiguous kind that could throttle a beautiful friendship and leave me trailing the field. I lowered my window an inch, tossed out my half-smoked cigarette and watched it flicker and dance as the rain carried it away. It was then I saw Potter, or rather heard the rim of his crash helmet as it tapped lightly against the glass.

'Thank Christ you're 'ere,' he said shakily. 'I've bin 'angin' around the car park for the last two hours.'

His face had gone a mottled chalky colour. Covered with a cerecloth he could have doubled for a week-old corpse. I said nothing. I watched the water drip from his visor and settle on his upper lip, watched his tongue as with an adder-like movement it flicked out and quickly soaked up the liquid irritation.

'I ain't goin' back to Chinhurst,' he stammered, 'I ain't goin' back . . . never. Stroudy's off 'is bleedin' rocker, Drakey . . . a nutter, I tellya.'

'Whatever's happened?' Kelly asked.

'Stroudy's murdered Paradise Kid, ain't 'e, that's wot's 'appened. He's butchered the poor bleeder . . . Oh, my Christ . . .'

Chapter Five

THE INSALUBRIOUS sight of my damp morning clothes lying in an untidy little pile by my bed was the first thing to hit me as I stepped into the chalet and snicked on the light. I hadn't been counting on having visitors, or returning quite so sober.

I peeled off my rain-impregnated Burberry and straddled a chair. Len Potter slouched his way in, removed his crash helmet, and finger-combed lank hair out of his eyes so that he could see me better. His hands had developed a definite tremor and he was saying continuously: 'Stroud's a raving nutter, I tellya, a raving nutter . . .'

'Take off your jacket and sit down,' I ordered.

'I ain't never seen nuffin' like it in me life . . .'

'Take it slow, easy, and try making sense.'

'Killed ole Paradise, ain't they,' he said at last.

'They?' Kelly queried.

'The Chinhurst mob. Duncan bloody Stroud—he done it. Clocks 'im wiv me own eyes, dun I? Blood everywhere there was. I nearly puked. I very nearly puked.'

'Where?' I asked.

'Penbury races, o' course. Stroudy dun for ole Paradise in the travelling box. Carved the poor bleeder up. Ain't 'uman is it, eh?'

I turned to Kelly. 'But you saw the box come back, why didn't you mention . . . ?'

'Because when the box returned to Chinhurst,' she said, anticipating my question, 'Paradise Kid was alive, unmarked, and kicking.'

'You're sure?'

'I'm very sure.'

'Don't ponce abaht,' Potter cut in. 'I sees wot I see and I

tellya Stroudy put the boot in. No 'orse loses blood like I see and lives.'

'How much blood?' I faced him squarely.

'Looked like gallons t'me. The box was smuvvered wiv it, all red and glis'nin' drippin' down the walls. Christ, it were 'orrible.'

Macabre was the word I would have used. What a flesh-creeping picture this kid Potter could paint. It triggered off wild thoughts and sent them skittering around my brain. Ostensibly the boy looked stunned and frightened and if it hadn't been for these visible signals I would have dismissed his story as claptrap and kicked his backside out of the door. Len Potter had seen something all right, something important and something that didn't make a lot of sense. I said, 'How come Stroud allowed you to watch this gory spectacle?'

He worried the pockets of his jeans, offered no comment. 'Got a snout, Drakey?' he said finally. 'I'm clean out and I'm sufferin' from withdrawal symptoms.'

I threw him my pack. I watched patiently as he selected a cigarette and lit it with stained fingers. Kelly suggested coffee and telephoned room service.

'I'd prefer a drop of the 'ard stuff,' Potter said.

'You'll get what you're given,' I retorted. 'Now quit with the requests for creature comforts and start talking about Stroud.'

'What d'yer wanna know?'

Harnessing my temper, I repeated my earlier question.

'Well we arrives at Penbury Races early, see. Stroudy says 'e wants a doze in the cab and 'e tells me and the box driver t'piss orf to the canteen fer an hour and an 'arf.'

'But you came back early.'

'Right on, Drakey. I creeps back after abaht ten minutes and wot d'yer know—Stroudy ain't in the cab 'avin' a quick forty at all. The sod's in the box wiv ole Paradise, ain't 'e.' He paused to pull nicotine into his lungs, then went on, 'So I walks round to the little door at the side and I pulls it open abaht an inch to 'ave a butchers. Well, holy shit—I 'ears this crash, I sees

74

ole Paradise buckin' and rearin' and all this blood . . .'

'And Stroud?'

'Well, 'e went crazy. I ain't never seen such a crazy look in a bloke's eyes before. Put the fear of Christ into me, I can tellya. I ran, Drakey, I ran like I'd bin sprung from trap six. When I reached the main road I started thumbin' and 'itched it back to Chinhurst.'

I unravelled myself from the chair, and did a quick walk to the door and back. I didn't need the exercise, but I was getting pretty sick of looking at Potter's pasty complexion, and anyway, I hoped the change of scenery might aid my concentration. Some kind of continuity was beginning to emerge from the kid's ravings, but just what it all meant in terms of solving the case was anybody's guess.

'Why go back to Chinhurst?' Kelly's voice penetrated my thoughts. She opened the door for the chalet maid, distributed cups of steaming coffee and parked herself opposite Potter.

'Well, it weren't thru choice, miss,' he told her, 'I went back t'swipe me gear and me scooter. 'Ad to leave me scooter though, might've bin seen.' He sucked noisily at his coffee and added, 'Luverly drop of Nescaff, I sure 'prishiate it.'

Steering the drift back to Paradise Kid, I asked him to explain how an apparently mutilated racehorse could gallop over a mile of Penbury turf and then arrive back at McQuillan's looking none the worse for its ordeal.

'Huh?' His mouth sagged at the corners.

'The horse ran in the three-thirty, Lennie,' I said. 'It didn't finish in the frame, but it ran nevertheless.'

'But it can't 'ave . . .'

'But it did.'

'Sod me.'

'And it certainly looked fit when I saw it only a few hours ago,' Kelly pointed out.

'You ain't callin' me a liar are yer?'

'We don't have to, Lennie,' I murmured mildly, 'you *are* a liar, that fact isn't in dispute.'

75

'Now look 'ere, Drakey . . .'

'No, you look, Lennie. Agreeing everything—Stroud, the travelling box, the gallons of dripping blood—Why, Lennie? What's it all about? You tell me.'

He looked at Kelly as though she should know all the answers. She looked at him as though she didn't. She said, 'I think I have half of the picture. It's obvious that Len disturbed Stroud at a critical moment, probably while he was administering the stimulant or whatever. Agreed?'

'Agreed.'

'Well, when things went wrong, Stroud was faced with either pulling the horse out or letting it run. As the former would presumably bring official enquiries, he kept his cool and went for the latter. We all know that on merit alone Paradise Kid didn't stand a hope of winning, but to allay any suspicions Stroud had to act naturally—even if the result was a disaster.'

I smiled in spite of myself. Grant would have been proud of her. I said, 'Any ideas about the blood?'

'Could Stroud have severed a vein?'

'He could have, but Paradise Kid would have bled to death before reaching the stalls.'

'A broken blood-vessel, then?'

'Another possibility, but it wouldn't produce anywhere near the quantity of blood that Potter described.'

She shrugged, sighed. Potter, who had been listening to Kelly's hypothesis with owlish interest, offered no comment, constructive or otherwise. He merely drained his cup of coffee, belched with feeling, and said, 'Oops, manners.'

I told him to climb into his jacket, said the conference was at an end. 'You got plans or sump'n?' he said.

'You're going back to London,' I said.

'I ain't goin' nowhere wivout me bike. I got plans of me own.'

'Like what?'

'Like creepin' back to Quilly's place when they're all kippin' and gettin' me bike.'

76

I smiled slowly. 'What's the matter with you. You got a death-wish or something?'

'Do wot?'

'A death-wish, Lennie. Stroud's no fool—he's going to expect you to come back for your bike—he's going to be waiting for you to put your grubby little bum on the saddle and then quietly, oh yes, ever so quietly, he's going to *slit your bloody throat!*'

He flinched, turned away. 'Gawd, do me a favour, will yer.'

I amplified my point by giving him a light but accurately placed straight-fingered jab in the vitals. This had the effect of recapturing his full attention. He made some sort of gurgling noise and he coughed a little, but he listened.

'Don't get me wrong, Lennie,' I went on, 'I wouldn't light a candle for you if you were discovered hanging by a head collar in the tack-room. In fact, I can honestly say that you wouldn't be a great loss to either me or the T.S.D. But what really makes me nervous is the thought of your overactive mouth during those few brief seconds that Stroud would allow before he screwed you.'

'Oh t-ta,' he said between coughs, 't-ta a lot.'

Experience had taught me that the racing game attracted more than its fair share of loudmouths. Freckles was a prime illustration. He only needed his larynx lubricated with a couple of drinks and he was spouting off about bent jocks and their various fiddles. Most of these had been picked up third or fourth hand, and all had been added to or sensationalized to impress the listener. Now Stroud wasn't the impressionable type. He was going to be after facts rather than fantasy, and Potter, like his counterparts, had the mouth to supply them.

'Start thumbing, Lennie,' I said, 'you've an appointment with Howard Grant.'

'I-I want me bike.'

'No chance, kiddo, start thumbing.'

'I want me bloody bike,' he said again, with more emphasis this time, 'and I ain't goin' nowhere till I git it.'

77

'Now listen . . .' I caught hold of his left ear and twisted it just enough to bring tears to his eyes. 'You clench your fist nice and tight, you stick your thumb up nice and high, and you make like you're pulling free beer at the Horse and Groom—Got it?'

'Ahh, leggo!' he squealed, 'you ain't gonna make me . . . you ain't!'

I looked at Kelly. She shook her head, said amusedly, 'You ain't you know, you definitely ain't.'

I reckoned she was right. I released my grip, sucked thoughtfully on a back tooth and said, 'Then we all go to Chinhurst to get his bike. We'll do it carefully and professionally, and while we're on the premises we'll take a look inside this famous travelling box.'

I didn't like impulse decisions or being forced into corners, but in for a penny, in for a pound, as the saying goes.

I raked out my old windcheater, flat cap, and rubber boots, telling myself that there was no moon and that the bad weather had put the odds in our favour. I began to brighten but it didn't stop me wondering just what or who it would take to sabotage this comparatively simple operation. My earlier fears began burrowing into my skull.

Stroud, I figured. If we weren't very damn careful, quite definitely Duncan Stroud.

It was five before midnight when we reached Chinhurst Stables. I'd killed a bit of time by stopping at a fish-and-chip shop, and Kelly and I made up for the lost meal at the Eclipse by gorging ourselves on cod, chips and peas. It wasn't *haute cuisine*, but it stopped those demanding rumbles from my stomach.

On arrival at McQuillan's, I bulled the M.G. into the under-growth and removed torches from the glove-box. I asked Kelly to wait in the car. I pointed out that a wall would have to be climbed and that the filthy October weather didn't exactly lend itself to this sort of precarious activity.

She didn't like the idea. The fact that she'd been born a

78

woman had never deterred her from rubbing shoulders with a little danger. If women jockeys could compete against men and win, she said, then she could climb walls along with the best of them. She could as well. Without any help from me she hoisted herself over the crumbling brickwork and dropped silently into the yard. Potter and I followed.

I snapped on the torch, said cautiously, 'Where's the travelling box?'

'Back o' the 'ouse,' Potter said, chewing intermittently at his skimpy lips. ' 'Ere, ain't we gettin' me bike first?'

'Later, Lennie, the bike comes later.'

'But, Drakey . . .'

'Now don't bloody start,' I wagged a finger in his face. 'If you start again I'll remove the sparking plugs from this bike of yours, toss them into the dung heap, and you can spend the rest of the night groping about for them.'

'Oh-kay, oh-kay.' He showed me his teeth, not the prettiest of sights.

'Let's go.' Kelly nudged us into action. Keeping tightly together we sprinted across the expanse of yard and took shelter under the overhanging eaves of the barn. I did a visual reconnaissance of the loose boxes, outbuildings and surrounding area. Everything appeared quiet, normal. The Lodge was in total darkness. The entire Chinhurst work-force was cocooned in a world of sleep. I hoped.

'Over there, see?' Potter indicated the hazy shape of the old travelling box.

'Seems peaceful enough,' Kelly said.

I told them both to stay put and to wait for my signal. Hunched in the wetness of my windcheater and choosing the most indirect route I could find, I cat-footed it to the box.

I peered into every dim corner. If some unfriendly guy was waiting in those gloomy shadows then I was offering myself like the fabled lamb to the slaughter.

Stealthily I approached the cab, satisfied myself that it was empty and worked my way round to the small side door. I'd reckoned on finding it locked, but the handle twisted in my fingers and it opened silently and easily. The beam from my torch illuminated the black compartment, exposing a tenantless interior. I released my reflexes a couple of degrees and flashed a signal towards the barn.

Kelly arrived first. I clambered into the box and hoisted her up. 'Glad you could make it,' I said.

She thumbed her torch into action and began sniffing at the stale air, like a puppy sniffs at its master's shoes.

'Bleach,' she informed me. 'Somebody's been using bleach.'

I was about to agree but got side-tracked by Potter as he levered himself in to meet us.

'Safe, is it?' he asked, adding, 'Stroof, stinks worse than a navvy's jock-strap.'

Kelly was down on all fours inspecting the floor. The grimy well-worn wooden boards were damp to the touch and had been bleached almost white in places.

'Stroudy's a fast worker, ain't 'e,' Potter said, reading my mind.

I asked him to reconstruct where Stroud and the horse had been standing during the episode with the blood.

'Ferchrissake, Drakey,' he whined, 'we ain't got time fer all this poncin' around. I want me bike and then I want out.'

'You'll get both when we've examined this box.'

'Waste o' time if yer ask me.'

'I didn't ask you.'

'No yer didn't, so I'm tellin' yer, ain't I. There's nuffin' 'ere, Drakey . . . you're gonna get us all dun over fer nuffin'.'

Kelly let out a squeak of delight and beckoned with the torch. 'Seek and ye shall find; knock and it shall be opened unto you,' she said eagerly, adding, 'I'm knocking but I'm going to need your help for the opening bit.'

Suppressing thoughts of manslaughter I ignored Potter's surly face and joined Kelly on the floor.

'It's a piece of glass,' she informed me, probing with a nail file between a gap in the floorboards. 'There's part of a label on it and if we're careful we might be able to salvage it.'

We were careful, and we did. The broken edges of the glass were encrusted with a brownish-red substance, which, if Potter's story held true, was presumably blood. The label was still soggy from the bleach that had leaked through the floorboards, but although washed out in places the wispy, almost juvenile, handwriting was still partially visible.

'Shouldn't be too difficult to decipher,' Kelly beamed her torch at the faded scrawl. 'I think it reads : *A sedative, September fourteenth.*' She looked at me, blinked those big brown eyes. 'Golly, could this be what's known in criminology circles as a lucky break?'

I studied the words on the label. They had been written in pencil and the brownish oversplash didn't improve their clarity. 'I figure it the same way as you,' I said, 'but a sedative . . . ?' I shrugged.

'A sedative has a tranquillizing effect, right?'

'Right.'

'Not the ideal drug to pep-up a racehorse.'

'Pep-down, more like.'

'Humph.' She mentally chewed on her thoughts for a few seconds, then said, 'Up a ladder and down a snake, I'd say.'

'Maybe. We'll let Grant decide that. Potter can take the label and the glass . . .' I stopped and instinctively swung towards the door, panning with the torch. 'Where the hell . . . ?'

The beam of light found no one. Len Potter had decided to go it alone.

Kelly tugged at her bottom lip. 'You don't think . . . ? The bike?'

I told her I most certainly did think. 'I'll break his bloody neck,' I said.

Leaving the sanctuary of the travelling box we headed for the garage. With the cold driving rain slanting pitilessly in our faces we scooted across the yard, paused briefly at the tack-room to catch our breath and negotiated the last twenty feet to our objective with deadly caution.

A minute elapsed as we crouched behind a battery of dustbins. Kelly clung silently to my arm, breath bated, peering into the pitchy darkness. The rain hammered relentlessly at our bent backs as we watched and heard the shadowy shape of Len Potter fiddling with his scooter, rocking the machine off its stand.

'What are we waiting for?' Kelly clutched my arm more tightly.

'You'll see,' I said.

Intuition, insight, sixth sense, you name it, told me that we weren't the only ones watching the boy's activites. They say you can feel these things in your bones, well all my bones could feel were wet trousers clinging to even wetter legs, but I knew all right, and discomfort or not, I was staying put.

It took no more than a couple of revolutions from the scooter's wheels before my hunch was proved right. Twin cones of light from what had previously appeared as an obscure lifeless shape, set the garage interior ablaze. I felt Kelly stiffen, saw Potter freeze in his tracks, as Duncan Stroud climbed from the driving seat of his very new, very shiny, Hillman Imp.

'He's got a crowbar,' Kelly whispered.

I nodded, eyes fixed unblinkingly upon Stroud.

'You'll have to do something soon.'

I nodded again, my breathing and pulse rate had quickened. It wasn't because I felt duty bound to save the kid's skin, but self-preservation told me I had to save his trigger-happy mouth.

An empty bran sack, hanging by a nail on the open garage door, offered a way out of my present dilemma. For obvious reasons I had to act without Stroud actually seeing me, and the sack, I figured, was my one means of achieving this. I told myself that the element of surprise was on my side, that Stroud had his back towards me, and that Potter wouldn't give me away because the Imp's headlights shone directly into his eyes. I clenched down on my teeth, broke cover, and inched my way towards the garage.

'I knew you'd come back,' Stroud was saying, swinging the crowbar in front of him, laughing as Potter retreated hastily to the far wall. 'You're so predictable, Len, so bloody predictable.'

'Take it easy . . . Listen, Stroudy . . . Fer Christ's sake . . .' Potter was gabbling, stuttering, talking in snatches.

Stroud advanced. The crowbar was now held like a fencing sword in his outstretched hand and with a sudden explosive movement he lunged forward, jamming the bent end under the boy's Adam's apple, pinning him against the wall. Potter gave a half-scream, half gurgle, and froze in submission.

'There's something I want to know,' Stroud said, the harsh pitch of his voice loud enough to cover my footsteps. 'When we were at Penbury . . .' He didn't finish the sentence. I ripped the sack from the nail and rammed it over his head knocking the crowbar from his hand with my forearm.

He cried out and struggled awkwardly, his entrapped arms threshing in anger and terror. As he tried frantically to get free, I spun him round and despatched my knuckles towards the piece of bone which jutted out invitingly below his squirming lips. It was an accurately placed blow—and, as this was the second time he'd found himself on the wrong end of my fist, it was a habit-forming one. He crumpled. His legs bowed like a couple of fruit-laden branches, and he collapsed at my feet like a tent with its guy ropes cut.

'Boy, that was close.' I found Kelly at my side. She stepped over Stroud's inert body and killed the Imp's lights.

'That was timing,' I grinned.

She didn't answer, just wrinkled her freckled nose at me.

Potter, still dazed by the chaotic sequence, wobbled his way towards us. 'Killed 'im, ain'tcher?'

'Stunned,' I said. 'He'll be all right.'

'Looks dead t'me.'

'Paradise Kid looked dead to you,' I growled. 'So before you issue any more of your bogus death certificates, I suggest you take stock of your own position and get going while I'm still in a merciful mood.'

Kelly asked how he proposed to get the bike out.

'No sweat. There's a gate in the wall, the key's on the inside.'

'Be careful,' she said.

He nodded, looked at me. 'See yer, Drakey.'

'I hope not, Lennie.'

He curled his lip in an unsavoury smile and taking a grip on his scooter, slouched off into the darkness. I felt my nerve-ends relax, but only momentarily. Stroud, breathing unrhythmically at my feet, soon jerked me towards the problems of the present.

'We'd better put him back in the Imp,' I said. 'With luck he'll sleep until morning, and with his sackful of obscure memories, he's going to have a hard time figuring things out.'

As I didn't want him to suffocate I removed the hessian restrainer, dusted him off, and with me taking a grip under his armpits and Kelly steadying his ankles, we manoeuvred his bony frame into the driving seat.

Kelly was grinning, she obviously found it all very amusing. I was far from happy with the way things had turned out. I suppose it had a funny side, and tomorrow when I recalled it I might grin too. At the moment I felt annoyed that Potter's stupidity had once again exposed me to what could have developed into a highly volatile confrontation. With Kelly and me committing the act of trespass, Stroud, I reckoned, wouldn't have needed any further excuse before putting the vindicatory boot in good and hard.

'There's something bulky in his jacket pocket,' Kelly murmured as the now snoring body slumped bonelessly into the upholstery.

I told her to investigate while I retrieved the crowbar from the garage floor. As I wrapped Stroud's inactive fingers around the iron weapon she pulled a large jar from his pocket and unscrewed the lid. She teased tiny white crystals into the palm of her hand and did an analytical probe with the tip of her tongue.

'A definite saline taste,' she announced, looking as though she had just swallowed an out-of-season oyster. 'Some sort of crystalline powder, but just what . . . ?' She shrugged.

I offered no comment, merely watched with amused curiosity

as she rummaged through back pockets, side pockets, and between breasts. Seconds later she produced a can of 35 mm film, tossed away the film, and proceeded to fill the empty can with crystals.

She dimpled at me. 'This is for forensic.'

'Or indigestion, maybe,' I grinned.

She laughed, poked out that analytical tongue.

'Let's go home,' I said.

The rain didn't feel nearly so wet as we retraced our steps to the wall. Funny how a return journey always seems quicker, simpler—but then we didn't have Potter's unamusing anecdotes to listen to. The going was now in our favour and the home stretch was downhill all the way.

Allowing for weather conditions and speed-limit signs, we made the Eclipse in good time. Nosing the M.G. into the hotel car park I flicked a glance at my watch. The luminous hands blinked 2 a.m.

The last person I expected to see as we entered the lobby was Howard Grant. But there, tucked in a corner, browsing through a copy of *Stud and Stable,* the Security Chief sat. He looked tired, wet, and not particularly friendly.

Kelly and I exchanged glances.

'Trouble?' I asked, upon reaching him.

'Trouble,' he affirmed, indicating that he wanted us sitting down.

I looked from Grant to the night porter, who appeared to be dozing, and then back to Grant again. I said that old classic line from a thousand Hollywood movies. 'Should we be seen talking together like this?'

'It doesn't matter now,' he grunted.

I didn't like the emphasis he put on *now.* I reckoned it was real bad news, and I reckoned right. He drew in a deep lungful of air and expelled five short but very meaningful words. 'You're both off the case,' he said.

Chapter Six

THE NEXT few seconds were rather like a cartoon strip without any speech balloons. I looked at Grant, who in turn looked at Kelly, who in turn looked at me. We all sat looking at each other, but none of us had anything to say.

'It's unfortunate, Simon,' Grant said shortly, 'but circumstances have forced me to make this decision.'

I lit a Chesterfield, brooding over the possibilities that could have prompted such drastic action. If I'd stepped out of line then I wanted to remember the when and the how. I wanted to have the perfect answer phrased correctly in my head so I could counter the 'why the hell did you do it?' when it came.

'Don't look so guilty,' he went on. 'I'm not taking you off the case as a disciplinary measure.'

'We're not responsible?'

'Of course not.'

'Then for God's sake, why?' The question spilled out tersely.

He pulled a hip-flask from the pocket of his raglan, poured himself a snorter of brandy and said with commendable casualness, 'Somebody is planning to kidnap General O'Hara—we're planning on stopping them.'

'Mrs Falloway's stallion?' Kelly gaped at him.

He nodded solemnly.

The reason was a stunner all right, but I couldn't quite follow the drift. Confused, I asked him to clarify whether he was dropping our present assignment, or us, or both.

'Shelving,' he said. 'I'm shelving your assignment and turning your talents towards the protection of General O'Hara.

The Division have made elaborate plans to ensure the animal's safety and you, Simon, have been selected as the General's personal bodyguard.'

'And Kelly?' I asked, a little baffled.

'Regrettably, Kelly must leave us.'

'Leave?' She caught her breath on a surprised little gasp.

'I'm afraid so.' Grant smiled at her. 'We're most grateful for the help you've given us.'

'But, sir . . .'

Grant politely reminded her of her obligation to the *Racing Times*, adding, 'As much as I'd like to, I couldn't possibly justify keeping you.'

Kelly looked downcast but brightened almost immediately. 'I've three weeks' winter leave due to me,' she said, sounding happier by the second. 'I was going to have a holiday in Scotland, but I'd far rather stay down here.'

Grant looked at me hesitantly.

'I'd like her to stay,' I said.

'As your assistant?'

'She's got a good head on her shoulders.'

'And a very pretty one at that.'

'Well, sir?' Kelly smiled optimistically.

Grant returned the smile. 'If your editor agrees, that's fine by me.'

With the perfect solution found, I piloted the conversation back to General O'Hara. 'The press can never agree on a valuation figure,' I said. 'They bandy the noughts about as though they were playing quoits. In hard cash terms, what's he worth?'

'Around the three million mark,' Grant attested. 'And he isn't insured.'

I flinched. 'Nasty.'

'It will be for us if anything goes wrong.'

'A colossal setback too for the breeding world and the improvement of British blood lines,' I murmured as the lugubrious facts sunk in. 'So how much do we know?'

'Not much, Simon. The Gaylawn Stables box driver was approached in a pub and given a map and a thousand pounds. The map shows the route that the would-be kidnappers want the box to take when the General is transported to the Newmarket Stud on Sunday. The route is fairly normal except for a cross-country detour at Royston.'

'And that's where they hit the box and snatch the General, uh?'

He quirked a sardonic eye at me. 'With four T.S.D. men inside the box and a car shadowing its journey, I hope we can prevent the "snatch" taking place.'

I smiled inwardly. Whoever had dreamed up this little one certainly deserved full marks for ingenuity. It was so easy, so very bloody easy, that I was left wondering why the hijacking of a valuable racehorse had never been tried before. A travelling box offered about as much security as a tin of biscuits and unlike the more usual *Homo sapiens* kidnappings, horses couldn't tell tales.

Kelly had a puzzled look on her face. 'Do you want us in the tail-car or the travelling box, sir?'

'Neither,' Grant said, smiling into his brandy. 'You'll both be miles away at a place called Buckfastleigh.'

'Buckfast-what?' It was my turn to look puzzled.

'Buckfastleigh, a village in South Devon. You'll be transporting the General there tomorrow.'

'But you said ... ?'

'Yes I know, but what I didn't say was that General O'Hara won't be in the box bound for Newmarket.'

'You're travelling empty?'

He shook his head. 'We couldn't do that. Everything has to appear normal, completely genuine. There could well be an accomplice working at the Gaylawn yard, so the box has to leave with General O'Hara—or should I say Boy Blue.'

'A substitute?'

'Exactly,' he affirmed, 'Boy Blue is almost a carbon-copy of the famous stallion. I say *almost* because there is just one subtle difference. Whereas General O'Hara has a large white star between his eyes, Boy Blue has one only half the size. This can be fixed with spirit dye, of course, and shouldn't present any problem.' He hesitated, then half smiled. 'Age, colouring, height, bodyweight, are identical. He walks like the General, has the General's bold arrogant head, and all in all he looks more like the General than the General himself.'

'One of Nature's miracles, huh?' I said, for the sake of something to say, watching Grant as he poured out another measure of brandy, listening as he launched into brief but explicit details of the ringer's history.

Boy Blue had run in Ireland as a two-year-old, shown definite promise and looked set on an auspicious future. These expectations were rapidly dissolved when it was later discovered that the animal had developed a heart condition. The horse was subsequently put up for sale and bought by a South Devon firm called 'Animals Unlimited'. The firm, a sort of private zoo-cum-safari park, specialized in hiring out to film companies anything from a performing flea to a full-blooded gorilla.

'You'll transport the real General O'Hara there tomorrow,' Grant wound it up. 'I'll be taking Boy Blue back to Gaylawn.'

Kelly said, 'So the duplicate horse goes to the Newmarket Stud?'

'Exactly. Anything could happen on the journey and we daren't risk the General's safety.'

I looked at him blandly. 'I take it you haven't overlooked the fact that the Gaylawn work-force are going to get suspicious tomorrow when we do all this shunting around?'

'No I haven't, and that's the reason why tomorrow was chosen for the switch.' Grant eyed the night porter, checked he was still dozing, then went on, 'Alison Falloway is holding a garden party at The Cedars to mark General O'Hara's retirement. Everyone at Gaylawn Stables is aware of this, and they also know that the horse is appearing as the surprise guest. When you arrive in the morning for the collection, no one will bat an eyelid.'

'It sounds like a good plan,' Kelly agreed. 'Have the police been informed?'

'They have, but they're leaving security to us. The less fuss the better. You'll be using a Rice trailer tomorrow and you'll be unescorted.' He leaned forward. 'Your M.G.C. has a towing bracket, hasn't it?'

I nodded.

'Then I suggest you dispatch yourselves towards the Motel. Try to get some sleep, you've an early start and a long day ahead of you.'

Kelly thought about that, then said slowly, 'You want us both to spend the night in the chalet?'

'Chalets,' he said, leaning heavily on the plural. 'Book yourself into one and charge it to expenses. It will save time in the morning if you're both under one roof.' He stood up, indicating the briefing was at an end. 'Well, I've a long drive ahead of me. Any final questions?'

Kelly produced the bloodstained label and film can of crystals, and I pitched in with an abridged version of our earlier activities. Grant appeared pleased with our spoils but stressed that General O'Hara's safety now took precedence over everything. Priorities had changed overnight and if I ran into the playboy son or anyone else connected with the previous assignment, I would just have to play it by ear.

Wesley, he said, was going to know anyway. As soon as this General O'Hara affair had been quashed, the T.S.D. would pursue open inquiry tactics into Falloway's wins in a final all-or-nothing effort.

When I told him that Potter was no longer with us, he smiled briefly and pronounced that if necessary the boy could always be found. 'Potter has a habit of popping up,' he added. 'I shall be very surprised if we've seen the last of him.'

'Well next time he pops up,' I suggested, 'either pop him down again or pay for him to have a personality transplant.'

Grant smiled good-naturedly and we shook hands. 'See you both at Buckfastleigh,' he said. 'Good luck.'

Kelly nudged the night porter into life, told him she would be away for a few days and went to pack some clothes. Forty minutes later we were back at the motel.

I thought it just possible that all the chalets might be taken, or that the guy who did the bookings might have deserted his post for a few hours sleep. It was just wishful thinking. The key to chalet eleven was handed over by an insomnolent desk clerk, so Kelly and I said our good nights and went to our respective doors.

I removed my wet clothes, took a shower, and donned a dressing gown. I lit a cigarette and sat on the edge of my bed listening to Kelly as she moved about in the neighbouring chalet. I wasn't one to let an opportunity pass me by, but I needed the right kind of entry-gaining ploy. Once inside, I figured, I could charm my way into being offered joint possession of her bed.

I picked up the telephone, spoke to the super-efficient clerk and ordered two cups of malted milk. There was nothing I hated more, but the sleep-promoting drink somehow had an aura of innocence about it.

'I thought you might like a nightcap,' I said, as she peered out from two inches of open door.

'For me?'

'For us.'

She looked unsure. My ploy suddenly seemed as transparent as the thin wispy material that covered her shapely torso. I felt sure she was going to shut the door in my face.

'Mm, come in.' The door opened, and gladly proved me wrong. 'I've just telephoned my editor,' she smiled suddenly. 'I can take my three weeks' leave.'

'You phoned your editor at . . .'

'I woke him up, but he's a very understanding man.'

'He's a saint,' I grinned, handing her the malted milk.

'I'm very sleepy.' She yawned, arching her body.

My eyes slipped over the inventory and I liked what I saw. I liked the shortie nightdress that showed an expanse of sun-kissed thigh beneath its deliciously inadequate length. The eye-teasing firmness of her breasts as her large, perfectly shaped nipples pressed provocatively towards me. I could feel the warmth from her body a few inches from mine, and I was getting hotter by the second.

'Things look exciting, don't they.' She fluttered her lashes.

'Very,' I said.

'It will certainly be a new experience for me.'

'That makes it all the better.' I was getting high on her perfume.

'Is it very risky?'

'Not if you take precautions, and most females do these days, so I'm told.'

She looked at me, frowned, 'Simon, what are we talking about?'

'Talking?' I was floating on cloud nine.

'Simon?'

'Uh-huh.'

'You're talking about *sex,* aren't you?' She gave adverse emphasis to the word.

I shook myself out of my narcosis. 'Who mentioned sex?'

'I was talking about the new assignment, about General O'Hara.'

'Yes, well . . . so was I.' I pegged back my libidinal forces. I thought about summer sun and lush green fields. Sweet pure wholesome thoughts, like the sweet pure wholesome drink I was now trying to swallow.

'Don't spoil things, Simon.'

'Spoil?'

'By letting desires ride rough-shod over feelings.'

I smiled, a little amused.

'We have a good relationship. Don't rush it. Let things develop naturally.'

I almost felt embarrassed. 'With you looking like that,' I said, 'it's hard to back-pedal.'

'I wasn't expecting company.'

'That doesn't make it any easier.'

'I'm not a prude.'

'I didn't think you were.'

She smiled with those big brown eyes. 'Duncan Stroud said I'd be as cold as ice in bed, remember?'

'I remember.'

'He was wrong.'

'Sure.'

'No, really, he was. It's not difficult to please a man. Only my man has to be special—very special. It's too easy to be a whore.'

'And am I special?' I asked, trying not to sound pompous.

'You could be if only you'd let the grass grow a little.'

I grinned. I'd been put in my place and I'd loved every minute of it. 'Would an old-fashioned expression of affection hamper its progress?' I asked.

She shook her head impishly.

I leaned forward to bestow a soft, brotherly kiss on her moist lips. At least that's how it started. The gentle peck developed into something a little more passionate and it lasted a full sixty seconds. It left me breathless and it confirmed Stroud's inaccuracy.

Kelly opened the door to show me the way home. I stood momentarily in the porch, watching as she snapped off the light and teetered towards the bed. 'Don't forget to set the alarm,' she said.

A few hours of spasmodic sleep later found me packing essential clothes and reflecting on the dramatic changes that had taken place in my life. Less than a week ago things had been very different. I'd gone to the occasional race meeting, knocked around with the boys, and led my usual happy-go-lucky existence. My time had been occupied with nothing more dangerous than trying to wallpaper a ceiling in my Wimbledon bachelor pad, and avoiding an elderly tenant who objected to my restorative activities, and more especially to young unmarried men with noisy sports cars. It was all very uncomplicated. Far different from playing guardian angel to a walking bullion van called General O'Hara. Three million quid on the hoof and my neck on the block if anything went wrong.

The rain had stopped and the cloud was high and moving fast in the sky as I snagged the gear lever into reverse and coaxed the M.G. towards the waiting Rice trailer at Gaylawn Stables.

Julian Ratcliffe looked the way one expects a prosperous racehorse trainer to look. Garbed in hacking-jacket with tartan waistcoat, jodhpurs, and elastic-sided ankle boots, he welcomed us warmly and carefully coupled the trailer to the car.

'Nasty affair, this,' he said as we crushed hands. 'It's a blessing I have an honest box driver, Drake, or heaven knows what might have happened to the horse.'

I looked into his coarse weather-beaten face, the skin of which resembled the texture of a pickled walnut. I gave him one of my easy smiles. 'Safety is our business,' I assured him. 'We'll be sticking to the General closer than a tout's binoculars on a promising two-year-old.'

The big horse looked the epitome of health as it was led from its loose-box into the trailer. This was apparent in its glossy, immaculately groomed coat; the strong muscular quarters and neck; the pricked ears constantly on the move like antennae, and those intelligent eyes that surveyed Kelly and me with guarded curiosity. The animal looked five-star quality all right and worth every last penny of its ritzy price tag.

Ratcliffe handed me a map showing the shortest way to Buckfastleigh and the exact location of the private zoo. 'I've also prepared a diet sheet,' he said briskly. 'The General is on reduced rations so my feeding instructions must be strictly observed.'

Assuring him they would be, I climbed back into the driving seat. 'How many people know about the switch?' I enquired.

'Apart from Grant, Mrs Falloway and yourselves, there's only the owner of Animals Unlimited and me.'

'Mrs Falloway knows, uh?'

'She had to be told, Drake. If anything goes wrong—'

'Sure.' I saw the implication. I wasn't worried about the old lady knowing all the ins and outs, it was the son and heir getting wind of the scheme that evoked uneasy thoughts.

We made our adieus and rolled out of the yard hauling our illustrious passenger behind us. We'd only covered sixty yards of narrow Gaylawn driveway before we made our first unscheduled stop. A Range Rover piloted by McQuillan's baby-faced jockey, Roy Biggs, blocked our exit.

'What on earth is he doing here?' Kelly looked worried.

'Complicating things,' I said, standing on the horn, signalling him to back up.

The Range Rover didn't budge, but Biggs did. With a wide affable grin tattooed on his face he strode over to meet us.

I said, 'Do you mind shifting that bloody wagon, we're in a hurry.' Rudeness wasn't in my nature, but then this was no time for naturism.

'Collecting a horse?' He appeared unmoved.

'The Range Rover, Biggs,' I said again. 'We'd like to pass.'

'Sure.' He gave the trailer the once-over. 'Hey, that's General O'Hara, isn't it?'

'Does it look like General O'Hara?'

'Yes it does.'

'Then I'd say it was, wouldn't you?'

'But what . . . ?' He narrowed his eyes.

I countered his half-question with a full one of my own. 'What are you doing here? I mean apart from blocking our exit.'

'My brother works for Ratcliffe.'

'So this is a social call?'

'Hey what gives, Preston?' The smile had melted into a suspicious scowl. 'What the bloody hell is a hack journalist doing with General O'Hara hitched to his car?'

I didn't like the remark. The fact that I wasn't a journalist, hack or otherwise, wasn't the point. The point was that Biggs thought he could call me one and get away with it—and that made me angry.

I climbed out of the car and resisted a retaliative urge that was begging me to shin up his skinny frame and pummel him into the tarmac with my fists. 'Shift that Range Rover,' I growled, 'and quick.'

He stood his ground, folded his arms. 'I smell something fishy and I'm not moving until you give me a damn good reason why General O'Hara should be in that trailer.'

The little guy had guts. I pulled my T.S.D. warranty card from my pocket and thrust it under his nose. 'The best reason in the world, Biggs,' I said. 'Now select reverse gear before I step over your prone body and do it myself.'

'But I thought . . . ?' His face crumpled like a soufflé caught in a blast of cold air. 'Christ, Security Division?'

'Nothing personal,' I said. 'It's the way I happen to earn my living.'

Looking stunned and confused he backed up to the entrance gates and offered us a clear exit. I didn't make with any explanatory spiel. Ratcliffe I figured, would satisfy part of his curiosity by telling him about the Falloway garden party, and as for anything else—well, the worried Mr Biggs was going to have sleepless nights working out his own answers.

We headed south. Three hours later found us at Animals Unlimited. It was an enormous set-up, far bigger than I expected, with large bushy compounds that housed large bushy animals. Strategically placed notices warned the pound-paying weekend public to stay in their cars and keep healthy, or get out and be mauled for free.

We found Grant in the tame sector. He introduced us to our host, a big, beefy Austrian in a fringed buckskin suit, scrolled cowboy boots and stetson hat with a leopard-skin band. I've never been one for limp effeminate handshakes, but Helmut Kruger nearly disintegrated my fingers as we went through the customary courtesies.

Kelly was taken to inspect our sleeping quarters and I helped with the unloading of General O'Hara. As Grant led the big chestnut horse towards the stable area, I removed the trailer from the M.G. and coupled it to the Security Chief's car.

'Well, what do you think, Simon?' Grant asked, reappearing a few minutes later with ... ?

My eyes did a double-take. 'Not Boy Blue?'

'None other.'

'It's bloody uncanny,' I said, and it was.

I did a once round, scrutinizing every twitching muscle, every inch of neat, firm flesh. I couldn't fault it. 'There's no difference,' I said.

'There's two million nine hundred and ninety-nine thousand differences,' Grant's smile was subtle.

'So he's worth only a thousand, huh?'

'Thereabouts. That's what he's worth to Kruger, and that's what we pay if anything happens to him.'

'The cosmetic treatment is perfect,' I said, looking at the large white star between the animal's eyes. 'I trust it's semi-permanent?'

'Stay-fast dye that isn't affected by rain or by sweating. It should see this case out with no trouble at all.'

We loaded Boy Blue into the trailer. As Grant slid behind the wheel of his car, Kelly reappeared to say that our rooms over the stable block were perfectly situated and very comfortable. Very separate, too, I reckoned.

'Good.' Grant adjusted his door mirror. 'I'll telephone you on Sunday from the Newmarket Stud.'

'That is always assuming you reach it,' I pointed out.

His voice held an edge of crisp assurance as he said, 'If they attempt a snatch, we'll be ready for them.'

We watched the trailer trundle away, then walked back towards the stable area. Kelly sighed and said, 'Oh well, Captain Grant has all the problems now. Our worst enemy will probably be boredom.'

'There's a dartboard in the garage,' I offered.

97

'I'm only very average at darts. I packed a pocket chess set though.'

'You play chess?'

'I was school champion for three years running.'

I grinned sheepishly. 'Double top to start?'

When I awoke it was ten minutes before three. It was a Sunday, the date was the 26th, and the month was October. Not that I was particularly conscious of any of these things at such an inhuman hour, but an impending encounter would shortly compel me to remember them, and remember them for a long time to come.

Four days had passed. Four time-dragging days and sleep-broken nights. Kelly and I had divided the nights into two-hourly intervals, taking it in turns to check the General's box at our appointed hour. The three o'clock stint was mine.

I ambled into the yard, felt the dank morning air spear my cheeks, creep uninvitingly through my hair. If my faculties weren't a hundred per cent functional at that moment, they were plunged violently into overdrive the milli-second I noticed the padlocks on the loose-box door were lying broken in their staples.

I sucked in my breath and listened hard. The rustle of straw, the faint tinkle of a head-collar buckle, the dull thud of a hoof as it clipped a water bucket. These were the sounds that pervaded the stillness. Familiar sounds. Sounds that told their own story.

A sudden movement flickered in the corner of my vision. I narrowed my eyes, peering into the darkness past an expanse of outbuildings and out into open country. I was vaguely aware of a vehicle, the hollow sound of a slamming door. It was a long way off, an innominate blur. Kruger's rangers patrolling the grounds, I thought. Christ, I hoped I was right.

I waited. Seconds passed. The intrepid side of my nature was telling me to act and act fast—my prudent side told me to retrace my steps and get help. Intrepidity won and I found myself homing in on the loose-box.

A voice now, soft, sibilant, breathing words of reassurance to the horse. I could hear the General blowing gently through his nostrils, swishing his tail impatiently. I stuck close to the wall, palming my way towards the open door.

Lady luck wasn't with me. I never reached the door. My foot connected with a reel of hose and sent it rattling off into the forbidding blackness. Spinning away from my outstretched hand. Broadcasting my presence like a loud-hailer in a Chapel of Rest.

'Freeze, brother!' The voice was harsh, designed to terrorize. Time hung suspended as I stood paralysed. I looked into the twin barrels of a sawn-off shotgun and they looked steadily back as if eager to spit in my direction. I tried desperately to think. My armpits felt damp. Sweat began rilling down my backbone.

'Inside!' The barrels beckoned me into the box.

I obeyed mechanically, feeling my way in, watching the forefinger of his right hand as it caressed the lethal pair of triggers. I could see the face now. The grotesque twisted features beneath the tight stocking mask. The flattened nose. The gleam of white teeth standing out starkly from malformed lips.

'How did you know the horse was here?' I muttered.

'No questions. Get over by the manger.'

'Somebody tipped you off, uh?'

'Git!' The barrels zeroed in on my chest.

If I'd heard the voice before, then I certainly didn't recognize it through the nylon covering. It was distorted, its harshness almost phoney. I backed up slowly until my hands touched the manger behind me.

'What do you plan on doing?' I asked tightly, stalling for time.

He chuckled. It was the kind of chuckle that told me exactly what he planned on doing.

I snatched a glance towards General O'Hara. The big horse

99

was getting restless. He didn't like being tethered to the wall, restrained by the head collar. He was beginning to sweat, drawing his sides in and out like bellows, as if sensing the impending danger. Suddenly he whinnied. It was inevitable and it was the chance I needed. As the animal jerked its head convulsively to and fro, I saw the masked man's eyes flicker from me to the horse. For the single space of a heart-beat he pointed the shotgun negligently downwards.

I gripped the manger tightly and lunged out with my legs. More by good luck than good judgement, my toe caught the tip of one of the barrels and the weapon somersaulted from his fingers, quashing his homicidal intentions. It spun up and over his head. I saw the butt club the floor, heard it clatter away into the darkness.

I was on him in a second. He let out a yelp of pain as I buried my fist into his abdomen. As he hit the floor I threw myself forward. He expected the follow-up move and twisted to meet me. We rolled over and over in the fetid straw, strength against strength, blow against blow, our bodies intertwined in a huddle of vicious intimacy. We fought under the belly of General O'Hara, amongst the frenzy of legs, the scuffle of hooves. We were conscious only of each other, blinded by fear and hate. We were totally unaware of the massive power in those hind feet and fore feet. Power that threatened to bruise, mutilate, and tear flesh from bone.

His fingers were in my scalp now. He grabbed a handful of hair with his right hand and levered my chin back with his left. Pain ignited in my midriff as he pumped his knee into my gut. I doubled up in a spasm of coughing and just managed to roll clear as he swung with a hell of a punch. The fist seared past my face and connected sickeningly with the wall. He screamed and clutched at his fingers in agony.

It was my turning point. I made a grab for his throat and began peeling back the stocking mask. The sound of my own heavy breathing prevented me from hearing the footsteps behind.

Something hard and heavy struck me with crushing force, sending pain slicing through my skull. I saw a few flecks of blood spatter across my hands. I guessed they belonged to me. I tried desperately to cling to consciousness, to hold back the black bottomless pit that bade me welcome. But my vision swam out of focus and bright fragments of psychedelic light danced hideously in front of my eyes—then melted into darkness. Darkness beyond darkness. Darkness and nothingness. I went with them. . . .

Chapter Seven

THE LITHE yellowish body, richly marked with round black spots, crouched spring-like in front of me. The eyes, large, wild, and unpredictable, fixed me with cool supremacy. The tip of tail twitched moodily to and fro and the muzzle creased back showing glistening pink gums and a perfect set of razor-sharp teeth. One hundred and fifty pounds of ferocious jungle cat. The fastest animal on earth. The cheetah.

I could have been dreaming, floating in a world of spectral fantasy. I'd lost a lot of blood, I knew that. I could feel the gummy wetness in my scalp, the solidified mess around my ears. But this cat was no apparition, this snarling baby was for real.

The inside of my head felt as though something had come adrift, but I wasn't suffering from the conventional loss of memory that usually accompanied a blow to the skull. I remembered everything that preceded the blow with uncanny clarity. Just how I came to be in a cheetah's dimly lit den, lying face down on a meat trolley, I didn't know. But then that was hardly my immediate concern.

My horizontal position restricted my field of vision. I tried to move my head, to seek out some means of escape, but pain lanced into my eyes like hot high-voltage wires. My limbs made a movement of retreat, but failed miserably. Weakness was to be my adversary.

The cat advanced, nostrils fluttering, picking up the scent of fear and blood. Waves of dizziness washed over me. I wanted to black-out. I felt my body go rigid, my ears start singing, as I clamped down hard on my teeth waiting feverishly for the *coup de grâce*.

They say that when death is imminent, pictures of your past life flash chronologically through your mind. Well, I figured I was as close now as I could ever be, but the pictures eluded me. The screen misted over.

'He's over by the observation window!' a voice rang out.

Observation window? I pulled my thoughts together, summoned awareness. I screwed my eyes as far left as I dared and saw the blurred hazy outline of a heavy-gauge window-frame. Kruger had told us earlier that the stable block backed on to the veterinary observation wing and my nerve-ends screamed with relief as realization dawned. I looked into the cheetah's gaping jaws, only inches away, saw its breath vaporize on the inside of the reinforced glass.

Anxious footsteps closed in. There were voices all around me. I went to turn my head but cancelled the action on remembering the pain that accompanied it the last time I tried.

'Lie still,' a voice ordered, Kelly's voice. I almost took a bite out of my bottom lip as she began swabbing the blood from my wound.

'The General . . . ?' The words came out feebly.

'Gone,' she said. 'Some of Kruger's rangers are checking the grounds, but I think it's pretty hopeless.'

'Christ.'

'It wasn't your fault.'

'It was all my fault. As soon as I saw the open box door I should have gone for help.'

'It's easy to be wise after the event.'

'But to walk into . . .' I shifted my head slightly. 'Hell, I feel giddy . . .'

'I can't stop the bleeding,' she said. 'You're going to need stitches.'

A husky male voice suggested the resident veterinarian for the job and added that I should be taken post-haste to the sick-bay. The thought of an animal doctor whose last patient probably died from anthrax sewing me up didn't exactly inspire confidence—but then I was in no fit state to protest.

'Can you stand?' Kelly asked.

'With help, maybe,' I said.

Two of Kruger's rangers hauled me effortlessly to my feet. The bones in my legs had liquefied and my head felt as though it had once belonged to a hangover, but with a little support I managed to remain vertical.

Kelly was crouching by the observation window and mumbling something about somebody warning us off. I watched as she removed eighteen inches of red sticky tape from the glass. Tape with letters indented on it.

'What is it?' I held out an unsteady hand.

She looked at me. 'Do you want to bleed to death, Simon?'

'Give,' I said.

'You're on your way to the sick-bay, remember?'

'*Give*,' I said again, in as firm a voice as I could muster.

Reluctantly she handed over the tape. I held it at eye level, waited for the letters to come swimming into focus. It ran : SECURITY DIVISION BE WARNED. ALIVE THE GENERAL IS WORTH MILLIONS. DEAD AND HE'S WORTH THE GOING RATE FOR DOG MEAT. ALIVE OR DEAD, SECURITY DIVISION?

'It's a God-awful mess, Simon,' Howard Grant said doggedly, pacing the length of the Falloway drawing-room, 'Lord knows how I'm going to explain General O'Hara's disappearance after our offering to protect the animal. The questions are going to be intolerable . . .'

I fingered the four stitches in my scalp and murmured thickly that it hadn't been all wine and roses at my end. I'd already given my version of the snatch to Grant on Sunday, and now it looked as though I would have to cover the ground again for the benefit of Alison Falloway. The three of us had been summoned to appear at The Cedars on Monday at 10 a.m. We'd arrived punctually. Now we were waiting for the grande dame of the turf to honour us with her presence.

Gilbert Bexson, the manservant, chauffeur, you name it, had met us at the door, gone through his 'Madam is expecting you' patter, and led us across a third of an acre of carpeting to the drawing-room. He looked far more at ease than when I'd seen him in the Horse and Groom, and if he recognized me, then he certainly didn't show it in his welcoming expression.

'You look a bit washed-out.' Grant stopped his pacing and decided to show concern for my welfare.

'I'm O.K.,' I said.

'Fit enough to carry on?'

'A bit weak, but mentally sound.'

'And what about Miss Meredith?' He looked questioningly towards Kelly. 'Don't you wish you'd taken that holiday after all?'

She shook her head.

'Things could get quite dangerous.'

'I'd like to see it through, sir.'

Grant grunted and tossed me a sealed manilla envelope. 'The lab report on the blood and crystals. Study it at your leisure and if you arrive at any conclusions, don't act, discuss them with me first.'

'Are you reopening the case?' I prompted him gently.

'No, the case remains closed until we find General O'Hara.'

'A negative report, huh?'

'Far from it. I think you'll find it very informative, but the Falloway stallion is priority number one, Simon, and don't you forget it.'

'My stitches will serve to remind me,' I murmured laconically, despatching the envelope to my jacket pocket.

Bexson reappeared and offered us refreshment. As he measured out the alcohol and mixed in the trimmings, I tried to relax by taking in the details of the elegant room.

It was spacious, but homely. The fireplace, a huge cavernous recess with a mammoth English oak mantel beam, dominated the whole of one wall. Above this hung an oil painting, unmistakably a George Stubbs, of a brood mare with foal. Fine Tudor doors, quaint mullioned windows, satinwood and mahogany fittings, and rich gold furnishings amplified the overall effect of good taste and good money. Antique porcelain figures, the kind you can't buy but have to bid for at Sotheby's, were all meticulously arranged in glass-fronted cabinets, and a permanent smell of expensive furniture polish lingered in the air. Yes, life was very baronial at the Falloway residence.

'Excuse me, please.' A distant humming sound had prompted Bexson to abandon his barman duties and sent him swiftly to open the door. Kelly and I took our cue from Grant and stood up. The humming grew louder. Bexson gave the discreetest of bows as Alison Falloway powered her way into the room on what at first glance appeared to be an electrically driven go-cart. She was wearing a double choker of pearls and an elegant black dress that was so unpretentious it just had to cost a fortune to buy.

'Sit down, sit down.' Her voice was disagreeable, school-marmish. 'Tuck your feet in, I don't want to be sued for breaking your toes.'

'What an incredible machine,' Grant remarked.

'Chairmobile,' she said testily, bringing the appliance to a halt in the centre of the room. 'An all-British invention the Japanese haven't yet copied, thank God.'

Bexson mixed the Duchess an intricate-looking cocktail, replenished our glasses, and finally made his exit. The stage was now set for discussion. The look on Alison Falloway's face told me it wasn't going to be particularly friendly. I watched her vein-traced hands as they gripped convulsively at the joystick control, saw the Chairmobile pivot on its own axis as it swung neatly towards me.

She looked me up and down, eyeing me as though I had just presented her with a bill that needed scrutinizing. Finally she said, 'So you're the young man who let them steal my handsome gallant General.'

I wasn't sure whether that was a question or a statement, or how she expected me to reply. I flicked a glance to Grant, looking for some kind of verbal support, but he merely lifted his eyebrows indicating that he had nothing to say.

'I didn't let anybody do anything, Mrs Falloway,' I spoke slowly, choosing my words with care. 'My job was to protect your horse and this I did to the best of my ability. I'm sorry that things went wrong.'

'*Wrong?*' she said scathingly. 'Hardly the most pungent adjective to describe the situation. Things are not *wrong*, Mr Drake, they are irredeemable.'

'Simon was brutally attacked, Mrs Falloway,' Kelly decided to jump to my defence. 'He did all he could do in the circumstances. The real mistake was in underestimating the intelligence of the kidnappers in believing that the travelling box was the target.'

The Chairmobile swung towards Grant. 'Who's this young woman?'

'Kelly Meredith,' Grant said. 'She's assisting Mr Drake.'

'She's far too pretty and far too young. They're both far too young. In my experience young people are usually headstrong, foolhardy and reckless.'

'But I'm afraid she's right.' Grant moistened his lips and looked a little sheepish. 'We did completely underestimate the kidnappers' guile. We concentrated all our strength and manpower in the wrong direction.'

She grunted and said, 'Do you intend keeping this Boy Blue at the Newmarket Stud?'

'I think it's good policy. As far as the public and press is concerned, General O'Hara reached his destination safely. We could release the truth, of course, but—'

'Don't you dare!' She abruptly cut him off. 'I couldn't tolerate being pestered by a lot of loathsome newspapermen.'

I took a long swallow of my drink and pulled a packet of cigarettes from my pocket. I scanned for an ashtray but there wasn't one nearby. A refectory table some five yards away held the necessary vessel, but the disapproving glare Alison Falloway was now giving me temporarily quashed my addictive pangs.

Grant said matter-of-factly, 'Now we must wait for the ransom demand.'

'How much?' The old lady whirled on him.

'I wouldn't like to hazard a guess. We could refuse to pay, of course. Call their bluff.'

'And risk losing the most celebrated horse ever to grace a race meeting in my colours?—that's out of the question.'

I said, 'If it is ransom then there's always a good chance of trapping them at the pay-off point.'

'*If it's ransom*.' She pounced on my words. 'What else could it possibly be?'

'Simon is referring to that irrational feeling called intuition,' Grant interjected. 'He feels there could be a more sinister motive to the horsenapping than just monetary gain.'

'Such as?'

'I've no idea,' I admitted. 'I'm probably wrong.'

'You're not a fool, are you? I've always said there's no fool like a young fool.'

'Old fool,' I corrected, smiling tolerantly. 'There's no fool like an old fool, Mrs Falloway.'

She lifted her head with great dignity. 'Don't try to be clever, Mr Drake. You can't be particularly profound or you wouldn't be sitting here explaining how you let three million pounds slip through your fingers.'

'*Touché*,' I said, and let it pass.

Kelly broke the tension by launching into her 'how the hijackers gained entry' theory. She drew the fire away from me as she explained why the early hours of Sunday morning had been chosen for the snatch. 'Animals Unlimited is open to the public at the weekend. It was easy enough for the gang to enter in the normal way on Saturday and hide themselves and their vehicle until everybody had either gone home or gone to sleep.'

'There were at least two of them,' I added, 'probably more.'

'And one of them struck you?'

'I was knocked unconscious and wheeled on a meat trolley to the observation wing. I was positioned in such a way that when I finally came round I found myself on intimate terms with a cheetah.'

'Either they have a flair for melodrama, or—' she thrust a bony finger towards me, 'you were suffering from hallucinations at the time.'

Grant handed her the strip of printed tape. 'They left this where they dumped Simon,' he said. 'It sounds far-fetched, I know, but Kelly can corroborate the cheetah story.'

For the first time I noticed a momentary softening of those stiff puritanical features. She propped a pair of *pince-nez* on the end of her nose, consulted the tape, then peered at me critically over the lenses. I reckoned I hadn't exactly made a good impression. Up to now I'd been described as a headstrong reckless fool with a fanciful mind. If I sat here much longer I'd begin to cultivate a complex about her not liking me.

She pondered. 'Why did they bother to wheel you anywhere?'

'To show they're not afraid to take chances. To frighten me off, maybe.'

'And have they "frightened you off"?'

'Yesterday I felt like quitting.'

'And today?'

'I don't know.'

She fixed me with courtroom eyes. 'What sign were you born under?'

'Ma'am?'

'Sign of the zodiac—your birth-sign.'

I gave it a few seconds' meditation. 'Scorpio,' I said.

'Then you're not acting in a typically Scorpionic way.'

Grant worried an earlobe. 'Mrs Falloway studies the movement of heavenly bodies,' he announced.

It struck me as funny.

'Astrology, Simon.' Grant saw my grin and clarified the point.

'Scorpio subjects are die-hards, Mr Drake. They are ambitious, vindictive, and purposeful. They are also obstinate, cynical and selfish. They have an abundance of both love and hate, and in turn they are either hated or loved. Did you know that de Gaulle was a Scorpio subject?'

Amused, I confessed that I didn't.

'I think you're a fighter, Mr Drake, and I like a fighter.'

Suddenly she liked me. I was beginning to like her a little better too. I said, 'Are you asking me to stay with this case, Mrs Falloway?'

'Scorpionics don't turn their backs and walk away.'

'Not all horses run true to form,' I pointed out.

'They might have their off days, but their characters never change.' She sighed, adding, 'My son is an Arien. He is wilful, impulsive and a gambler. All ineradicable traits of his birth-sign.'

I could have added arrogance, wiliness, and villainy to the list but I wanted to stay on the right side, so I smiled pleasantly and dredged up that frayed-at-the-edges adage about how boring the world would be if all our personalities were the same. I didn't believe it, of course. The world, I felt, could well afford to lose its quota of Wesley Falloways. Not a very brotherly feeling, but then my Scorpionic vindictiveness was rearing its ugly head.

'Is Wesley away?' Grant asked, tentatively.

'Until tonight, yes. He took advantage of a free weekend to go on a fishing trip.'

'He chose a bad time.'

'My son and I don't get on, Captain Grant. We tolerate each other only because we have to. I don't need Wesley's or anyone's shoulder to lean on in moments of anxiety.'

That I believed. The fearless Mrs Falloway was as hard and indestructible as the multi-carat chunk of pure carbon that glinted at me as it nestled on her index finger. A rich gutsy lady who'd inherited a waster for a son and an electric wheelchair for those thin inoperative legs.

She moistened her lips, regarded me speculatively. 'I want you and Miss Meredith to move in at The Cedars. That way I'll be kept abreast of any developments.'

Kelly and I said simultaneously, 'Here?'

'Do you find the house objectionable?'

'Well, no . . .'

'Then that's settled.'

'But I haven't—'

'Said "yes"?' She cut across my words. 'Say "no", and I'll sue the Security Division for negligence.'

Grant gave a nervous little cough and Kelly grinned broadly. It took me a few seconds before I could say anything. Then I said, 'Funny, but earlier I had the distinct impression you didn't want me on the case.'

'That was earlier.' Her eyes flickered indifferently. 'I didn't have a very high opinion of you then.'

'And now?'

'Now I discover we both share the same birth-sign, I am confident you won't let any harm come to my horse.'

I saw the logic of her reasoning, if you could call it that. I said, 'So we both have a sting in our tails?'

'Don't be flippant, Mr Drake.'

'There will be a bonus in it, Simon.' Grant dangled a carrot in front of my nose.

'And I'm not ungenerous,' the Duchess added.

Money was suddenly pouring on the table and I was finding it hard to look a Falloway gift horse in the mouth. The money aside, I knew I couldn't just ignore the last few days, and bid the case farewell. It had nothing to do with birth-signs or character traits, or if it had, then I wasn't aware of the fact. All I knew was I had a responsibility to finish what I'd started.

'Well?' she demanded.

'I'll get General O'Hara back,' I said, and I hoped I meant it.

I didn't bother to open Grant's manilla envelope until after we'd eaten lunch—a very vintage affair, served with subtle dexterity by Gilbert Bexson and cooked, I imagined by the as yet invisible Emily Byford. Feeling decidedly well fed, I took myself and the envelope upstairs, joined Kelly in her brass-bedsteaded boudoir, and together we studied the typewritten lab report.

Firstly the blood and the label. We sifted through the forensic biologist's jargon for anything that would clue us up on what really happened to Paradise Kid in the travelling box at Penbury Races.

We'd been wrong in our interpretation of the blood-smeared handwriting. We'd both read it as: 'A Sedative', but tests had shown it to read: 'A negative'. An easy mistake to make, but a vital one to miss. I had assumed, and rightly, that the fragment of glass and label had once belonged to a bottle—but far from containing a tranquillizer, it had accommodated the same fluid that had smeared the label. *Blood*.

The report went on to say that it wasn't human blood, and pointed out that 'A negative', without going into the complexities of serology, was a simple grouping classification and this tallied with the bloodstains found on the label.

Next came the analysis on the crystals that Kelly had found in Duncan Stroud's pocket. This was brief and easy to follow. The salty crystalline powder was sodium citrate, an anticoagulant chemical. It was used in the treatment of kidney infections, sometimes added to the milk of infants to prevent the formation of curds—*and* . . . when mixed with a small quantity of sterile water it prevented blood from clotting during a transfusion.

Kelly looked at me, fluttered her lashes. 'Blood everywhere, Len Potter said. Stroud could have dropped the bottle while he was giving Paradise Kid a transfusion.'

'Same thoughts,' I admitted soberly.

'You don't sound exactly sold on the idea.'

'Blood groups, transfusions, it sounds a bit science-fiction, doesn't it?'

'Stroud has had the veterinary experience,' she reminded me.

'Yeah, but what's it all about? Why the hell should he give a horse a transfusion prior to a race?'

'To help it win, maybe. It would, you know.'

I looked at her. 'Say that again?'

She did. It sounded the same the second time around.

I said, 'O.K., expound, clarify, tell me how you've just solved the case.'

'The Olympics,' she said shortly.

I felt she was about to lose me again. 'You mean like the world Olympics, track events, that sort of thing?'

'Mm, I should have twigged it when Potter first mentioned the blood. After all, horses are no different from athletes, right?'

I told her I followed her meaning and sank back into the well-sprung mattress. I looked up into those big brown eyes and wondered what the hell I was doing discussing a case that Grant wanted shelved when the moment and the brass bedstead lent themselves to a much more pleasurable pastime.

She went on : 'I worked for *Sport International,* right? Well you can't work for a mag like that without hearing about the various drugs used by athletes for improving their performances. They all try them at some time or another. The trouble with drugs, as you know, is that they can be easily detected, but with the blood-boost—'

'Blood-boost?'

'Mm, a blood transfusion with an athlete's own blood just prior to racing. A pint of blood which has been donated by the athlete several weeks before and kept on ice until the event. Remember the date on the label?'

'September fourteenth.'

'The date Stroud must have taken the blood from Paradise Kid. Quite a few weeks, in fact, before the scheduled Penbury race.'

'That figures,' I said, 'but the ratio of extra blood would be far greater for a horse than for a human.'

'So how much blood does a horse carry around?'

'Seven, maybe eight gallons.'

She whistled softly through her teeth. 'Then Stroud would need to transfer about eight pints. It could be taken out in easy stages over a period of time. The actual putting back, which he does presumably in the travelling box at the course, would only take about an hour.'

'So the horse runs with nine gallons instead of eight, uh?'

'That's my theory, Simon.'

'And the effect of all this?'

'Powee!' She jetted her fist through the air. 'Wesley Falloway's second-rate horses are suddenly equipped with a supercharger.'

'Never mind the dramatization,' I said, 'what happens in the physical sense?'

She dimpled at me. 'It immediately pushes up the red blood-cell count. It would give a horse more wind, more stamina, and a lot more energy. It wouldn't last long, of course, but long enough for the horse to pick up the race.'

There was a fairly lengthy silence, during which I tried to digest this almost Frankensteinal piece of conjecture. I didn't like it very much, but then I didn't have to. I reminded myself that this sort of freakish power booster was a taste of things to come. The T.S.D., like other security forces, was living in a scientific age where conventional techniques were dying fast.

The more I thought about it, the more it seemed to fit the facts as we knew them. Len Potter, with his 'gallons of blood running down the walls' story, didn't seem such a gross exaggeration any more. And the negative result on the blood samples taken from the suspect horses made fools of the veterinarians. After all, they were looking for something in the blood, not the blood itself.

I hitched myself off the bed and took a meditative amble to the door. I had a sudden impulse to see Stroud. I wanted to face him and tell him we knew all about his illegal blood-bank, and I wanted to find out how deeply Falloway and McQuillan were implicated in the running of it.

Kelly eyed me circumspectly. She knew what I had in mind. 'I've seen you look that way before,' she said. 'You're debating whether or not to go to Chinhurst Lodge, aren't you?'

'No chance.' I felt myself smiling. 'Grant would crucify me.'

She narrowed her eyes, weighing me up.

'See you later,' I said.

'Oh no, you don't.' She leapt from the bed. 'I know how your mind works, and I'm not letting you out of my sight.'

'Suit yourself, I'm going to the loo.' The statement stopped her in her tracks. Still smiling, I stepped out of the room and closed the door quietly behind me.

The M.G.C. was parked out front on the macadamized forecourt. I felt sure my departure from the house had gone unnoticed—that is until I stabbed the ignition.

'Some walk to the loo, huh?' Kelly arrived breathlessly and snuggled herself into the passenger seat.

'It's not that I don't want you along,' I explained, 'but you'd be safer back at the house.'

'Safe and bored,' she said. 'I don't want to be safe and bored.'

I grinned. 'You definitely would have found Scotland dull in October.'

We headed for McQuillan's. I wasn't in any hurry, so we talked. By the time we turned off the main highway and on to the narrow lane that would take us to Chinhurst Lodge, we'd discussed everything from Olympic athletes and boosted-up racehorses, to star-gazing old ladies.

I suppose my concentration on the road ahead wasn't all it should have been, but then I wasn't expecting to meet a speed merchant in a red XJ 12 Jaguar. I saw the fast-approaching car filling the carriageway, in the fleeting second it takes to flick a steering wheel and avoid a full frontal collision.

With its air-horns spitting a piercing warning, the Jaguar loomed towards us. I spun the M.G. clear, and burnt half-an inch of rubber off the tyre treads as I nearly rammed into a solid wall of earth.

'Bloody Wesley Falloway!' I snarled, as the M.G. lurched to a halt.

'I didn't see the driver's face,' Kelly said.

'I didn't have to,' I told her, jamming the shift into reverse. 'He's the only guy with a Jag like that for miles.'

Swearing with some fluency under my breath I manhandled the M.G. back onto the road. As we got under way, I noticed I'd lost my nearside wing mirror, so by the time we reached Chinhurst Lodge, I was far from good humoured.

'I want to see Duncan Stroud.' I faced McQuillan over the contents of his shabby desk, watched as his lips twitched involuntarily into a smile.

'Mr—er . . .' He stood up, hesitated. 'Preston . . . ?'

'Mr Drake and Miss Meredith,' I said tightly. 'I'm an investigator for the Security Division—as I'm sure your jockey Roy Biggs was very quick to tell you.'

'Roy did mention it,' he admitted, concealing his metal hand in his jacket pocket. 'I was dumbfounded when he told me— and, of course, disappointed.'

'Disappointed?'

'I had hoped the *Racing Times* was going to give us the publicity we so badly needed, but presumably that was only a cover for the purposes of surveillance.'

'You catch on fast, McQuillan,' I said.

'So this stable has been and still is under T.S.D. investigation?'

'Right again.'

'But why?' he asked almost apologetically. 'I don't understand . . . ?'

'Chew on the Falloway horses,' I growled.

'Wesley's horses?'

'He tells you when he wants them geed-up and you do the geeing, uh?'

'I'm not a puppet, Drake. I don't dance to Wesley Falloway's or anyone's tune.'

'He's just left, hasn't he? What were you doing, checking blood supplies?'

'Wesley, here?' His expression of bewilderment would have done R.A.D.A. proud. 'I haven't seen Wesley in days.'

'Oh come off it, McQuillan, his car nearly piled into ours.'

'He passed us in the lane,' Kelly put in.

'I'm sorry.' He shrugged. 'I can only repeat I haven't seen him.'

I hadn't time to argue. I said, 'Take us to Stroud.'

Pleading innocence and looking completely nonplussed, he escorted us out of the office and across the yard. Stroud, he said, was helping him out by working in the barn. 'It's officially a rest period,' he told us, 'but we had a rather messy delivery of straw this morning, so Duncan being conscientious—'

'When I need a character reference,' I cut in, 'I'll ask for one. For the moment I just want to ask him a few questions.'

We reached the barn. McQuillan used the hook-like attachment on his metal hand to effortlessly pull open the heavy wooden door. Sunlight streamed in. There was no sign of Stroud.

Several bales of straw were strewn untidily behind a wooden partition. I looked roofwards, saw several gaps high up in the neatly stacked wall of straw. There were five gaps and five bales at my feet. As one bale had broken free of its retaining strings it didn't take a lot of brains to figure out that the bales had either fallen or had been pulled from the stack.

Kelly took a couple of steps forward and leaned over the partition. I heard her say, 'Jesus God . . .' and then I saw Stroud.

He was lying face down behind one of the bales. As I approached I stepped on a piece of broken pitchfork—the harmless wooden half. The pronged end wasn't far away either. It was embedded deep into Stroud's back. His face rested in a pool of half-dried blood. The blood had oozed through the gaps of his very white teeth, congealed obscenely round his twisted lips.

I didn't bother to check for his breathing. When two sharp fingers of steel had pierced through the lung, then breathing became a thing of the past.

Kelly clutched tightly at my arm. 'Jesus God . . .' she said again.

McQuillan felt obliged to vomit. He staggered to the door, retching helplessly.

I turned away from the bloody spectacle and stepped out into the fresh air. The travelling head lad wasn't going to answer my questions, now or ever. He had the best excuse in the world for not listening—the eternal excuse.

Chapter Eight

It was 4 p.m. before I finally reached Howard Grant at his London number.

'Dead?' The word emerged softly and with very little emotion behind it.

'The police seem to think it was an accident.'

'But you think otherwise.'

'I find it hard to swallow. Nobody as experienced as Stroud would lean a pitchfork, prongs uppermost, against a partition and then fall and impale himself on it while stacking bales of straw.'

The line fell silent. Through a background of static I could hear Grant's breathing quicken as he mulled over my words.

I carefully lifted the telephone from the Hepplewhite cylinder desk upon which it rested, and sat cross-legged on the floor. I was alone in the Falloway study but knowing how voices carried, especially in old buildings, I wasn't going to risk being overheard. Waiting for Grant to speak I idly perused the collection of hard-cover volumes that occupied shelf space in the sizable bookcase. There was quite a range of subjects but the gee-gees came out on top. Reference data on training and breeding methods, bloodstock sales analysis, and various autobiographies nestled on the shelves. There was even an Argentine Jockey Club publication on the control of doping. I found myself smiling.

'What were you doing at McQuillan's?' Grant said at last, his words wiping the smile from my lips.

'Kelly and I went to see Stroud.' I braced my ear for the verbal blitz. 'I know you're going to bawl me out, but we've rumbled how the Falloway horses are being hotted up.'

'But I was most emphatic...'

'I know, but Kelly came up with this brilliant piece of deduction—'

'She worked out the blood-boost, is that it?'

I sighed weakly into the mouthpiece. My one and only line of defence had just blown up in my face.

'We might only be desk jockeys to you,' I heard him saying, 'but we're not completely ignorant where new methods are concerned. We knew it was only a matter of time before somebody put this into practice with racehorses.'

'*You* might have known,' I murmured bitterly, 'but it's the first I've heard of it.'

'We didn't know anything for sure until you supplied us with the fragment of glass. The label confirmed the method and all we needed then was a confession. Given time we would have got it. But now with Stroud gone...' he dribbled off.

'If only I'd been put in the picture—'

'You were left out of the picture for two very good reasons. Firstly the picture hadn't fully developed, and secondly, by the time it had, you were no longer on the case.' The statement crackled so forcefully over the wire that it was almost as if he was blaming me for the tragedy.

I made a few placatory noises and held the receiver at arm's length while he blew off his excess steam. When he'd cooled down, I said, 'It's pretty damn obvious Stroud was acting under Wesley's instructions.'

'Obvious to us perhaps, but where's the motive?'

'Playboy turned killer, even,' I added. 'He was in the vicinity at the time.'

'I repeat, where's the motive?'

'I don't know,' I said weakly. 'Besides, I'm not even on the case.'

'No, but you're in a good position to keep an ear to the ground. You're under the same roof as Wesley, probably sharing the same table for breakfast...'

It seemed he was knocking me down with one hand and

helping me up with the other. I said, 'So you want me to dig for this motive?'

'It's a logical move in the circumstances. Just don't let it interfere with your main task of finding General O'Hara.'

'Any leads?'

'None. I've a couple of men questioning people in the Buckfastleigh area and we're checking hire firms who rent out large vans, trailers, and suchlike. It's routine and so far it's proved fruitless.'

'It will be. The General's tucked safely away in virgin territory by now. The operation was too carefully planned for conventional slip-ups. Somebody leaked our location details, and I want to know the who and to whom.'

He grunted approvingly and began to sound like an anxious father as he reminded me of his responsibility for Kelly's safety. He was looking towards me to shield her from any danger, he said, and then he wound it up: 'Keep in touch,' he ordered crisply, 'and I mean regularly, Simon.'

'Naturally,' I said as I broke the connection.

I found Wesley Falloway in the indoor swimming pool. He was lying on a steamer-chair applying oil to his well-muscled torso, and tanning himself under a bank of ultra-violet lights. I'd learned over lunch how water exercises had been suggested as a beneficial means of strengthening the old lady's legs, and how an extension had been built on to The Cedars to accommodate a pool. The son appeared to be making full use of the facilities.

As I approached, my eyes roamed over the Beverly Hills inventory: the high glass-domed ceiling supported by marble pillars, the elaborate carpet of mosaic tiles which washed across the floor, the extravagant fitments. Falloway stared back at me unblinkingly. Apart from today's episode with the Jaguar, we hadn't faced each other since our virulent *tête-à-tête* in the Eclipse bar—and if he knew I'd been driving the car he'd nearly run off the road, then he wasn't giving the fact away in his dead-pan expression.

'Quite a pool you've got here,' I began conversationally.

'We like it.' His smile made its fleeting appearance as he adjusted his sun goggles and lay back under the lights. 'I understand you're our guest,' he said, adding slowly. 'Which one of your *noms de plume* are you adopting today? Is it Preston or Drake?'

'Drake,' I admitted soberly.

'The man who works for the Security Division?'

'The very same.'

He smiled a little crookedly and reached out to adjust a dial on a wall-mounted control panel. This action increased the wattage from the overhead lights and caused me to notice that the fingers of his right hand were heavily bandaged.

'Are you swimming?' he asked.

My mind was swimming all right, swimming between masked men with shotguns and playboy actors with strapped-up fingers. I was doing a mental comparison. Matching build for build, height for height, feature for feature. Falloway seemed taller, I concluded, but I couldn't be sure. 'Mother forgot to pack my trunks,' I quipped.

'No problem.' He reached under the steamer-chair and tossed me the necessary article. They were blue and embroidered with a little silver serpent and the initials W.F.

'Thanks, but I'm not in the mood.' I tossed the trunks back, aiming deliberately at his right hand. He winced as he caught them.

'For Christ's sake!' He showed me his pained expression.

'Sorry,' I said, tongue in cheek. 'I didn't realize . . .'

'You could see my fingers were bandaged!'

'It's the lights,' I apologized, adding: 'A recent injury?'

'Very recent and extremely painful. I pitted my wits against a conger eel and lost. If you know anything about sea fishing then you'll know it isn't advisable to catch your fingers in the wire trace while trying to land something as big as a conger.'

I didn't, but it sounded convincing. I said, 'You were away when General O'Hara was snatched?'

'In Looe, yes.'

'Doing what?'

'I've just told you. I was on a fishing trip.'

'Pitting your wits against a conger eel.'

'Look, Drake . . .' He sat up, snatched off the sun-goggles. 'I don't think I care for your tone . . .'

'And I don't care for your story.' I decided to dispense with the niceties and rock the boat a little.

'What the hell is that supposed to mean?'

'It means I don't trust you, Mr Falloway. I know all about your blood-boost activities and anyone who can put that into practice must be more than capable of a little horse-thieving.'

He didn't like my analogy. I watched the perspiration break out on his upper lip, saw it run across his wide shoulders, trickle its way down his naked backbone.

'Blood-boost?' he snapped. 'What on earth are you talking about now?'

'Don't play games,' I growled, 'Why do you think I've been sniffing around at Chinhurst Lodge, passing myself off as a journalist? How come we've been talking for several minutes and you haven't asked me once about the deception?'

'I thought McQuillan must be under suspicion for some malpractice—'

'And you figured it wasn't any of your business.'

A nerve fluttered beside his wide mouth. 'That's exactly what I thought.'

'You deny any knowledge of illegal methods being used to improve your horses' performance?'

'Of course I deny it.'

'Then you also tell lies.'

His eyes narrowed. 'Be very careful . . .'

'Sure,' I smiled tolerantly, 'I'll be as careful as Stroud must have been when he stuck the needle into Counterfoil's jugular vein and transfused the blood. I'll be as careful as you were when you discovered the boy's weaknesses, when you tapped his veterinary knowledge, when you bought him the car . . .'

'That's a slanderous remark, Drake!' He thrust a finger in my face.

'It's only slanderous if it isn't true,' I snarled.

'You have a statement from Stroud?'

I shook my head.

'Then you'd better get one before—'

'Where do you suggest I go,' I cut in, 'the mortuary?'

'Mortuary . . . ?'

'Stroud's as dead as yesterday's news.'

'My God.' He slumped limply back into the chair, the deep facial tan blanching under the ultra-violet lights.

I reminded myself he was an actor by profession—not a very good one judging from the reviews, but an actor nevertheless. A convincing expression of shock-stricken ignorance was an elementary exercise learned by all.

'How did it happen?' He snicked off the lights and pressed a neighbouring button. A bell, somewhere behind me, tinkled faintly.

'A pitchfork pierced his lung,' I said.

'An accident?'

'A carefully constructed one, maybe. I'd hoped you'd be able to tell me.'

'Me?' he said roughly, 'why should I?'

'Because you were at Chinhurst,' I replied just as roughly.

'What?'

'Are you denying you visited the stables today?'

'No . . .' He hesitated. 'But I didn't have anything to do with Stroud's death.'

Gilbert Bexson appeared on the scene pushing a drinks trolley. Falloway looked relieved. He asked for a brandy, drank it in two quick gulps and then asked for another. The alcohol helped him regain his composure, the colour filtered back into his cheeks. I sipped a Barcardi-and-Coke and listened as he fed me a string of words which protested his innocence. He spoke with his hands too. They moved fluidly, expressively, almost pleadingly. He told me how he'd called at the stables on his

124

way back from Looe. How he'd wanted to see McQuillan to discuss prospects of running Paradise Kid over hurdles this winter, and how he'd looked for the trainer without success. He'd heard nothing and seen nothing, so he said, and I found myself almost believing him. An error I was quick to rectify.

'Why call on McQuillan when you could have telephoned?' I asked quickly. 'No, Mr Falloway, you didn't go there to discuss trivialities. You went there to see Stroud.'

'That's not true.'

'Was he becoming too much of a risk? Putting you through the squeezer, asking for more money? Or how about blackmail?'

'You're crowding your luck, Drake.' He balled his left hand into a fist, but opened it again. 'I could have you thrown out for—'

'And I could tell your mother how you've been manipulating your racehorses. I'd tell it with such conviction that you'd end up being thrown out with me.'

'You're a bastard.'

'Just so long as you're not a killer,' I said, adding, 'now let's try and keep it friendly, huh?'

He ran a tongue over his lips and smiled nervously. 'I didn't kill Stroud.'

'Somebody did.'

'Not me.'

'Stroud was gee-ing up your horses on your instructions.'

'Prove it.'

'Oh, I will,' I said, 'I've a very persistent nature.'

'Why don't you check my bookmakers' accounts?'

I grinned. Obviously he had a sense of humour. And why shouldn't he spit in my eye? With Stroud on his way to the abode of the blest, Falloway knew only too well that we were floundering. There was no way we could positively implicate him. We couldn't call a corpse as a witness, and yet we didn't have a motive. I was on a hiding to nothing and he was safe. And he damned well knew it.

'Let's talk about General O'Hara,' I murmured mildly. 'Were you aware that we'd switched horses?'

'My mother told me just before the garden party. She thought I might notice the difference and she didn't want me commenting on the fact.'

'Who else did she tell?'

'No one as far as I know.'

'What about Bexson or the housekeeper?'

He shook his head.

'And you,' I probed, 'who did you tell—Stroud?'

'We're back on that tack again, are we,' he grunted impatiently. 'I suppose that over-fertile mind of yours has fabricated yet another conspiracy. Stroud and I stole the General, is that it?'

'The thought had crossed my mind.'

'Well you're crazy. I didn't tell Stroud. I didn't tell anyone. I was miles away when it happened.'

'Fishing in Cornwall.' I met his gaze levelly. 'But can you prove it?'

He hesitated. 'I was with Vicky Annesley.'

It seemed he could. A dirty weekend for an alibi. It wasn't bad, it wasn't bad at all.

Falloway's eyes widened suddenly as he looked from me to the door. I followed his gaze. The superbly proportioned body of Kelly Meredith picked its way towards us, her soft young breasts billowing over the top of a silver minissima bikini.

Falloway didn't waste much time shovelling himself out of the chair. 'Well, hello,' he said, a welcoming smile arching obscenely over his face.

'Hi!'

'Do you want to use the lights or the water?'

'The water looks tempting.'

'Seventy degrees all the year round.'

'Mm, fabulous.' She paddled across to me, took my hand. 'How do I look, Simon?'

'Desirable,' I said.

She smiled in that infectious little-girl way of hers and squeezed my fingers. The squeeze spoke sentences. Things were right between us. The grass was progressing nicely. It helped balance the effect of the bikini, but it didn't stop me wanting to see her even more *au naturel*.

'Enjoy your swim,' I told her, consulting my wristwatch.

'You're going out?' She eyed me quizzically.

'Don't wait up. I'll be late.'

'You don't want me along?'

'Uh-uh. Any time now the horsenappers are going to make clear their demands, and I want one of us here when that happens.'

The news of my intended departure had a brightening effect on Falloway. As far as he was concerned I had already left. He had me counting the moles on his shoulder blades as he administered his how-I-sweep-the-dames-off-their-feet formula to Kelly.

'Don't forget to tell her about conger eels, wire traces, and damaged fingers,' I said satirically. 'Women find fishermen's tales fascinating.'

He whirled on me. 'Everything I've told you is true, Drake. If you choose to believe otherwise, then that's your prerogative. But utter malicious libel in front of a witness and I warn you . . .'

I turned, began to walk out, not even bothering to let him conclude his threat-making speech.

'I mean it, Drake!'

'Sure.'

'Don't push me . . . I won't be pushed around . . .'

I pushed the door instead, and walked out.

Vicky Annesley's bungalow was tucked discreetly away in the Quantock Hills. It was of modern ranch-style design with big bay windows, sliding patio doors, and a decorative sun-trap garden. An elaborately carved nameplate on the gate announced: *Serendipity*.

On my way to the door I weaved a course around a flashy-looking motor-bike and an early-sixties Ford Consul. I guessed she had company. I leant on the bell-push and activated a melodious peal of chimes.

'If it's insurance we don't want any,' a male voice proclaimed. 'If it's encyclopedias, we've already got a set.'

'And if it's the man from the pools company?' I countered.

'Then you're at the wrong bloody house, mate. The only draws we're interested in have a subtle difference in spelling— and they usually end up round ankles during rag week.'

A chorus of voices laughed heartily as the door opened to reveal a broad grin on the face of brother Eddie. He stood before me wearing a Mickey Mouse T-shirt and a pair of striped bell-bottoms loud enough to break the sound barrier. A couple of what can best be described as 'the beautiful people' stood with him. I'm not up with campus lingo but if I categorize them as long-haired weirdos of indeterminate sex, then I guess you'll get the picture.

'I know that face—wait a minute—' Eddie snapped his fingers enthusiastically. 'Last Tuesday evening in the Eclipse bar, right?'

'Right.'

'You've come to see my sister.'

'Socially,' I said. 'I never sell insurance this close to Christmas.'

His blue eyes crinkled in amusement, emphasizing the scar tissue around his left eyebrow. It looked like an old boxing scar, but then Eddie didn't look like a boxer. His body was tough and compact, but his face was good-looking almost to the point of being pretty. Just as Vicky Annesley had turned many a man's head, so little brother, no doubt, had made many a girl's heart flutter at Wroxford College.

'You'll have her all to yourself.' His smile deepened as a plug of chewing gum flipped from one cheek to the other. 'C'mon, fellas, my sister's got company.'

'Don't let me break up the party.'

'Nothing to break up, man,' said a longhair, pulling a pack of tobacco from his denim shirt and expertly rolling a cigarette one-handed.

'Peace,' said the other, showing me the ingrained dirt on his palm.

'Peace,' I echoed, smiling inwardly.

With a twist of the throttle Eddie gunned the motor-bike out through the wrought-iron entrance and off down the track. The Consul rattled its way after him. I watched the dust settle, then stepped in to meet Vicky.

She was calling her brother's name and saying something about dinner. I heard a door open and the sound of approaching sandals clacking across the parquet flooring.

'Remember me?' I asked as she came into view.

'Surprise, surprise.' I could feel the warmth emanating from those clear blue eyes as she showed me that gift-wrapped smile of hers.

'Eddie's just left,' I told her.

'He was supposed to be staying for dinner,' she shrugged her slim shoulders. 'Still, that's Eddie all over.'

I asked her if he lived at the bungalow. She pulled a face and put two fingers to her temple. 'Don't wish that on me. It's bad enough when he drops in unexpectedly. He has a habit of bringing the strangest people with him.'

'Neolithic men,' I grinned. 'I'd noticed.'

'You weren't exactly expected either,' she added, still smiling.

'I'm sorry if I'm intruding—'

'Don't be sorry. You weren't expected but that doesn't mean you aren't welcome.'

I thanked her and followed in the haze of her perfume as she led me into a bright, nicely furnished lounge. The room smelled quietly of leather and log fires. The fittings were modern but elegant, unquestionably feminine. She told me briefly how she'd bought the house when her parents died and how she tried, sometimes unsuccessfully, to keep a sisterly eye on Eddie's activities. I liked her breezy manner, the way she bubbled when she talked. She slipped some music on the hi-fi and brought forth a bottle of vodka and two crystal glasses.

'I am right about the vodka, aren't I?'

'The lady has a good memory.'

'You made quite an impression the last time we met.'

'Likewise,' I said.

She settled next to me on the sofa, arranging her body to its best advantage. My eyes ran over the low-slung hipster slacks, the cute halter top which made no pretence of covering her navel. The broad band of bare flesh was designed to whet the appetite, and from where I was sitting it was having the desired effect.

'I think I can guess why you're here,' she remarked softly.

'Guess away,' I said.

'Wesley Falloway?'

'You've played the game before.'

'I know you work for the T.S.D.'

'Word gets around.'

'Wesley told me. I think Roy Biggs told him.'

I was sure he had. I smiled blandly.

'You don't look like a racing investigator. I thought they were all old men in trench coats.'

'They are. I'm a nonconformist.'

She laughed. The action caused her midriff to ripple deliciously. She was giving me a hard time.

'It's Wesley's horses, isn't it?' she asked finally.

I nodded. 'For animals that were once the debris of the turf they've made miraculous progress.'

'I guessed as much.' She bit down on her bottom lip. 'When Wesley told me you worked for the Security Division I put two and two together. We quarrelled about it in Cornwall—we had the most terrible row—it's all over between us . . .'

The flurry of words—especially the last five, were music to my ears. Somehow I'd broken up their relationship, but just how I'd managed it I wasn't too sure.

'I could tell he was lying to me,' she continued. 'I'd felt all along he was cheating in some way or another. He was very thick with Duncan Stroud—always giving him money—'

'So when you discovered my real identity—'

'It all fell into place. I wouldn't have minded if he'd told me the truth, trusted me enough to confide in me. But he got angry, very angry. He told me it was none of my concern and that I was to keep out of it. He showed me a side of his nature I never want to see again . . .'

I chuckled internally and topped up the glasses. She padded out to the freezer, filled up the ice-bucket, then sat staring reflectively into her drink. I didn't try to restart the conversation. I turned the L.P. over on the turntable and narrowed the segregative gap between us as I sat back on the sofa.

'Will Wesley be arrested?' she asked hesitantly.

'I doubt it. We can't press charges because we haven't any evidence that directly connects him with anything that's happened.'

She asked whether Stroud would testify.

I shook my head and told her briefly about the tragedy. When the initial shock had subsided, I said, 'And apart from all that, I'm no longer officially on the case.'

'Or any case?' She looked at me interrogatively.

'I've moved on to bigger and better things,' I hedged. 'Something that needed you to corroborate an alibi, hence the visit.'

She looked vaguely surprised.

'Like you spending the weekend with Wesley in Cornwall.'

'But I didn't.'

'But you said—'

'We'd planned a long weekend together, yes. We left early on Friday and arrived in Looe around midday. The row developed shortly afterwards.'

'You walked out on him?'

'He walked out on me. He stormed off with his stupid fishing tackle and left me at the hotel.'

'So you came home.'

'By way of a hire car, damn him. I was so angry, Simon. I haven't seen or heard from him since—and I want to keep it that way.'

She sounded as though she meant it. Having wrangled with female fickleness before and lost, I wouldn't have bet money on it. Shirts come expensive.

Time melted away as air replaced alcohol in the vodka bottle. We drank, we talked, and I found myself invited to dinner. It was all very romantic. Just us, candlelight, and smoochy music. I glided through the meal becoming more intoxicated by the second. It wasn't the drink. Vicky radiated such intense sexuality that it was making me heady just watching her movements. She could use her body as a mute uses his hands. She was tigerish yet totally feminine, promising an infinite reward.

We ended up back on the sofa. I had a hand round her shoulder. Her skin felt cool, creamy smooth.

'I've a lot to thank Wesley for.' I moved closer, almost touching my face with hers. 'Without him we might never have met.'

She blew in my ear. 'And I really thought I was in love with him.'

'People make mistakes.'

'He's involved in something else, isn't he? Something that happened over the weekend.'

'He could be.'

'And I was supposed to be his alibi?'

'That's the way it looks.'

'Well, what—'

'Hey.' I put a finger to her lips. 'We're not going to spend the evening talking about Wesley, are we?'

'Well you brought him up. You said—'

'I know,' I grinned, 'and I'm beginning to regret it. I'd far rather talk about you.'

She snuggled tighter. 'I'm the sort of girl who goes through life making mistakes where men are concerned. Am I making another one now, Simon?'

'Now?'

'You're married, aren't you,' she said with sudden seriousness.

'Am I?'

132

'You have all the signs. I think you're the kind of man a girl can depend on.'

'I had a wife once,' I said. 'It seems a long time ago.'

'It ended in divorce?'

'Barbara died of an incurable disease . . .' I found myself hanging on to the words. The memory still hurt.

'Was she very pretty?'

'She was beautiful.'

'I'm sorry.' She flushed slightly.

'You talk too much.' I cupped her face in my hands and kissed her. It seemed the most natural thing in the world—as if I'd been doing it for years.

'You've been hurt.' She shivered slightly as she mussed my hair, her fingers tracing the stitches in my scalp.

'A battle scar,' I told her. 'My current assignment.'

'Somebody did that to you?'

'I got in the way.'

'Don't . . .'

'Don't?'

'Oh, Simon . . .' Her eyes were wide and anguished.

'Yes?'

'Why are things always so complicated?'

'I live a complicated kind of life.'

'I'm glad we've found . . .' She stopped suddenly.

'Each other?' I supplied.

'Mm.'

'Well, say it then.'

She did, adding, 'Please be careful.'

'I'm always careful.'

'Always?'

'Always.'

Her tongue was skidding round my teeth as she murmured with breathy excitement. 'Now I know you're the kind of man a girl can depend on.'

I didn't answer. My mind was drugged, my thoughts uncoordinated. I was unaware of anything except the now naked breasts that moulded themselves against me. I took a nipple in my mouth and teased it to erection on my tongue. I felt her fingers flutter beneath my shirt as, like a kitten starved of affection, she dug her nails into my shoulders. Her eyes were closed, her breathing coming in jerky little gasps 'Simon Simon Simon,' she moaned softly, as her slacks swished to the floor, her shoes tumbled against the sofa.

I worked my thumbs inside her pants and began peeling them over the round swells of her hips. My hands kneaded the firm flesh of her buttocks, explored the damp creases of her thighs, pulling her on to me, gently . . . reassuringly . . .

We made love three times that evening. I didn't arrive back at The Cedars until well after two. I felt tired, dehydrated, and my floating head promised a beaut of a hangover in the morning. In short, I felt wonderful.

Chapter Nine

'I TRUST you have a valid reason for your lateness, Mr Drake.
Unpunctuality is a weakness I cannot tolerate.'

It was the following morning and Alison Falloway's voice
was astringent. I walked a little unsteadily into the drawing-
room, found the nearest chair, and sank into it. She eyed me
as though I was a late delivery which should have been un-
packed before breakfast. A clock on the mantelpiece took sides
and struck eleven times.

'You've kept us both waiting.' She gestured vaguely behind her. 'Are you all right? You look a trifle liverish.'

Somebody chuckled and a voice declared, '*Omne nimium
vertitur in vitium.*'

'Every excess becomes a vice.' Alison Falloway acting as
translator.

I hardly heard her. The suave voice delivering the Latinism
had had a devastating effect on my optic nerves. My eyes
rapidly panned and focused on the crossed ankles, the mirror polished toe-caps, which protruded from behind the Chairmobile. The machine moved forward to reveal a pair of im-
peccable trouser creases, a fine worsted jacket with a flourish
of crimson handkerchief, a fleur-de-lis silk tie and . . .'

'Christ,' I groaned audibly as I spotted the carnation button-
hole. 'Not Nick bloody Barron?'

'At your service, old love.' His eyes flickered with amusement.

I sighed feebly and fumbled out a cigarette. Of all the
people I could have done without seeing, Nick Barron, racing
correspondent for the *Sunday Globe*, was number one on my

card. His name was synonymous with slick racing *exposés*—owners, trainers, jockeys, if there was any dirt to be thrown, then Barron would do the throwing. He used a spade, not a pen, and if any of the dirt happened to fall in your court then you could either sue, which was a foolish and expensive road to take, or you could melt quietly away, which was what most of his victims did.

Scandal attracted Barron the way a bonfire attracted Boy Scouts. He was insincere, ruthless and mercilessly ambitious. He also liked himself. We'd crossed paths many times, but these encounters hadn't exactly endeared us to one another.

He brushed up the ends of his moustache and said, 'You look decidedly rough, Simon. I've seen healthier faces in a geriatric ward.'

Alison Falloway wrinkled her forehead and asked bluntly, 'Where were you last night?'

I didn't consider my movements were any of her business, but being in an unmilitant mood I mentioned Vicky Annesley's name and murmured something about furthering my enquiries.

She didn't approve. She tut-tutted and said, 'I don't know why you've been questioning that woman, but I'll tell you the same as I've told Wesley. She's a temptress, a fortune hunter, and best avoided.'

'Simon never could resist a good-looking female,' Barron chuckled.

'Well on this occasion he'd better try. They're totally unsuited.'

Her words made me angry. Not angry enough to risk upsetting her with a quick-tempered remark I'd later regret, but angry just the same. I took a calming pull on my cigarette and let it pass.

'Vicky Annesley's a Sagittarian,' the Duchess went on. 'They're ambitious creatures and renowned excitement chasers. A relationship between her birth-sign and yours can only prove disastrous.'

'Thanks for the astral warning, but there's nothing between us,' I lied. 'I went there on business.'

Barron gave me a straight-lipped smile and said, 'But the poached eggs under your eyes tell a different story, eh, old love?'

I considered that a rhetorical question and ignored him.

'I'm an avid believer in astrology.' He turned to the Duchess, buttering her up, switching on that professional charm. 'I've always found it a wonderful guide to a person's character, their motivations and inner emotions.'

He was lying through his teeth but Alison Falloway welcomed the contrived enthusiasm. I didn't relish getting bogged down with the intricacies of soothsaying, so I decided to turn the conversation. Knowing the Duchess considered newspapermen 'loathsome creatures', I wanted to know why the hell she was rubbing shoulders with someone of Barron's notoriety. 'You didn't come here for an astrological forecast, Nick,' I said, 'so why?'

His eyes were on me humorously. 'To act as go-between, old son.'

I looked at him obliquely.

'If you'd been here last night, explanations wouldn't be necessary.'

'Well I wasn't and they are, so—'

'General O'Hara.'

'You know?'

He nodded smugly.

'The iniquitous people who stole my horse have contacted the *Globe*,' Alison Falloway explained. 'They want Mr Barron to act as an intermediary.'

I closed my eyes and drew a deep, calming breath.

'It's not unusual for a newspaper to be used in cases of kidnap,' Barron went on. 'A neutral third party can provide a buffer and have a calming effect on all concerned.'

'And end up with a gigantic scoop,' I murmured.

'I admit it has its compensations.'

'You're too damn right it has.' I turned to the Duchess. 'You realize the *Globe* will play this up to the hilt. It's a gift from the heavens as far as they're concerned.'

'I want my horse back, Mr Drake,' she said calmly. 'I'll do anything just as long as he's returned alive and unharmed.'

Barron showed her his sincere face as he picked at a neatly manicured fingernail. 'Rest assured, Mrs Falloway, the *Globe* will do everything in its power to retrieve the General and put an end to this miserable business.'

I found his tone sickening. Barron and the publishing organization he represented were interested in the sale of newspapers, nothing more. If negotiations went smoothly and the stallion was returned unharmed, then they had a great front page. If things went badly wrong and the stallion wasn't returned at all then they had a sensational front page. Either way the *Globe* would have the exclusive, the presses would roll, the circulation figures would soar, and Barron would ride in on the glory.

'It's a pity Grant's decoy scheme didn't work out,' I heard him saying. 'It would have saved Mrs Falloway a lot of anxiety, not to mention a great deal of money.'

I didn't like the dig. I reckon the Security Division would be made to look incompetent fools when Barron hit the typewriter keys. 'How much?' I asked tightly.

'Sorry, old son?' He frowned, decided to act dumb.

'The horsenappers, how much are they demanding?'

'A figure wasn't mentioned. My instructions were to drive to The Cedars, assure Mrs Falloway the horse was in good hands, and await a 7 p.m. telephone call.' He sniffed derisively and added, 'Ask me later this evening.'

Suddenly he was running the show. I didn't like it one bit. I told him in no uncertain terms that the T.S.D. had no intention of playing second fiddle to the *Sunday Globe*. I also told him that no private deals or arrangements could be made without first being vetted by us.

He gazed defiantly at me. We were like a couple of

warriors who had just locked swords. 'The Division hasn't any more say in the matter,' he replied glibly. 'The kidnappers have stated that if you persist in your enquiries or attempt to interfere—'

'Are you telling me to lie down and play dead?'

He inclined his head. 'Until the General is returned, that's exactly what I'm telling you.'

'Well you can go to—',

'Mr Barron's right,' Alison Falloway interjected. 'As much as I dislike pandering to these people, we cannot and must not take chances.'

I sighed weakly. Nick Barron had taken the initiative away from the T.S.D., and it looked as if the old lady was opting for the easy way out. 'And I thought Scorpionics were diehards,' I submitted roughly.

I saw her fingers twitch nervously on the joy-stick control as her shrewd eyes held mine. 'Twenty years ago, Mr Drake, they didn't die any harder than Alison Falloway. If these circumstances had occurred then, I would have willingly gambled with the General's life rather than let anyone dictate terms for his safe return.' She smiled wistfully, her mind reliving the past. 'The fire still smoulders but the flames went out a long time ago.'

She could have fooled me. I said doggedly, 'So you're going to close your eyes and hope I'll go away.'

'And will you?'

'No.'

She glanced at Barron. 'Mr Drake has the bit between his teeth and I don't think we're going to shake it loose.'

'He'll jeopardize everything,' Barron snorted.

'Then your newspaper should be able to make capital out of my bungling,' I said patiently. 'How the Division fluffed it—not once, but twice. That's quite a headline.'

There was a slight quiver of his mouth, but he controlled it instantly; with his self-discipline he'd learned the art of harnessing give-away expressions.

139

'Then you must adopt the role of the chameleon, Mr Drake,' the Duchess compromised. 'See all, but be seen by no one.'

'I respect your wishes, of course,' Barron said grudgingly, 'but I still think——'

'I'm staying, Nick,' I said, and he knew I meant it.

Alison Falloway powered the Chairmobile forward and handed me an envelope. 'Miss Meredith left this for you. I believe it's important.'

'Is Kelly out?'

'Wesley's taken her to lunch.'

'Oh.'

Barron grinned as he saw my face drop. He lifted himself from the chair, adjusted his tie with micrometric precision and announced that he too would be eating out. I made a similar statement after I'd read Kelly's note. The message was brief but explicit. It told how last night had been fun night for everyone. The playboy actor had made full use of my disappearance to woo Kelly away from the house and out into the country. They'd stopped at the Horse and Groom where Kelly had run into Freckles. The boy wanted to see me urgently and she had suggested the pub at midday today for the rendezvous. She'd signed the note 'With love'. A pure formality, I convinced myself, glancing at my watch, trying to disperse a mental playback of the obscene grin on Falloway's lips the afternoon he'd watched her enter the swimming pool. I wasn't sure why I felt so bitterly jealous. I couldn't really equate my feelings for Kelly with my feelings for Vicky Annesley. I told myself they were paternal. We'd formed a partnership and I felt a responsibility towards the girl, to watch over her, to protect her. That's what I told myself, but I knew I was wrong. I remembered the way I'd felt when I kissed her. No father ever felt that way about his child.

I made my way outside. There was very little breeze and the sun felt hot on my cheeks. Mercifully I'd parked in the shade of a large oak which still battled valiantly to preserve what few browned leaves it had left. I wasn't alone. The M.G. and the old lady's Daimler were rubbing noses. Gilbert Bexson, sleeves rolled, brow agleam with perspiration, was working in earnest. I could see the muscles flexing in his thick arms as he applied polish to the resplendent coachwork. Emily Byford stood by his side.

'Good morning,' I began traditionally. 'Is this to keep the demon rust away, or purely a labour of love?'

'Both, sir,' he smiled very genially, showing large white teeth. 'I try to keep it in showroom condition. The master was very fond of this car.'

'The late Mr Falloway; you got on well, uh?'

'He was a gentleman, sir. The finest employer I've ever worked for.'

He sounded as though he meant it. I doubted whether he held Wesley in the same esteem. I said, 'That's thirsty work. You had your hand round a lager the first time I saw you.'

He stopped polishing and regarded me blankly.

'The Horse and Groom, about a week ago.'

'A week ago . . .?' He pinched his nostrils.

Emily Byford offered no comment, just gazed at me pensively. I decided to give their memories a few seconds for recollection, then plunge straight in and hustle them hard.

'Did she ever find out?' I asked shortly.

'I'm sorry?' Bexson frowned.

'These thousands of pounds or whatever. Did Mrs Falloway ever find out?'

'I—I don't follow you.' He feigned ignorance.

'That's because you're not trying. How about Mrs Byford—how's her memory?'

They looked at each other. They understood my meaning all right and it was worrying them. I could sense their thoughts triggering inside their heads, searching, questioning. Bexson's complexion had lightened a shade. He wiped his forehead on the polishing cloth. 'What's on your mind, Mr Drake?'

'A certain questionable conversation I overheard in a pub,' I said. 'I've a restless curiosity which keeps asking why a chauffeur and housekeeper should be discussing large sums of money and be worried in case the lady of the house should get wind of it.'

'Gilbert—' Emily Byford snatched a glance towards Bexson. He avoided her eyes. 'You're some sort of private eye, aren't you?' he asked.

'Some sort,' I said.

'And you're connected with horseracing?'

'That's right—now have you something to tell me?'

'No, I . . .' He hesitated, seemingly undecided how he should reply. 'No, I've nothing to tell you . . . Nothing that's relevant,' he finished weakly.

'You deny the conversation?' I challenged him.

'You shouldn't have been listening,' the housekeeper piped up. 'You've taken a handful of words out of context and placed the wrong construction upon them.'

'And what is the right construction?'

'It doesn't concern you. Haven't you ever heard how curiosity killed the cat?'

I grinned at that. 'My favourite maxim,' I said.

Her dark eyes held mine with controlled irritation. She didn't like me very much and it showed. They were pretty close, these two, and I reckoned I'd have to go in for some melodramatics if I was to stand any kind of chance of opening them up. I lost the opportunity the moment Alison Falloway's voice came floating across the tarmac. She was calling for Bexson and he was more than pleased to receive the call.

'If you'll excuse us,' he smiled with effort, 'but we do have other work to attend to.'

'Duty comes first,' I said.

'Good morning, Mr Drake.' Emily Byford brushed past me with a distinctly audible sniff.

I watched them walk towards the house and stood for a moment pondering on Bexson's words. He'd queried my occupation and then stated he had nothing to tell me. Nothing that was relevant, he'd said. But relevant to what? I guessed he meant horseracing. I wasn't thinking too clearly this morning and as I didn't want to burden my brain with worthless conjecture I decided, for the moment at least, to forget it.

I reached the Horse and Groom late. I found Freckles propping up the bar, staring despondently into an empty glass. 'I thought you weren't coming,' he said.

I told him I'd overslept and felt lousy and that I hoped he wasn't going to waste my time.

'Is it true you work for the Security Division?'

I told him it was.

'Then I'm going to do you a favour.'

For a moment I thought he was about to elaborate on his previous characterization of bent jockeys in cheating kits, but he abolished my fears by adding quietly, 'Stroud's death wasn't accidental.'

I looked at him. 'Have you told that to the police?'

'I don't want to get involved with the dicks, besides—' he grinned engagingly, 'I kind of thought . . .' He handed me his empty glass.

I figured it was going to cost me and it did. I ended up parting with a tenner and my promise to buy the beer. The boy certainly knew how to drink. He downed two pints faster than I could pay for them and as he hadn't mastered the ventriloquous art of talking and drinking at the same time, I wasn't getting value for money. Finally he stopped, wiped his mouth on his sleeve and said, 'Stroud was blackmailing someone and that someone killed him.'

The statement acted as a shot of adrenalin to my brain. 'You're sure of that?'

'Sure I'm sure. If I wasn't you wouldn't be ten quid light.'

'So tell.'

'Well . . .' He rearranged his young face into a philosophic expression. 'I went to the barn as instructed. When I reached—'

'Hold it. Who gave these instructions?'

'Stroud. We'd had a delivery of straw and McQuillan wanted it stacked. It was our rest period, see, and Duncan was moaning like bloody hell because he'd been told to do it. McQuillan had collared him, so he collared me. I was supposed to help him out.'

A very different version from McQuillan's 'conscientious worker' patter, I thought. In the one I'd been served up, Stroud had been featured as the stable benefactor who'd volunteered for the job. I said, 'So you lent Stroud a hand.'

'Did I buggery. Stacking bales is bloody hard graft. No, I waited till I reckoned he'd finished and then I went round. I was gonna make some excuse—say I'd hurt my wrist or something.'

'And?'

'Well, the barn door was shut. I thought that was kind of odd seeing as how warm it was. Anyway, I heard voices—or rather Stroud's voice. He was talking and laughing. Not a funny laugh, more a sarky sort of chuckle, follow me?'

'So you listened?'

'Copped a right earful, didn't I? Stroud was saying he knew too much and that that was worth money, a lot of money.'

'Those were his words? He knew too much and he wanted buying off?'

'Yeah, more or less. Either you cough up or I'll blab to the law, that's what he said.'

I'd intended to stay away from alcohol but my throat had grown dry. My theories were fast becoming realities and I needed something more potent than ginger ale to perk up the grey matter. I bought Freckles another pint and sipped meditatively on a vodka. 'Who was he putting the screws on?' I asked optimistically.

He wriggled his bony shoulders. 'If I knew that I'd have tapped you for a score.'

I grinned. 'So you didn't recognize the other voice?'

'Couldn't hear it properly. Stroud was doing most of the talking. He was still heaving the bales about, and laughing,

144

and saying something like, "If I don't get what I want, I'm going to walk to the office, pick up the phone, and shop you".' He paused for thought, adding, 'I think there was a scuffle but I can't be sure. I slid back to my quarters a bit sharpish. Fifteen minutes later you arrived.'

'You panicked?'

'S'pose I did a bit. Copper started neighing and trying to kick his door in. Whenever that happens, McQuillan comes skittering across the yard. I didn't want to be caught so I bolted for it.'

I felt he'd lost me. I asked him to back-track a dozen or so words and tell me about this door-kicker called Copper.

'Dunno what his racing name is,' he explained, 'we just call him Copper 'cause all coppers are bastards—and this one's a right 'un. He dropped out of the blue over the weekend—nobody knew he'd arrived until Quilly announced the fact on Sunday morning. We have a new arrival from Ireland, he tells us at breakfast. Coughed its guts out on the flight over, he says. Equine 'flu. Equine bloody 'flu, would you believe, and he brings it into the yard.'

I straightened up, studied him critically. 'Describe this horse to me.'

His pale eyes puckered. 'You're not going to believe this.'

'Try me.'

'I've never seen it.'

When I asked him to explain, he drew in a long breath and told how McQuillan had isolated the animal in an odd box at the far end of the yard. The area was taboo to all except the trainer. He alone did the feeding, watering and mucking out. During the day the horse was confined to its box and both halves of the door were kept shut. At night they were padlocked. 'If Quilly doesn't want the virus to spread,' Freckles scoffed, 'then why the bloody hell did he take the sod in?'

My mind had slipped into overdrive. I said quickly, 'What about your mates? Somebody must have seen something?'

He wagged his head doubtfully. 'Riddle says he caught a

145

glimpse of his rump one morning. A chestnut he says he was —but I wouldn't take it for gospel.'

Knowing Riddle, I knew what he meant. It was probably nothing more than a string of crazy coincidences, but it didn't stop me adding *Sunday* to *isolation* to *chestnut*, mixing them all together, and coming up with a General called O'Hara.

Freckles lifted a quizzical eyebrow. 'How come you're so interested?'

'Let's say I've never grown up. I'm still intrigued by mysteries.'

'Bullshit, you're on to something.'

I murmured. 'Keep your voice down. I haven't seen the horse so how can I possibly be?'

'You figure Copper is in some way connected with Stroud snuffing it, don't you?'

I said nothing.

He considered. 'The killer was being blackmailed by Stroud. Why should a sick horse . . . ?' He flicked me a glance.

'You're writing the closing chapter,' I said quietly, 'not me.'

'Copper's a mean one all right,' he went on reflectively. 'I've laid awake at nights listening to the pig clout his door. Bang, bang, bloody bang. He kicks up one helluva racket at times.'

'Restless, uh?'

'Not bloody much.'

'An infirm animal?'

'Huh?'

'Well how frisky do you feel with 'flu?'

He met my gaze levelly, moistened his lips.

'Precisely,' I said.

We stared at each other, silent thoughts passing between us. Finally I jerked my head towards the door. 'I want to take a look,' I said.

He made worried noises. 'No chance. Quilly would hang me up by his hook.'

'Point me in the right direction, that's all.'

'It's too risky. The box is in full view of the office.'

'I'll take that gamble.'

'If you get caught . . .'

'I'll carry the can,' I promised.

There was a brief silence during which he drained his glass and chewed on a broken thumbnail. Finally he murmured his assent.

I felt vulnerable and highly conspicuous as I left Freckles at the barn and ambled across the expanse of yard. My progression to the suspect box was slow. I had one eye on the office, watching for any sign of movement, ready to change direction if McQuillan was even to think about stretching his legs.

With or without Freckles' help I would have found the box. I could hear the animal fretting. The quivering exhalation of air through nostrils echoed feverishly from within. Obvious distress signals, I thought, listening as a hoof scuffed rhythmically at the stone floor.

Wire had been twisted around the bolts to make sure they couldn't be shaken loose. I cursed silently. This I hadn't anticipated and it was going to be a fiddling business getting them undone. I snatched a last look around the yard. Nothing human stirred. My solitude offered confirmation that I had reached the box without apparent detection. I held my breath and began unwrapping the wire.

I worked quickly and it was only moments before the first bolt slid smoothly from its keeper. The second wasn't so easy. I became so engrossed in the elaborately twisted wire that I hardly felt the little burst of air as it caressed my cheek. I got the full message a split second later as McQuillan's hook embedded itself into the mouldering timber, the stainless steel tip missing my fingers by millimetres.

'That's a sick horse!' he growled, the hook squirming in the woodwork as it wrenched itself free. 'Who the devil . . . ?'

I turned quickly to face him. 'Drake,' I said, 'and I don't like the dramatics.'

He wasn't alone. I caught a glimpse of Nick Barron emerging from the tack room. What the hell was Barron doing here? I steered my mind away from the gouged hole in the box door, smiled thinly, and added, 'That's a lethal piece of ironmongery, McQuillan.'

'I'm sorry, Drake,' he began, 'I thought you were some yobbo who'd wandered into the yard—'

'He does need a haircut,' Barron chuckled.

I needed the reporter's humour like a heart case needed a blocked artery. 'This animal is going box crazy,' I said, ad-libbing quickly, 'I heard it thrashing about and as no one was around . . .'

'A trifle neurotic I grant you,' McQuillan's tone was acidy as he re-fastened the wires. 'But I do know how to tend sick horses, so I'll ask you not to interfere.'

'How sick?'

' 'Flu virus—hence the isolation.'

'The dreaded bug, eh?' Barron sounded amused.

McQuillan smiled tolerantly and steered us away from the box. He removed a splinter of wood which had impaled itself on his hook, and then concealed the metal implement in his jacket pocket. 'Can I help you in some way, Drake?' he enquired as we reached the office. 'I assume you're here on official business?'

I'd had a question floating around in my head since yesterday. As I needed an excuse for my presence, this seemed like a good time to air it. 'What precisely were you doing prior to Stroud being found?' I asked.

He looked at me blankly. 'I was working on the owners' accounts.'

'In here?' I indicated the office.

'Of course. You found me at my desk when you arrived.'

'And how long had you been there?'

He paused. 'I can't remember exactly.'

'Minutes, hours—?'

'About an hour and a half I suppose. What are you driving at?'

'Wesley Falloway tells a different story. When he arrived about fifteen minutes before us, you were nowhere to be found.'

I saw a spasm of anger ripple across his face. 'He's a damn liar. I was bogged down with paperwork and never moved from my desk. If you're going to side with a renegade like Falloway then you're a poor judge of character.'

I looked at him impassively, made no comment.

'I've told him to remove his horses,' he went on bitterly. 'You and the Security Division have already indicated that something underhand has been going on in these stables and I want an end to it. I don't know what it was and I don't wish to know. Falloway is trouble as far as I'm concerned and I want rid of him.'

'Something underhand?' Barron snatched at his words. 'Something underhand has been going on in these stables? My, my, Mr McQuillan, now you have aroused my newsmongering instincts.'

The trainer squared his shoulders and muttered, 'I have nothing further to say. If you'll excuse me I have work to do.'

'Come, come, old sport.' Barron didn't quit that easily. 'The work can wait a few moments—If Wesley Falloway has been a naughty boy then the *Globe* would like to hear about it.'

'No comment.' He was adamant.

'Was Falloway friendly with Stroud?'

'I said no comment! If you're so damned interested why don't you ask Drake? He seems to know most of the answers.'

He threw me a hostile glance and lurched into the office slamming the door hard behind him. Barron grinned, pursed his lips, and whistled a few bars of *Softly as I leave you.*

'What the hell brought you here anyway?' I asked.

'Duncan Stroud's accident. My editor thought there might be something in it—and it looks as if he was right, eh, Simon?'

'I don't owe you any favours,' I grunted. 'You tried to cut me out—'

'Only my fun, old love.' He wrapped a let's-make-it-up arm

149

around my shoulder. 'Of course I'll keep you in touch with negotiations. We'll both get the General back. I was playing along with the old girl, that's all.'

'Do me a favour, Nick?' I removed the offending arm.

'Such as?'

'Take your bloody oar out of my business.'

'Now that's not nice.'

'That's the way it is.'

'You're not going to tell me about Stroud or Falloway?'

'You're clutching at non-existent straws.'

'McQuillan seemed to think differently.'

'McQuillan was wrong. You're wasting your time.'

'What about that box?' He peered past me and into the yard. 'What's so interesting about a sick horse?'

'I didn't know the horse was sick. I heard it whinnying and was doing my samaritan bit, that's all.'

'I thought McQuillan over-reacted, but . . . ?'

'You're guessing. It was nothing I tell you, nothing.'

'Simon, old lad . . .' His lips curled into a cunning smile. 'For a man with a handful of nothing, you certainly play an excellent game of poker.'

That evening I buried myself away in the library. I rested my chin on my hands and my elbows on the Hepplewhite desk. I had a cigarette between my fingers, a pad and pencil in front of me, and I stared impatiently at a white telephone which refused to ring. It was ten minutes past the appointed hour. Ten interminable minutes. The horsenappers were employing sweat tactics.

I was beginning to feel tired, not tired in the physical sense, just tired of being manipulated by other people. A lot had happened since that first briefing at Newmarket Racecourse. Many people had come in and gone out of my life.

I watched my cigarette smoke wreath its way ceilingwards. I thought about Potter who had unconsciously started the ball rolling; about Stroud who had ended his days like a piece of skewered mutton; about Vicky Annesley who had given love and warmth and the things a guy needed; and about Kelly who had suddenly attached herself to Wesley Falloway . . . I blotted that one out. It was beginning to get between me and my peace of mind.

The shrill from the telephone turned the mental images into broken fragments. It gave half a ring then stopped. Barron's reflexes were sharp. I snatched up the receiver, heard the rapid pips of a pay-phone, and covered the mouthpiece. A male voice whispered through a background of static:

'Mr Nicolas Barron?'

'Yes.'

'Does your client wish to purchase the livestock in question?'

'Yes, she does.'

'Good. Then it will cost her a quarter of a million pounds.'

I heard Barron's sharp intake of breath. He said a little shakily, 'That's an awful lot of money.'

'It's an awful lot of horse. The animal's total prize money is all we're asking, Mr Barron. £250,000 to be paid as instructed.'

'And if my client—'

'Doesn't pay? Then that would be tragic, wouldn't it? The General would be gelded and thus rendered useless.'

'I see.'

'Now ask your client, Mr Barron—and please make it brief.'

I could hear muffled words being anxiously exchanged between the reporter and the Duchess. Finally Barron said, 'It would take at least a week for Mrs Falloway to raise that figure.'

The voice laughed weakly. 'Don't make jokes, Mr Barron, your client could raise double that amount in twenty-four hours, but we're not asking for the total sum in cash. Even in notes of high denomination it would be far too cumbersome to handle.'

'Then . . . ?'

'You're taking this call in the drawing-room?'

'Yes?'

'Hanging over the fireplace is a painting of a brood mare with foal by George Stubbs. It's valued at £200,000, I believe?'

He hesitated to consult the Duchess. 'It is,' he admitted.

'Then after you've removed the canvas from its frame and rolled it up carefully, purchase a large pair of saddle-bags. Make sure they're big enough to hold both the painting and fifty thousand in unmarked notes.' He laughed again. 'You see how cleverly we've arrived at my original figure.'

'And the time and place?' Barron asked stiffly.

'The Roebuck Tavern at Axford, this coming Saturday at 9.30 a.m. It's a picturesque little spot. Do you know it at all?'

'I'll find it.'

'Good. There's a triangle of green outside the pub with a seat on it. Leave the saddle-bags on the seat and go home. If everything is in order then you'll be contacted and told the location of the goods. Do I make myself clear?'

'Perfectly.'

'And no tricks, Mr Barron. You do realize the merchandise is perishable?'

'I understand.'

'Excellent. Until Saturday then.' There was a click and the line fell silent.

I gave it a few seconds, flipped the rest, and dialled Howard Grant's number.

Chapter Ten

VICKY ANNESLEY looked nothing short of tremendous when I saw her on Wednesday. She leaned barefooted against her door-jamb, smiling at me, sleek arms folded over her breasts.

'Hi! What took you so long?' The smile turned into an elfish grin.

I grinned back, my eyes gliding over the skinny-rib jumper, the figure-hugging denims which marketed every peak and contour of her body. It fired my blood. It made me want to cast aside the plan I had shaped in my mind. I remembered how good she'd felt, and like a bear who'd discovered the taste of honey, I wanted more.

'I'm so glad you're here.' She pressed hard against me, her lips clinging wetly to mine. 'I've missed you, darling.'

'It's only been a day and a half.'

'Seems ages.'

I laughed contentedly. 'I'm taking you to lunch.'

'Just the two of us?'

'Of course just the two of us.'

'No Wesley Falloway?'

'Huh?'

'He always seems to come between us. He's a shadow which looms up whenever we talk.'

I kissed her gently. 'I'll try to keep him hidden.'

'We'll both try. We'll make a pact to only talk about *us*.'

I sighed. 'Now that's going to be difficult.'

She eyed me quizzically.

'I need your assistance,' I went on, suddenly feeling selfish. 'I'm sorry, Vicky, it's this damned case . . .'

'Simon Drake—' She looked up at me, traced a finger over

my lips. 'Somebody ought to tell you how to treat a lady when you ask her out.'

'I'm sorry.'

'So I should think.' She rolled her blue eyes, adding, 'But this case of yours did bring us together, so we'd better see it through together. How can I help?'

'By keeping Neil McQuillan talking for five minutes or so.'

She blinked at that. 'Is Neil doing something illegal?'

I explained about the sick horse and my previous abortive attempt to view the animal. I told her I couldn't make with the whys and the wherefores because I didn't want to get her involved. I realized how illogical the statement was the moment I'd said it. Getting her involved was exactly what I was doing.

She tugged at her underlip. 'I don't understand, Simon. What on earth are you hoping to find?'

'Would you believe me if I said three million pounds?'

'I'd be incredulous,' she murmured, 'but yes, I'd believe you.'

'Thanks.'

'Poor Neil.' She gave a sympathetic shudder.

'Are you sure you still want to help?'

'Mm, I'm sure. I'll be helping *you* and that's what matters.' She looked at her feet, wriggled her toes. 'Give me a few minutes to throw on something decent and I'll be right with you.'

She could have thrown on a saddle blanket and still looked fantastic. I watched her sway into the bedroom and then I turned and walked back to the car. I wanted to be completely honest with her. I had a crazy urge to tell her about General O'Hara, the kidnap, and the ransom demand. God knows I felt a need to talk to someone who didn't have an axe to grind, someone I cared for, someone who cared about me.

Lowering the hood, I reminded myself that the less she knew the safer it would be. It wasn't going to be easy bluffing it out, parrying her questions, but it was necessary. I'd said enough already, and for her own protection it was vital I shouldn't say any more.

I slipped behind the wheel and lit a cigarette. She picked her way towards me wearing a simple print dress with a deep-plunge neckline. Her hair was tied back with a ribbon. The sun burned mellowly in an azure sky. It seemed more like June than the end of October.

'That was fast,' I said.

'All models are quick-change artists.' She smiled but her voice held an edge of uneasiness. I sensed a sudden coolness.

I shook my gaze from the golden cleavage, and said, 'Are you O.K.?'

She nodded vaguely.

'Sure? You look a little melancholic.'

'It's nothing . . . really.'

I looked at her. 'When a lady says it's nothing really, it usually means it's something really—so give.'

'Hold me, Simon,' she said suddenly, snuggling herself close. 'Tell me things won't change between us. Tell me we'll always feel like this, no matter what.'

'Hey,' I grinned. 'What's suddenly brought this on?'

'Sometimes people aren't always what they pretend to be,' she said gently. 'Sometimes pretence and realism get mixed up with emotions and while you think one way you really feel the other. What I'm trying to say . . .' She faltered.

'You're a silly little fool.' I brushed strands of blonde hair from her cheeks. 'You think that when this business is over I'll just drive out of your life?'

'I thought . . .' Her body shuddered against me.

'You're in my bloodstream, Vicky. I'm hooked.'

I felt her cool fingers on my hands. Her mouth came up to be kissed.

'You said I was the kind of man a girl could depend on, remember?'

'I remember,' she breathed, her lips clinging briefly, meaningly. 'I was right, wasn't I?'

I unhitched the handbrake, jammed the shift into reverse.
'All the way,' I said.

It was fifteen minutes past one as I brought the M.G. to rest
outside Chinhurst Lodge. The timing was perfect. McQuillan,
I figured, would have taken up residence in his office, and the
yard would be free from sharp-eyed stable lads.

Vicky and I had lunched at a nearby hotel. We'd had an
omelette, a steak, and shared a bottle of red wine. I'd hardly
tasted the food, or noticed the waiter. With a woman like Mrs
Annesley for company, food and the way it was served came
a very poor second.

'Feel confident?' I asked.

'Uh-huh.' She tidied her hair in the rear-view mirror.

'Talk about your horses, talk about anything, just give me
ten minutes from the time you reach the office.'

'Right. Be careful, Simon.' She squeezed my hand.

I watched those long legs swing clear of the door, sweep
their way confidently across the yard. I consulted my wristwatch,
allowed thirty seconds to elapse, and then followed.

Everything appeared peaceful. The familiar noise of flesh
rubbing on wood as an inquisitive neck craned, the methodic
grinding of teeth on hay, were the only sounds to greet my
ears. I reached the box, pulled pliers from my pocket, and began undressing the wire from the bolts.

·The interior was uncannily quiet. There were no discomfort signals, no anguish, nothing. I listened hard as I worked.
Perhaps the horse really had been sick and was now respond-
ing to treatment. Or perhaps it was so exhausted it was beyond showing signs of physical misery. Or perhaps there
wasn't any horse at all. These were the unsettling thoughts that
clawed at the edges of my mind as I drew back the bolts. I
glanced quickly round, made a brief check to see whether I
was being observed, satisfied myself I wasn't, and gently eased
open the top half of the door.

I didn't find General O'Hara. The big liquid eyes that

peered out at me didn't belong to the classic-winning stallion who had found immortality on the turf. They belonged to a rather heavy-shouldered grey which viewed my gate-crashing tactics with indifference as it rubbed its tongue against a salt-lick.

There was something odd about the animal, something which grated against my practised experience with horses. All the visible 'flu symptoms were apparent. There were dark patches of sweat running along its back and its quarters, and its nostrils were clogged with mucus. A perfect illustration of the virus at its worst. Perhaps a little too perfect.

I looked closely. The eyes were bright and the ears pricked forward as I snapped my fingers. There was no drooping neck, no languid movements, no sign of listlessness. It was almost as if somebody had taken a perfectly healthy horse and externally doctored it up to look feverish.

I closed the door and pushed home the bolts. Numerous questions careened across my brain as I laced up the wires. Had McQuillan expected me to return and therefore boxed clever by switching horses? Had I really been looking at a sick horse or merely a cleverly constructed sham? Surely Riddle wasn't that colour blind? I shrugged off the questions and returned to the car. I didn't know what to think any more. With so much happening of late, I wasn't even sure if my addled brain knew the difference between reality and illusion.

'No three million pounds then, Simon?'

I guess I must have looked like a prototype for dejection as Vicky snuggled herself in the passenger seat.

'Nope,' I said.

'So what did you find?'

'A sick horse—maybe.'

'Maybe?'

'Forget it.' I forced a smile. 'Ever had the feeling things just aren't going your way?'

'Often.' Her soft eyes lingered for a moment. 'But not to-day, Simon. Today I'm incredibly happy.'

I took hold of her hands. 'And I'm being bloody selfish. guess I'm all screwed up with this case. Forgive me?'

'You're forgiven,' she said expansively.

'So is it my place or yours?' I asked.

'Mine if you like, but Eddie—'

'Might just drop out of the blue and bring the "in-crowd" with him. No way! It had better be . . .' I paused, meditated. On the one hand I had brother Eddie, and on the other I had the Duchess, Nick Barron, Kelly . . . That was worse, much worse. 'How about the motel?' The sudden flash of brilliance struck me. 'I'm paid up until the end of the week, and there's a bar—'

'And it's very private. Just us.' She wrinkled her nose.

I grinned, pulled the chalet key from the glove-box, and dropped it into her lap. We looked all set for a pleasurable afternoon and a long, long night, and this prompted a thought. 'I've some unfinished business with Alison Falloway. O.K. if we stop briefly at The Cedars?'

'Oh.' She lowered her eyes.

'Wesley?'

'I'd rather not.'

'He probably won't be there.'

'Can you go via the motel—drop me off?'

'If you're sure you'll be all right?'

'I'll be lonely—but I'll be waiting.'

I looked at her, held her eyes for a moment as unspoken thoughts and feelings passed between us. I was acutely aware of her. I could see the rhythmic rise and fall of her breasts, the slim silver-tipped fingers as they toyed with the motel key fob; I could feel the powerful magnetism of her body, hear the softness of her breathing. Our chemistry was unchallengeable.

We parted company at Chalet Ten. Traffic was no more than a trickle as I barrelled the M.G. through the afternoon sunshine and towards Fransham. What few cars there were I passed. I even risked my clean licence by crashing a red light. I wanted a quick turn-round at The Cedars. I had a lot to hurry back for.

Mrs Alison Falloway clasped her arms tightly around Bexson's thick neck as he lifted her from the Chairmobile to the sofa. As he lowered her wisp of body towards the upholstery I watched his eyes stray upwards to the mantelpiece, to the vacant rectangular space that had previously displayed an expensive piece of canvas. He stood momentarily transfixed.

'Down, Bexson, down!' The old lady ordered testily, not enjoying being suspended a few inches from comfort. 'What's the matter with you? Are you unwell?'

'The Stubbs, madam . . . ?' His words were almost inaudible.

'Well, what about it?'

'It's missing, madam.'

'I know it's missing. Mr Barron removed it this morning. I-I'm selling it, Bexson,' she temporized. 'Now for God's sake put me down!'

He dropped rather than put. His jaw went slack and he took two steps backwards, still looking at the empty wall.

I said levelly, 'Is something bothering you? Is there some reason why it shouldn't be sold?'

He remained motionless. I waited for an answer to my question. I had to wait a long time.

'It was the master's favourite painting,' he said finally. 'Brood mare with foal, signed and dated 1774. I remember the day he bought it—'

'You're a sentimentalist, Bexson,' the Duchess broke in. 'I've grown tired of the picture. It's high time we had something new.'

The observation seemed a trifle out of character, but Bexson made no comment. He probably didn't hear it. He still appeared mesmerized, unable to hear or see anything except the contrasting rectangle of emulsion paint which betrayed the painting's absence.

'Stop moping and bring Mr Drake a drink,' Alison Falloway continued. 'And while you're at it, you had better pour yourself one. You look as if you're about to collapse at my feet.'

He made apologetic noises, bowed briefly, and brought forth the drinks trolley.

He had me worried. Worried enough to watch his reactions closely as he dispensed alcohol and its additives into three glasses. There was a slight tremor in his fingers. Ice cubes rattled nervously against the hand-cut crystal.

'There's nothing wrong with the Stubbs, is there?' I asked shortly.

'Wrong, sir?'

'You appeared a little unnerved when you found it missing. Unnerved rather than upset, I'd say. As if it meant something more than just a sentimental loss.'

'I—I thought it might have been stolen,' he replied without conviction. 'I was shocked when I saw the bare wall. Living with something for so long and then find . . . Well, you must know how I felt . . .'

Alison Falloway and I exchanged glances. 'Thank you, Bexson,' she said. 'That will be all.'

'Madam.' He had regained his composure. The bow was a little crisper this time.

'I don't like it,' I remarked as he made his exit. 'He knows far more than he's letting on.'

'Nonsense, Mr Drake,' she dismissed my words. 'Gilbert Bexson would never indulge in Machiavellism. He's too loyal to the Falloway name. I trust him implicitly.'

I could tell by the irrefutable tone of her voice that I wasn't going to shatter her faith in the guy. With that and the possibility I could be wrong, it seemed pointless to pursue the tack. I lit a cigarette without asking permission and decided to get down to fundamentals.

'You're going ahead with this quarter of a million pay-off?'

'I am.'

'You realize the Security Division will have the area staked out.'

She nodded solemnly. 'I don't suppose I can stop them.'

I leaned forward, clasped my knees. 'Mrs Falloway, given the inclination I think you could stop the whole damned world from turning. If you brought one milligram of your influential weight to bear on the T.S.D. then there wouldn't be a single security man within miles of Axford on Saturday.'

A smile touched her lips. 'You overrate my persuasive powers, Mr Drake.'

'I don't think so. Your teeth have lost most of their bite, I know that. You've smothered that vigilante spirit and become almost complacent about the whole business. You accepted Nick Barron a little too readily, virtually agreed with him when he told me to keep my finger out of the pie. First you wanted my help and then you didn't. Your behaviour has been nothing short of erratic, and it's got me worried. Whatever happened to that tough resolute lady who verbally tore me limb from limb the first time we met?'

She mulled over my words, then said, 'I've come to terms with the situation. I'm not so—' She stopped as I slowly shook my head.

'Please don't feed me your line about the fire having gone out. I'm past the age for fairy stories. Something significant has happened to change your attitude, Mrs Falloway—what?'

She glared at me but said nothing. I'd told her how I felt and reckoned I hadn't been very diplomatic about doing it. I looked at her pale face, at the weariness around her eyes, the thin spidery lines on her forehead and mouth which cosmetics couldn't conceal. I waited for a reply, for a single embittered sentence that would bury my doubts and put me very firmly in my place. None came.

'Mr Barron has gone to purchase some saddle-bags,' she said finally, deliberately going off at a tangent. 'He's a Geminian you know. They're very industrious people, always in a hurry. He's extremely capable at his job I should imagine.'

'Extremely,' I murmured, letting alcohol slide down my throat until my glass was empty. It just wasn't my day for getting straight answers.

'My late husband was a Geminian too,' she went on reminiscently. 'He was a tower of strength, Mr Drake, always knowing what to do in a crisis. I only wish my son's disposition was comparable in that respect.'

'Does Wesley know about the pay-off?'

'He doesn't know a thing.' She glanced down at her hands, fingered her diamond ring affectionately. 'He's been a great disappointment to me. He's weak and totally unreliable. I'm only glad Clement had the foresight to acknowledge these weaknesses in his will.'

Presumably she was referring to the size of her son's monthly allowance. I decided to act ignorant. I said, 'So your husband made sure his money wouldn't be squandered?'

She nodded. 'He did it in a slightly unorthodox manner, but an effective one nevertheless.'

'Unorthodox?' I queried.

'On Clement's death the house and half of his estate passed directly to me. The other half was invested in securities and held in discretionary trust. This means the Trustees have an unfettered discretion as to dealings with both the capital and the income it produces. Wesley cannot demand as a right any of the money; it is entirely up to the Trustees whether they pass any of the income or capital to him.' She paused, adding slowly, 'Clement knew his son was work-shy and a waster and he made provision for these traits. Only if Wesley can legitimately earn fifteen thousand pounds in any one year, and produce satisfactory evidence that he has done so, are the Trustees obliged to pass the whole of the trust fund to him.'

I liked it. Her words activated a switch in my brain and the word 'motive' lit up like the tilt sign on a pin-ball machine. I stood up so I could think better, took a final pull on my cigarette, and stabbed it to death in an ashtray. 'How much does Wesley make as an actor?' I asked.

'Not enough, Mr Drake.'

'Not fifteen thousand a year, I know, but what—four, five, six . . . ?'

'Acting is an unpredictable profession. Certainly no more than five, and that only if he's lucky.'

'Five thousand, huh . . .' I was thinking back to the figures in the dossier. I was doing mental calculations, adding his blood-boost winnings to his earnings. I made him about twelve hundred short of the old man's target. If Paradise Kid had won its race he would undoubtedly have made it. Duncan Stroud and that broken bottle had cost him plenty. 'Would the prize money earned by his racehorses count under the terms of the will?' I suggested.

She inclined her head. 'As long as it was legitimately accumulated and he had receipts for the prize money, yes. The only exception is gambling. There's a clause which states that the trust fund cannot be passed to Wesley if any part of the fifteen thousand was obtained with money won by betting.' She gave a hint of a smile, more to herself than at me. 'You're not seriously suggesting that my son's insignificant horses could nett ten thousand pounds?'

'You should study the results page more closely,' I said.

'But they've always been . . .'

'Small beer? I know. Remarkable how they've improved, isn't it?'

'Are you trying to tell me something, Mr Drake?'

'There's always next season,' I went on musingly. 'He'll do it too, unless he's stopped.'

'You're not making much sense,' she snapped impatiently. 'Will you please tell me what's been going on?'

'I'd like an answer to that one too,' I said. 'But people aren't very co-operative when I ask them. They usually change the subject—talk about saddle-bags and birth-signs and such-like.'

I had my hand on the door when she spoke again.

'Where are you going?' she demanded.

'The complications are crowding in and I need room to breathe. I'm also keeping a lady waiting.'

She shifted forward in an attempt to stop me, but she didn't get very far. I heard her curse silently, damning the legs that refused to carry her weight. I felt a twinge of sympathy but swallowed it, reminding myself she was tougher than an old goat. I left her ringing the bell for Bexson.

As I crossed to the M.G., I saw Kelly lounging against the wing of Falloway's Jaguar. She was sporting a pink safari-style trouser suit and holding a pair of sunglasses in her hand. A small travelling case rested at her feet. The case told its own story. At the sight of it, anger welled up inside me. For not the best of reasons I felt betrayed. I should have walked on by, but I didn't.

'Going for a drive?' I enquired cynically.

'Yes, I am.' She flushed slightly.

'How long will you be away?'

'I'm not sure,' she said vaguely, not looking at me. 'Wesley will be filming for two or three days. He's invited me along.'

'Thanks for telling me. I might have worried.'

'Sorry, but I haven't seen you to tell.'

'You're pretty good at leaving notes.'

'And you're pretty good at sleeping off hangovers.' She turned her back on me.

I caught hold of her wrist and spun her round to face me. 'Like him, do you?'

'Yes, I do. He's very good fun.'

'I wouldn't have said he was your type.'

'Then you'd be wrong.' She wriggled herself free. 'He's a very gentle person when you get under the skin.'

I laughed at that. 'You crease me, Kelly,' I said. 'You know he's an out-and-out villain. You know all about his fraudulent racing wins and his long sordid history with other women. Why the hell...?'

'You're jealous of him, aren't you?'

'Jealous? I'm not jealous of *him*, I'm disappointed in *you*.

I didn't think the virtuous Miss Meredith went in for dirty weekends.'

She said nothing.

'Listen, baby,' I pressed on incensed, 'I'm trying to tell you the facts of life about a con-merchant called Falloway. It's on the cards more than ever that he murdered Duncan Stroud. You ought to bear that in mind when he puts his arms around you. You ought to notice the blood on his hands when he's groping at your clothing, when he's—'

Her open hand slapped me hard across the mouth.

She packed quite a blow. It brought water to my eyes and maybe shook a little calming sense into my tired brain. I fingered my stinging lip. I reckoned I'd begged for it and got my just desserts. 'I really believe you've fallen for him,' I murmured thickly.

'Maybe I have,' she said.

I looked at her. 'You've changed, Kelly. You're not the girl I met in the Horse and Groom a couple of weeks ago. The one who gave up her holiday to help me find General O'Hara. I feel I don't know anybody any more. Am I going bloody crazy, or what?'

'Simon . . . ?' There was concern in her eyes.

'Yes?'

'Nothing.'

'Still here, Drake?' Wesley Falloway's breath caressed the back of my neck. 'Shouldn't you be out looking for my mother's horse, or something?'

I turned to face him. My eyes followed the line of his immaculately cut suit. He looked like a dummy in a Savile Row window.

He stroked a lapel affectionately. '*Dormeuil* cloth,' he informed me.

'I wouldn't know,' I quipped. 'I work for the Security Division, not the *Tailor and Cutter*.'

His lips twisted. 'Then don't let us keep you. I'm sure somebody is in line for a multitude of your misguided questions.'

'I've one or two for you,' I growled.

'Go to hell!' His long arm swept out and whisked Kelly's case into the boot. 'God knows I've done my best to help you, but there comes a time—'

'Does Vicky Annesley tell lies?'

'What?' The question stopped him in his tracks. He looked at me shrewdly, the boot lid poised half-way to its fastener. 'What trap am I supposed to fall into now?'

'The weekend you'd planned in Looe,' I reminded him. 'I say had planned because it didn't really materialize, did it? At least not with Vicky Annesley.'

'You've been checking up on me, Drake,' he smiled crookedly. 'O.K., so we had a row, and she walked out on me. What does that prove? I was still there.'

'You're minus an alibi—and get your facts right. She didn't walk out on you, it was the other way around.'

'She told you that?'

'Yes, she did.'

He slammed the boot shut. 'Then she does tell lies. She was bitchy on the journey down—the route, the way I drove, the hotel, nothing was right. We hadn't been there five minutes before she said she felt unwell and wanted to go back. I told her I had no intention of going back. That was the last I saw of her. I think she took a hire car.'

I smiled slowly. 'I prefer her version.'

'Which is?'

'That she talked about your mysterious wins, and how the Security Division had suddenly arrived on the scene. She began to put two and two together and you didn't like it.'

He looked incredulous. 'That's completely untrue.'

'Is it? I doubt it.'

'I've had enough of this—' He yanked open the passenger door for Kelly. 'Come on, darling, I'm not going to waste time listening to this drivel—'

'I know about the will,' I said matter-of-factly, as he slid behind the wheel. 'So near and yet so far, eh?'

'Damn you, Drake!' His lower lip quivered as he wetted it with his tongue. I'd caught him below the belt and it showed.

As he stabbed the ignition, Kelly looked anxiously across at me. I leant against the driving door, said through my teeth, 'Kelly's a good kid—the best. Break her heart and I'll break your back.'

He slammed the automatic in drive and gunned the motor hard. I swayed in the slipstream as the big car lurched forward, loose chippings peppering from its tyres. A remnant of blue smoke still hung on the breeze as I climbed into the M.G. I melted into the thin tributary of southbound traffic and headed back to the motel.

'Simon?' Vicky's voice was barely audible above the drone of cascading water. I closed the chalet door quietly, smiling inwardly on seeing her cotton dress hanging in the wardrobe, the neat little pile of underwear on the bed. 'Simon . . . ? It is you, isn't it?' She peeked round the edge of the shower curtain.

'It's me.' I threw off my jacket and stretched out on the bed.

'You don't mind, do you?'

'Mind?'

'Water for the use of?'

'Be my guest.' I clasped my hands behind my head and gazed longingly at the shimmering blur of nakedness which stirred my glandular impulses. 'Is there room in there for two?' I asked.

She laughed—a laugh which suddenly turned into a hideous ear-splitting *scream.*

It had happened fast. A shadow flickering across the room. The fleeting vision of a car outside. The swish of tyres. A brief tortured squeal as somebody touched the brakes. A loud crack as the chalet window burst into fragments. Slivers of glass cascading everywhere.

I rolled off the bed as the bottle broke. It careered across the room, bounced off the padded headboard and shattered against the bedside cabinet. A litre of instant arson. A Molotov cocktail.

'Simon!' Vicky shrieked out my name as the interior erupted into flame.

I scrambled feverishly to my feet. I realized my shirt had been spattered with petrol and was burning. I tore off the garment, forcing my feet over the circles of smouldering linoleum, eyes rooted on the smoke-enveloped shower cubicle.

'Keep wet! Don't move!' I suddenly felt very calm. I had to keep a hold on my nerves for both our sakes. I glanced briefly left and right. A creeping line of fire was outflanking me. A plume of sparks spurted upwards as the imitation wood panelling ignited into a sheet of flame. I didn't look back.

Vicky screamed again. I could hardly hear her above the crackle of timber, the hungry roar from the now blazing structure. I certainly couldn't see very much as I fought grimly against the hot choking particles of soot. She began to cough. I stumbled on blindly—a cold sweat moistening my hands as a tongue of orange flame crept imperceptibly past me, licking at the shower curtain. Suddenly it caught. It hissed and it spluttered as droplets of water tried vainly to stunt the fire's progress. I felt globules of molten plastic dripping on my shoes. I saw Vicky huddled in a corner of the cubicle. Her hair was all over her face; her naked flesh wet and glistening and trembling uncontrollably.

'Sim . . . Please . . . Oh, God!'

'Easy, baby, easy.' I let the water wash over my back, soak through my trousers. It felt good, almost healing.

I knelt beside her, wrapping an arm around the small golden hairs on her thighs, the smooth brown skin of her waist. Her head hung limply forward as I hoisted her towards me. I felt the fullness of her breasts against my chest, her whole body began to shake convulsively under my hands.

'Please God . . .' she whispered numbly, the two monosyllables echoing my own silent prayer for salvation.

I turned and struggled drunkenly forward. The floor was a sea of orange flame beneath my feet. My chest had grown tight. I pulled polluted air into starving lungs and headed for where

I thought the door should be. I could hear distant voices, the faint garble of excited tongues. I could feel the heat searing my ankles, smouldering my trousers, promising to take away my legs and smother me in its calescence.

'Not far,' I breathed reassuringly, more to myself than to Vicky; hugging her close, shielding her vulnerable body from the splinters of glowing debris. 'Not far now—we'll make it.'

Somebody began kicking at the door. The jamb gave way under the strain and the structure lurched inwards. Fanned by the sudden draught, spouts of flame leapt waist-high in front of me, blocking our exit. Vicky gave a frightened little gasp and I bit so hard into my lip that I could feel a dribble of blood ebb its way down my chin.

'Two people!' A voice shouted frantically.

I could see hustling bodies in the doorway, someone was struggling with an extinguisher. My shoes felt as though they were melting, my feet as though they were no longer capable of supporting the added weight.

'Hit it!' The extinguisher erupted into life, cutting through the wall of fire, sending a carpet of foam bubbling over my ankles.

Three steps. Two. One. I staggered out into the clean, pure air.

People were milling around in a seemingly inextricable chaos. Helping hands were everywhere. I suppose I should have been concerned with the bruises and burns, but I found myself shunning help and futilely trying to conceal Vicky's nakedness from gaping onlookers—a situation saved by the arrival of two blankets.

We were bustled to safety. A chalet maid brought two glasses filled liberally with brandy. I gagged mine down, fighting the rising nausea. Vicky choked a little on hers, too, but it helped bring the colour back in her cheeks. She almost smiled.

'The shower was your saviour,' I said raggedly, 'both our saviours. If you'd been wearing that cotton dress—'

She shuddered and wiped a smut of soot from my cheek with the corner of her blanket.

'I must have been followed. Somebody tailed me either from McQuillan's or from The Cedars.'

'Who, Simon . . . ? Who would want—oh, it's too awful . . .'

'The somebody I've pushed a little too far,' I murmured, kicking off my scorched shoes. 'In my search for the truth I've unearthed a pyro-bloody-maniac.'

'Stop now—please.'

'Stop?'

'For my sake.'

I kissed that little upturned nose. 'That's exactly what they want me to do.'

'And is that so impossible?'

'I hurt when I burn. They should have asked me nicely.'

We clung to each other—blankets, bare feet, bruises and all. We were two very tired people. Grateful people. We listened to the distant wail of sirens, and watched the pall of black smoke as it drifted higher and higher into the sky.

Chapter Eleven

HOWARD GRANT ran a forefinger and thumb around the saturated brim of his trilby. His eyes flickered upwards as he listened to the drumming rain echoing against the roof of the van.

'Vicky Annesley?' he muttered, breathing heavily down his nose.

'You sound surprised.'

'I am, just a little. Obviously the opposition have no qualms about who they kill or maim—just so long as Simon Drake is disposed of.'

Grant and I were sitting on bench seats at either end of the Division's mock Post Office van. The vehicle was one of a fleet which had been converted for surveillance purposes. It was nine-twenty on the Saturday morning and we were parked outside a telephone kiosk some eighty yards from the Roebuck Tavern.

'They used a damned crude method,' he added. 'It couldn't have been planned. Almost an act of desperation.'

'Burned half the bloody motel down, nevertheless.'

'Have the police . . . ?'

'No chance. Nobody saw a thing.'

'It was an instant decision,' he went on reflectively, 'a decision prompted by your actions on that day.'

'I figure it that way too. I could have given three people cause to throw that bottle—McQuillan, Bexson, and Wesley Falloway.'

'So who had the strongest motive?'

I shrugged. 'I'd like to say Falloway, but Kelly was keeping him company when he left. Gilbert Bexson knows far more than he's letting on, but I reckon he's more at home decanting from bottles than hurling them through windows.'

'Which leaves us with McQuillan.'

'The guy with the metal hand,' I murmured. 'The guy who brings sick horses into his yard and keeps dead travelling head lads in his barn.'

Grant sniffed thoughtfully but said nothing. A burst of static suddenly spluttered from the two-way radio at his elbow. *'One to control, one to control, do you read?'*

He snatched up the hand mike, 'Control—go.'

'Yellow Vauxhall approaching pay-off point, sir.'

'Thank you, one. Maintain surveillance.'

As Grant reached for his field-glasses, I slid back the observation panel and peered out into the gloom. Nick Barron's car was pulling into the forecourt of the Roebuck. Little flurries of drizzle were being carried on the wind, sheeting against the van, and causing us considerable visibility problems.

'Damn weather!' Grant abandoned his glasses.

'Where are your men located?'

'Two campers, and a motorist with a fan-belt problem.' He indicated a tent perched on a distant ridge and a car with its bonnet up parked outside the local garage.

'They're getting wet.'

'So is your Mr Barron, by the look of it.'

The *Globe* reporter was lugging the saddle-bags from the Vauxhall to the seat. He was fighting every step of the way, the bulky satchels proving cumbersome to handle in such filthy conditions.

Grant said quietly, tonelessly, 'My theory is they'll use a horse and rider, and make off across the moors to a waiting trailer. There's a lot of country out there. A horse can go where a motor-car can't.'

I grunted.

He looked at me. 'Is everything all right?'

'These boots are bloody tight.'

'Jodhpurs fit? Riding mac O.K.?'

I grunted again. I wasn't over grateful at being chosen for the job of tracker. Any initial glamour I might have felt was now marred by the fact that I was going to ache like hell and get a soaking into the bargain. 'I've tethered the horse at the side of the smithy,' I said.

'Are you clear on what you have to do?'

'I follow at a safe distance and report any developments by radio.'

He handed me a walkie-talkie. 'The money collector will probably cut across country to a main road. We've got three mobiles at points where a road divides the woodland. They'll be waiting for your call.'

'One to control—yellow Vauxhall departing.'

Grant acknowledged, then said, 'That's Barron out of our hair. Now all we have to do is wait.'

The waiting was physically painful. Thirty minutes passed in almost total silence. I sipped at some bitter-tasting coffee from Grant's vacuum flask and gazed miserably out of the observation panel. The plan was a neat one, I thought, but one that relied heavily on my competence as both rider and hunter. I hoped I was up to it.

'A Land-Rover's pulling in at the pub.' Grant moistened his lips expectantly.

'It's filled with people,' I said.

'What the devil . . .' An expression of bewilderment passed fleetingly across his face. 'It's some sort of gathering . . .'

They were locals not tourists, heavily mackintoshed farmers and agricultural workers, talking, enjoying a joke, sheltering under the Roebuck's eaves, as if anticipating the start of some big event.

Grant looked at me, raised an eyebrow.

'Smallholders' meeting?' I offered.

'They're coming from all directions.' He quickly shut the observation panel as rubber-booted feet tramped past the van.

173

The radio crackled an announcement that scattered groups of people were heading in the direction of the Roebuck. Horse-boxes were beginning to arrive and several cars towing trailers had been spotted on the outlying roads. 'This is madness, Simon! Either the hijackers are being very clever or—' He broke off as somebody rapped smartly on the back doors.

'Are you in there, old loves?'

I winced inwardly.

'Get him in,' Grant audibly ground his teeth.

I released the lock and hauled the reporter into the dry.

'Thank you, Simon.' Little droplets of rain glistened on his moustache as he offered me a smile as impermanent as a debt collector's. 'The weather is absolutely appalling. I'm drenched right—'

'Why have you come back?' Grant's tone was cutting. 'Your instructions were to leave the saddle-bags and return to The Cedars.'

'I'm well aware of my—'

'You realize you've probably been seen? You've given away our location and put our entire plan at risk.'

'I've done no such thing.'

'I'll be the judge of that.'

'Captain Grant . . .' Barron slid back the observation panel. 'Take a look at the people out there. They're arriving in droves. I was careful. Who on earth do you think noticed me among so many?'

I lifted the field-glasses to my eyes. I said, trying to ease the tension, 'There's nobody near the bags. The rain seems to be easing a little.'

Grant muttered, 'Why are they here? What possible attraction could a small Devon village hold for so many people?'

'Intriguing, isn't it?' Barron sounded pleased. 'This offers masses of colour for my story, of course. Far better that the public should be unwittingly involved. Brings the whole thing to life, don't you agree?'

Grant grunted. He was in no mood for irrelevancies. 'I don't give a damn about your sensation-seeking news coverage,' he said. 'All I know is I don't want a wall of people between my men and the money.'

'You think innocent bystanders might get hurt?'

'Of course not. There'll be no risk to the public.'

Barron pulled a slightly soggy notebook from his pocket and jotted that down. 'Tell me, old son,' he said grinning benignly at me, 'how does it feel to be the Security Division's first line of attack?'

'There won't be any attack. I'm here to tread on the collector's heels, that's all.'

'And if the collector is a little too quick for you?'

'Then I'll lose him, won't I. What a bloody stupid question.'

He was about to retort, but the radio beat him to it.

'Motor coach pulling up at pay-off point, sir.'

Grant swung to the panel, narrowing his eyes. 'It's full of young people—students by the look of it. Good God, there are thirty of them at least!'

Barron and I followed his gaze and contemplated the flow of cavorting humanity as it poured from the coach.

'They're erecting banners,' Grant said.

'Some kind of demonstration,' Barron added.

I focused the field-glasses on the nearest placard. I read aloud, 'Ban bloodsports—long live the fox.'

Grant and I exchanged glances. 'Christ,' I said.

'Of course!' Barron jabbed me with his pencil. 'It's November the first—the start of the hunting season. This alters the situation considerably.'

Grant wasn't grateful for his perceptive advice. 'Shut up, Barron, I'm trying to think. You'll have to get out and mingle, Simon. There's bound to be a clash between demonstrators and huntsmen, and that's when they'll try to make the pick-up.'

'Indubitably, old love.' Barron grinned his approval.

I ignored him and unlocked the back doors. I glanced towards the Roebuck. A group of locals had approached the students and judging from the gesticulations, trouble was already beginning to brew. I pulled my flat cap over my eyes and headed for the gathering.

Banners were everywhere. Undeterred by the drizzle, students littered the forecourt. They had organized themselves into small predominantly male groups. A stringy youth sporting a Zapata moustache and wearing an old army greatcoat flitted from group to group apparently giving instructions. Every now and then he would stand on the pub wall and address the gathering collectively. He was performing the function of a comedian at a TV warm-up. He kept spirits high and aroused feelings to fever pitch. When he'd finished, the small concentrations of people would show him their strength by coalescing into an ugly slogan-shouting mob.

I shouldered my way through the jabber of voices:

'Use the aerosols to confuse the hounds . . .' 'I'll ram this bleedin' pole in his face . . .' 'Grab for the legs and pull . . .' 'Pacificism will achieve sweet F.A. . . .'

Farmers looking dazed and confused watched the spectacle at a safe distance. Two or three had ventured to voice their disapproval but their protests were hopelessly drowned in a chant of abuse. I skirted round them and across to where I could get a clear view of the seat. The saddle-bags were intact.

'Do you want a banner?' a young voice asked breezily.

I turned and looked into a pair of dark eyes. She stood with one hand on her hip, clad only in ragged jeans and a T-shirt. I could see the little pink stems of her nipples as they pressed against the wet translucent material.

'You have a choice,' she indicated the neatly painted slogans. 'Down with the hunt', or 'Bloodsports are barbaric.'

I grinned.

'I take it you're anti?' she said.

'Do I look anti?' I asked, amused.

'I don't think you're pro. You have too kind a face.'

'Thanks, but carrying banners isn't really my style.'

She looked down at my boots. 'Without one you could easily be mistaken for the opposition.'

'I thought student demos were peaceful nowadays?'

'Ours usually are, but—'

'Judy, are you bloody coming.'

The voice cut through the bawdy background chatter and the girl's eyes swivelled towards the crowd. A guy was beckoning with his banner. She spotted him and responded by waving back. 'I have to go, are you sure you don't want to stand up and be counted?'

'Some other time, maybe.'

'We don't cover fox-hunts all that often.'

'But when you do it gets a little violent, huh?'

'Carlos is organizing this one, and he's got everyone pretty wound up.'

'Judy for Chrissake!'

'Carlos being the thin guy with the tash?' I probed.

'Uh-huh.'

'JO-O-O-O-DY!'

'Bye.'

With the students breaking into a chorus of *Hey Jude*, she held her banners high and marched towards the throng.

The rain had stopped and things were rapidly coming to the boil. Horses had been unloaded from trailers and men and women garbed in immaculate black coats and white breeches were standing with their mounts, adjusting girths, trying to ignore the verbal bombardment. I saw Zapata look at his watch and did the same. It was ten-thirty.

The signal was given and students poured out of the forecourt. They began forming themselves into two columns at either side of the pub entrance. The columns stopped only a few yards short of the saddle-bags.

At the back of my mind I was beginning to wonder whether all this wasn't just a little too well organized, whether Zapata wasn't manipulating his troops just a little too carefully. The banner carriers were getting the taste for vindication and liking it, but perhaps Zapata was getting the taste for money and liking it even more.

Keeping one eye on the seat, I dodged round the demonstrators and joined ranks with a group of farmers. Four women carrying trays of drinks and sandwiches emerged from the Roebuck. They stood in the middle of the forecourt, waiting. They looked nothing short of terrified.

'Gaffer'll 'ave to run gauntlet,' said one farmer.

'On 'is arse he'll be. Ought to gid drinken a miss,' another pointed out.

' 'Ark at theirn buggerin'. Tom'll fetch constable.'

There was the distant yapping of hounds, horses were being mounted, hooves began to clatter on the roadway. An impassioned silence fell over the assemblage. The calls from the whippers-in grew louder, their cries cutting through the stillness and echoing in the damp morning air. Faces tightened, fingers took a firmer hold on banners. Time stretched like a piece of elastic, ready to snap at any moment.

'Stand aside, young man!'

The Master of Fox Hounds, a bulky, red-faced guy in scarlet, looked down at Zapata from beneath shaggy eyebrows. His horse, a lengthy grey, remained motionless. The youth, who stood between the two columns, folded his arms defiantly and said nothing. Hooves were silenced as the huntsman, the whippers-in, and the field lurched to a halt.

'I'm asking you to stand aside.' The Master moderated his tone.

Zapata shook his head. 'No deal, Commander. There'll be no fox killed today.'

'Now look, you've made you're point. We've read your placards—so why don't you go home?'

'Yes, go home!' shrilled an elderly woman riding sidesaddle.

He smoothed both sides of his moustache and grinned.

'You're nothing but a young thug,' the huntsman shouted.

'And you're nothing but an upper-class Philistine. An ungentlemanly gentleman who gets his kicks at a defenceless animal's expense . . .'

178

As the arguments raged, I glanced along the line of riders. They were standing two and three abreast and stretched in a long phalanx from the pub to a cluster of cottages. I counted at least forty faces. The pick-up man was either amongst them, I figured, or very close at hand. I had a brief qualm about whether I could reach my horse quickly if trouble started. In normal circumstances I would have taken up a position midway between horse and money, but with heaving flanks and protesting bodies blocking my view, these circumstances could hardly be called normal.

'Keep these blood-thirsty mongrels under control!'

Zapata wasn't pleased at having the hounds jumping and frolicking around his ankles. They were giving the occasional tug at his jeans and forcing him back through the tunnel of people. To stop his regression he kicked out viciously with a plimsolled foot. A hound yelped and limped clear of the pack.

'And you preach to me about defenceless animals . . . !' The Master jabbed his heels into the big grey's flanks.

'Aagh!' The youth screamed as the horse cannoned into him. He seized hold of the bridle to keep his balance and was dragged along the tunnel.

The mayhem button was pushed. The Master rose in his stirrups and began clubbing at the boy with the butt-end of his whip. Banners became lances as the students surged forward. Suddenly there was chaos.

I just managed to dodge clear as the columns fanned out and a mammoth of haunch reversed towards me. The Master was still flourishing his whip, being pulled bodily from his horse. The big grey was snorting in terror. Banners were being thrust at the soft flesh of its neck, hands were pulling at its plume of tail, fingers were clawing at its rider's red tunic . . .

'Bloody bastards! Bloody bastards!' A girl screamed hysterically as the whipper-in came to the Master's aid.

The red-coated riders bored in and began dragging students from the grey. A youth with a stranglehold around the Master's neck let out a shriek of pain as a hunting whip sliced brutally across his face. He fell backwards but didn't release his grip. The Master lost his hat and his balance as he was wrenched from the saddle. He toppled heavily to the ground. A stirrup leather had snapped and the stirrup itself was jammed over his boot. I could see his legs threshing wildly as a crazed mêlée of student bodies bundled on top of him. The grey was no longer a target for violence. It shook its sweat-flaked neck and galloped confusedly off, reins streaming in the wind.

People were scattering in all directions. Riderless horses bucked and reared, blundering into demonstrators, trampling hounds underfoot. In the confusion I'd lost sight of the saddle-bags. I regained my bearings and fought my way towards the seat. The pouches were undamaged. A student, clutching his stomach with one hand and a banner with the other, knelt vomiting helplessly nearby.

'Pigs,' he groaned. 'Soddin' socialite pigs.'

I extended the hand of assistance, then wished I hadn't. His eyes widened as they latched on to my jodhpurs and boots. With a sudden uprush he rammed the banner into my groin.

Luckily there wasn't much power behind the lunge. There was enough to bring me to my knees, but not enough to paralyse me with pain. I saw the canvas shoe long before it reached my face. I grabbed it, twisted it, and sent its occupant spinning into the regurgitated mess left by the banner-thrower.

Students were all around me now. I climbed awkwardly to my feet just in time to receive a clubbing blow from a piece of brick as it bounced off my shoulder. The huntsman wasn't so lucky. Caught in a hail of stones his chestnut mount shied sideways and stumbled. The sheer mass of horse crashed cumbrously earthwards, dislodging its rider, gouging through grass and soil as it furrowed to a halt.

'Get him!' bellowed a voice as I helped the huntsman to his feet.

I turned, saw Zapata thrusting an indicative finger in my direction. I had no intention of being 'got', not now—

especially not now. A horse and black-coated rider were at the seat. A gloved hand was reaching for the saddle-bags . . .

'Go! Go!' Zapata dispatched three students at me.

A banner lay at my feet. I reached for it, swung with it, and upended the first guy by scything his legs from under him. The second hurled a big bony fist at my face. It didn't connect. I blocked it with my left and pitched a double right into his abdomen. As his head went down I grabbed at his sideburns and brought my knee up hard. He catapulted backwards. Blood began pumping from his nose as he collided heavily with student number three.

I stood for a moment recovering my faculties. The black-coated rider had managed to haul the saddle-bags over the animal's withers. Reins were being gathered up and a trouble-free escape route was being sought. I held myself in check. I wanted to grab those reins and take a hard look at the features which shielded behind an upturned collar and a black silk hat. The walkie-talkie rubbing against my thigh gave me a gentle reminder that I was expected to follow instructions.

Reaching my horse was out of the question. I scanned for a substitute and saw the huntsman's chestnut thrashing unsteadily to its feet. Apart from a broken throat-latch its tack appeared undamaged. I approached cautiously, caught hold of the reins and mounted.

The money collector had already made his exit. He'd weaved a course through the confusion of limbs and was now making off at full gallop across the moors. I whirled the chestnut round, felt it respond to the pressure of my heels as I pushed it on in pursuit.

The way ahead was like a battlefield. Hounds were scouring to and fro, riderless panic-stricken horses were zigzagging in and out of limping, bleeding, mud-spattered people. I got snagged behind a loose black mare and momentarily lost my balance as we bulled into the animal's quarters. I'd just cleared the horsy obstruction when I ran into the more resistant human kind.

'That's Rupert's gelding!' a big-bosomed woman in hunting garb shouted accusingly.

'He's not one of us,' declared another voice.

I heard the sound of lumbering hooves and just managed to rein in as a steaming bay hunter swept past me, taking up my ground.

'Get off that damned horse!' The whipper-in veered his mount round and took hold of my bridle.

'You don't understand—' I began.

'Get off or be pulled off!'

He was so close that I could see the fine mappings of blood-vessels in his bulbous nose. I hadn't time to argue so I hit him. The nose squashed like an overripe plum as it sunk into my knuckles. He cried out, released the bridle, and toppled clumsily from the saddle.

The action didn't achieve very much. It extricated me from the grasp of the hunting community, but brought me face to face with Zapata and the student brotherhood.

'That's the pig!' rasped the youth who'd jettisoned his breakfast.

'Screw him, Carl,' said another.

'Fascist! Fascist! Fascist!' shrieked a girl, pulling off a shoe and hurling it towards the chestnut's face.

The heel clipped the animal's poll. It baulked, stood back on its haunches, and gravity sent me sprawling to the ground. I balled myself up and rolled. I felt the thrust from those lethal hind legs as the horse skidded in the mud, righted itself and galloped heedlessly off.

'Fascist!' the girl said again, adding a little more potency to the noun by pursing her lips and spitting in my face.

I climbed to my feet, wiped the warm saliva away with my sleeve, and pushed her to one side. I wasn't the friend-liest of people at that moment. I'd just lost a quarter of a million pounds and I hurt. I wanted a little vengeance of my own.

Zapata decided to chance his arm. He moistened his moustache with his tongue and in a single convulsive movement he threw himself at me. I glimpsed the word L-O-V-E tattooed across the knuckles of his right hand as he jabbed two stiff fingers into my eye sockets. I turned to deflect the impact, but accuracy was on his side, and timing wasn't on mine.

Backwards was the only place to go. I went, grabbing at the wrist, bending back the fingers in an effort to alleviate the pressure. Somebody wrapped me in a waist-hold from behind and this gave me the necessary leverage. I pumped my knee into Zapata's soft belly with all the force I could muster. All the frustrations of the morning went into that blow. I prised open my sore eyelids and saw his hard, pitted face twist up in pain as he sagged feebly to the ground.

What happened next happened quickly. I released myself from the waist-hold by grabbing a handful of my assailant's genitals, and was ready to pay back in kind anything anyone had to offer—but there weren't any takers. A great burst of spontaneous cheering sent the students scattering. I was vaguely aware of two policeman on bicycles bumping unsteadily over the turf. I dragged myself to the seat, collapsed on to it, and began nursing my sundry bruises.

'What a tragedy, Simon.' Barron's overloaded tones found their way to my ear.

I looked up at him. He was still weaving patterns in his notebook and he looked cooler than a pint of iced lager.

'Absolutely catastrophic, old love,' he added. 'I still can't believe it . . .'

'You're referring to the money?'

'Money? Good God no. I'm referring to a photographer. I should have brought one along. If only I'd known there was going to be a pitched battle—'

'If only *I'd* known,' I sighed heavily.

'You'll heal.'

'Thanks for nothing.'

'*Nil desperandum*, old son.' He put a patronizing hand on my shoulder.

'It was a set-up,' I said bitterly. 'This anti-bloodsport demo was laid on for the collector's benefit.'

'That's conjecture.'

'But reasonable conjecture.'

'I think you're wrong. I think the horsenappers knew there was going to be a clash and made capital out of the fact—anyhow that's how it'll read in tomorrow's edition of the *Globe*.'

'Should make a wonderful story.'

'I think so,' he said smugly.

'Real action-packed Sunday breakfast reading, uh?'

'True, true.'

'A brief life though?'

'Brief?'

'On Monday it'll get covered in grease when they wrap fish and chips in it.'

His lips retracted. 'Hadn't you better call Grant up—tell him how you're *not* on the collector's heels.'

I reached into my pocket and pulled out the broken remnants of the walkie-talkie. 'I'd better do it in person,' I said.

He grinned thinly and began to walk off, talking as he went. 'Tell him I'll see him later. I want to interview the Master if I can find him, get some first-hand comments from the students, and see if the police can . . .'

A riderless sweat-drenched mare, its girth dangling loose against its flanks appeared out of nowhere. Barron, intent only on listening to the sound of his own voice was walking directly into its path. He was oblivious of either my shouts or the sound of pounding hooves. The animal clipped his shoulder as it cantered past, bowling him neatly into a little pile of freshly dropped manure.

I don't think he saw the funny side. I did. I had one hell of a grin on my face as I walked back to the telecommunications van.

Chapter Twelve

I FELT Vicky's lips moving deftly across my cheek, her teeth nibbling gently on my ear. I was a little slow to respond. I dragged open bleary eyes and waited for the hands of my wrist-watch to materialize. It was 9 a.m. I'd slept for twelve hours—well no, that wasn't quite true. I'd been to bed for twelve hours, I'd slept for maybe . . . ? Slim fingers fluttered along my thigh, canvassed a lot of ground on their way to my chest. I'd slept for maybe . . . ? Hell, who was counting anyway?

We brushed tongues. 'Love you,' she whispered.

'And leave you,' I whispered back, unhooking her arm from my neck.

'Must you?'

' 'Fraid so.' I levered myself upright, reached for my cigarettes. 'The Duchess has a thing about being kept waiting—specially by yours truly. She's likely to lecture me on the alluring capabilities of a certain Jezebel in the Quantock Hills.'

She smiled.

I took her chin in my hand and rained little kisses on her mouth and neck. 'And of course she'd be so right.'

'Simon?'

'Yes?'

'What will you do when it's over?'

I considered. 'Live happily ever after,' I said. 'Isn't that the traditional ending?'

She lowered her eyes. 'You're mocking me.'

'Mocking myself maybe.' I gave her a cigarette and lit it with mine. 'In a storybook world that's exactly what I'd do. In reality . . .'

185

She rubbed her face against my chest. 'I love you, Simon.'

I wanted to tell her I loved her too; I wanted to wrap her in my arms and talk about the future, plan the good times ahead, indulge in the idealistic 'dreams' of escapism, the childish love-talk that can lift a guy over the moon. I stroked her cheek and slid free of the silken sheets. Soon, very soon, I told myself. For the moment I had bitter memories of Molotov cocktails—the kind that told me it didn't pay to plan too far ahead or to share innermost feelings.

I zipped up my trousers and went through to the bathroom. Cobwebs were clinging to my apology for a brain. I shook them loose with soap and hot water. With Grant, Barron and the Duchess all gathering for this morning's meeting, I figured I needed all the sagacity I could muster. Vicky came and leant on the doorway. A copy of yesterday's *Globe* dangled from her hand.

'Do you think Nick Barron's wrong?' she asked softly.

'Wrong?' I fumbled for the towel.

'About General O'Hara being returned unharmed.'

I shrugged. 'We've had no word since the pay-off. Everybody's beginning to sweat.'

She read Barron's words aloud: '. . . and the horsenappers assured me that if their demands were fully met, then the illustrious superstar of the turf would be reinstated at the New-market Stud forthwith.'

I grunted and took a razor to my stubble. The reporter's story had lifted the lid off the O'Hara affair. It had spelled out to the *Globe*-reading public everything from the duplicate horse to the student demo. It had asked the question: 'Why was the horsenap allowed to take place?', and had laid the blame firmly at the Security Division's door. It had also complicated the facile relationship I shared with Vicky by prompting her to ask a host of awkward questions.

'You *will* be off the case once the General's returned, Simon?'

'That depends on Grant,' I hedged.

'Don't you have the choice—being freelance, I mean?'

'I could opt out.'

'Then—'

'I want to get them, Vicky. It hasn't anything to do with playing hero. It's a simple case of retribution. My own private brand of justice for the indignity of having my scalp sewn up by an animal doctor—for being punched, kicked and spat at. But mostly for what they tried to do to you . . .'

'No, Simon, no.' She took hold of my hands and moulded her warm body against me. 'Don't make me the reason—please. I don't want to be part of your private justice. I know you've been hurt and you want to hurt back—but not for my sake, darling. I don't want it. I want you—as you are now. Simon Drake, twenty-eight years of age, all his own teeth, and no visible scars except . . .' She stroked a finger across my nose. 'Remember?'

I grinned. 'You left out the bit about being unattached,' I said.

'Mmmm.' She threw her arms round my neck and we indulged in a little lip to lip resuscitation. Shaving lather never tasted so good. 'Mm, yes I did, didn't I,' she said.

'Must go, baby.' I reluctantly broke the clinch, reached for my shirt.

'Promise me, Simon?' She lowered her voice to a persuasive purr.

'We'll talk about it over lunch.'

'Will you be able to get away?'

'A guy's entitled to a lunch hour, isn't he?'

She brightened at the prospect. As she straightened my collar, fussed over the knot in my tie, I arranged a one o'clock rendezvous in Fransham. I left her curled up on the bed, still drinking in every word of the *Globe*'s front page.

'Nick Barron mentions you several times,' she remarked. 'I think he likes you. It certainly comes across that way in the story.'

I took a last lingering look at what I was leaving behind, and pushed open the door. 'Never believe everything you read in the newspapers,' I said.

There was an air of funereal solemnity at The Cedars. Barron was tapping his pencil in a slow meditative tattoo against the arm of his chair; Grant was staring dreamily at the ceiling, twirling an unlit cigar in his fingers; and Alison Falloway seemed unable to take her eyes from a circle of intertwined flowers which formed a centrepiece on the refectory table.

I stood looking at their faces. Nobody spoke. I'd had a hazardous drive through fog to get there and I tried to lighten the atmosphere by commenting on the fact. Nobody gave a damn. I shrugged and crossed to an armchair.

'We followed instructions . . . so why? . . . Why?' The words spilled staccato fashion from the Duchess's lips. A little black-edged card fluttered from her fingers.

I retrieved it from the carpet, my stomach constricting as I saw a tiny embossed silver cross and the words: *In loving memory of your beloved General.* I followed her gaze to the centrepiece.

Grant pursed his lips. 'The wreath was delivered fifteen minutes ago by a florist in Fransham, Simon. According to the driver an envelope containing a fiver was pushed through the shop's letter-box last night. This address and the message was dictated by phone this morning. No possible trace, I'm afraid.'

'Could be a crank.' Barron put his fingertips together. 'Some practical joker who read my story—'

'Unlikely,' Grant said crisply, 'they went to too much trouble to protect their anonymity—no, whoever sent it has the General all right.'

'My money, my painting, *and* the General,' Alison Falloway pointed out bitterly. 'God, I need a drink . . .' She spun the Chairmobile round and powered herself out through the door, calling for Bexson.

Grant exhaled loudly. 'O.K., Simon—what have you got, what do you know, and what are your theories?'

I glanced hesitantly at Barron.

'Speak freely,' Grant continued, 'and that goes for Mr Barron too. We can't afford secrets at this juncture.'

Barron smiled his quick insincere smile.

'I've a few hunches,' I said, 'nothing more.'

'Something we can act on?'

'Depends if you want to stick your neck out.'

'McQuillan?'

'Right. I think the General's been at Chinhurst since the hi-jack. A horse has to be fed and watered regularly so the chances are he's still there. I've pussyfooted around, but Mc-Quillan's no fool. A full scale search is the only way.'

'I take it McQuillan had assistance?' Barron queried.

'Probably Duncan Stroud when he was alive, and possibly Roy Biggs.'

'Biggs?'

'It's a long shot but we can't rule him out. He did see us moving the horse.'

'He could have tailed you,' Grant agreed. 'Ratcliffe certainly didn't see him after you'd left. Neither did the jockey's brother. We checked. He was away sick on that day.'

'Now let's get this clear . . .' Barron made a few foppish hand movements, then knitted his fingers together delicately. 'The General was napped on the Sunday and Stroud was found dead on the Monday . . .' He flicked me a glance, 'Captain Grant tells me you think he was murdered?'

I nodded.

'By whom?'

I looked at Grant.

'It's all right, old love,' Barron put in, 'I know all about this blood-boost business.'

My brain baulked at that. Grant said nothing. Obviously the *Globe*'s front page had caused a lot of embarrassment with the department, and he had employed come-clean tactics in an effort to stave off any more bad publicity. I said, 'At first I thought Wesley Falloway killed Stroud.'

'Blackmail?'

'Right. I haven't completely ruled that out, but in the light of this sick-horse caper, and the bottle through the motel window, I'm leaning heavily towards McQuillan.'

'Same motive?'

'Stroud was squeezing the trainer for a bigger cut.'

'Sounds plausible,' Barron conceded.

'We're running a check on your student leader, Simon,' Grant said, 'and it looks as though you were right. Fox-hunts don't really seem in his line. Higher forms of disruption—housing, immigration are more his style. Mass battles with the London police—that sort of thing. He's got quite a record.'

'Bloodsports to order, uh?'

'Could well be. If there are no further developments by this evening, we'll pull him in for questioning.'

'Any more thoughts on the money collector?' Barron asked.

I shook my head. 'He was far taller than Biggs, and it wasn't McQuillan either. This guy had fingers.'

The Duchess trundled back into the room. Gilbert Bexson followed wheeling the drinks trolley. He parked it and motioned towards us.

'Some refreshment, gentlemen?'

We ordered. The Duchess got to grips with an ultra-large gin and waved away the bottle of tonic in Bexson's outstretched hand.

'Tell me, Mr Drake,' her eyes, sharp, analysing, peered at me over the rim of her glass. 'Will I ever see my gallant General again?'

'I don't think they'll harm the horse,' I said, trying to sound convincing. 'Kidnappers invariably keep their word.'

'But the wreath . . . ?'

'A cheap bit of dramatics, maybe.'

'More likely a forerunner to another monetary demand,' Barron interjected.

'What more do they want!' She swung angrily towards the fireplace, projecting a finger at the naked wall. 'They've had my beautiful Stubbs, plus fifty thou—'

'Look out, man!' Grant cut across her words as his measure of brandy slipped from Bexson's hand and shattered against the drinks trolley.

There was an uneasy silence. All eyes were on the man-servant.

'Something you want to tell us, Mr Bexson?' I murmured mildly.

He made some inarticulate noise and lowered his head. Finally he said, 'Yes, perhaps I have . . . Something I should have told you long before this awful moment . . .'

'Oh, for God's sake stop blithering—' Alison Falloway began.

'The Stubbs, madam.' He looked briefly towards the vacant space. 'It isn't . . . I mean it wasn't . . .'

'Oh, God!'

'Are you trying to tell us it was a fake?' Grant prompted him gently.

'Y—yes, sir.' He slopped whisky into a glass and sucked it down. 'I had no idea it would be used in payment for the General. I suppose the wreath . . . If anything's happened to the horse . . .'

'Oh dear, oh dear.' Barron made worried noises and picked at a spotless fingernail.

'Fake!' The Duchess whirled on him. 'I had it valued only last year—'

'It was switched only recently, madam.'

'You stole the genuine Stubbs?'

He gave his head a mournful shake. 'Not I, madam—Mr Wesley.'

I thought she was going to explode. Her neck turned puce, her eyes widened with something akin to horror, and her mouth fell open. I could see a little vein pulsing in her temple.

'My son? Are you telling me that my son . . .' She dribbled off.

'I think you had better explain, Mr Bexson,' Grant said.

He did. He spoke slowly, picking his words with care, telling how the housekeeper had first become suspicious of Wesley's intentions when she had seen him taking photographs of the painting.

'That was several months ago,' he added. 'When Emily told me, I was stunned.'

'Go on,' Grant said.

'Well, sir, a few weeks ago Mr Wesley arrived with a package and locked himself in the drawing-room. I could hear him tampering with the picture frame. I didn't have to be a detective to know what he was doing.'

'But can you be positively sure?'

'I'd pencilled my initials on the back of the original canvas.'

'So you checked and found them missing.'

He nodded. 'I had sleepless nights wondering what to do for the best. Emily and I found ourselves talking of nothing else . . .'

'Even in the Horse and Groom,' I grunted.

'Yes, even there. You see we had to consider the family name. We didn't want anybody to get hurt, so we agreed to keep silent. Everything will eventually go to Mr Wesley anyway . . .' He glanced hesitantly at the Duchess. 'Madam, can you ever forgive our stupidity?'

'Damn your misguided loyalty!' she snapped.

'I was only—'

'Leave us, Bexson!' A flick of her finger dismissed him.

He looked distressed. He managed a brief bow and a rather strangled 'Excuse me, gentlemen' and made his exit. The Duchess powered her machine to a neutral corner and faced the wall. She took a calming swallow of her drink and held the glass at arm's length to check her fettle. The contents rocked unsteadily.

192

I looked at Grant. 'What do you give for the General's chances now?'

He sighed heavily.

'Nick?'

'*Dum spiro, spero*, old son.'

'In English; you're not still in the sixth.'

He grinned. 'Where there's life there's hope.'

'But we don't know if there is any life,' Grant said. 'That's the whole damned point.'

Bexson reappeared in the doorway. His eyes settled on the Duchess and he coughed discreetly. She whirled the machine around to face him.

'I'm sorry to disturb you, madam, but there's a young person at the tradesman's entrance. He's asking for Mr Drake.'

She squinted at me.

'I'm not expecting anyone,' I said.

'A Mr Potter, sir,' he provided.

I groaned.

'Tell him to stay put,' Grant said. 'Mr Drake will see him outside.'

'Secrets, Mr Drake?' the Duchess enquired.

'More of a burden,' I grunted.

'I've met him, Mrs Falloway,' there was a slight note of panic in Barron's voice. 'If it's the Mr Potter I think it is, then he's not at all the type of person for your drawing-room.'

She was unmoved. 'Show him in, Bexson, a little diversity might do us all good. And Bexson—'

'Yes, madam?'

'I regret my behaviour of a moment ago.'

She had collected herself well. The words came out in a tumble and they must have cost her plenty. It wasn't every day she apologized, or every day she was told she had a thief for a son. She gained a big chunk of everyone's respect at that moment.

Len Potter slouched his way in whistling a few untuneful bars of lord knows what. He hadn't changed his shirt since the night we'd visited Chinhurst. His hair was a little greasier, his nails a little dirtier and he was wearing that jubilant grin of his.

'Well if it ain't Drakey, the Captain, and ole Nichol-arse 'imself,' he said in that endearing way of his. 'Nearly didn't get 'ere. That fog's real clampers.'

I smiled tolerantly. 'How did you find me, Lennie?'

'Motel said y'might be 'ere. Motel? I gotta be jokin'. That'll teach yer t'smoke in bloody bed.'

Grant glanced briefly at Alison Falloway and raised his eyes. Barron gave an embarrassed little laugh.

'Talkin' of smoke,' Potter went on, 'anybody got a ciggie?'

Nobody offered.

The Duchess cleared her throat, gestured. 'There's a silver cigarette box on the mantelpiece, young man.'

'Oh ta. Ta a lot.' He was over to her in three quick strides, extending an unwashed hand. 'Mrs Fallerway, ain't it?'

'Mr Potter.' She shook it.

'Leonard Maximillian, ma'am. I once 'ad the 'onour t'look after yer son's arthritic nags—Oops, beg pardon, I mean class 'orses.'

'My God . . .' Grant sounded feverish.

'You were right the first time, Mr Potter,' the Duchess agreed. 'Arthritic nags is a far more suitable description.'

'Is it?' He looked unsure.

'Far better.'

'Yeah it is, ain't it.' He convulsed with laughter.

'I think she likes him,' I breathed.

Grant's mouth twitched.

'Nice 'ouse you've got 'ere,' Potter continued, surreptitiously filling his pocket with the contents of the silver box. 'Fireplace is nice too. Bit bare, mind. Look better wiv a picture over it.'

Barron cringed, looked at me. 'Can't you shut him up, Simon?'

Who was I to interfere. The Duchess actually looked amused.

'What do you suggest, Mr Potter?' she asked.

He considered, rasping the bristles on his chin. 'Dunno really. A naked bird stretched out on one of them shaggie longies nightn't look bad.'

'Try to moderate your language, Potter,' Grant said weakly.

'Did I say summick wrong?'

'Everything,' Barron muttered.

'Wouldn't say no to a sherbet.' His eyes flitted to the drinks trolley. 'Fog's got down me throat,' he coughed phlegmily to emphasize the point, adding, 'Parched I am.'

The Duchess told him to help himself. He did. He squatted down and began rummaging through the assortment of bottles. 'You've got everythin' 'ere,' he beamed. 'I'm gonna 'ave an 'ard job choosin' from this lot.'

'Get on with it, Potter,' Grant grunted.

The Duchess was studying him. 'You're Pisces, aren't you?' she said suddenly.

He emerged with a bottle of Campari, looking indignant. 'No I ain't, ma'am. Sober as a brewer's drayman I am.'

Even Grant had to smile at that. He was about to qualify the question but the appearance of Bexson stopped him short. The manservant looked flustered as he advised the Duchess of her son's and Kelly's return.

She said with sudden emotion, 'I'll deal with him in here.'

'We'll use the library if we may.' Relief swept over Grant's face as he ushered us out.

I released Potter's fingers from the Campari and steered him towards the door. We met Wesley coming in.

'I know that face . . .' He bristled at the sight of Potter.

'And I can 'ardly forget yourn,' the boy replied cockily.

'What's going on, Drake?'

'We were discussing art,' I said. 'Len suggested a nude reclining on a chaise-longue, but I expect you'd prefer something more tasteful—a Stubbs for instance?'

He didn't reply, but he went a little pale around the gills.

'Wesley!' the Duchess shrilled out.

He turned his head. 'I've had a long journey, Mother. I'm tired, I'm—'

'In here—now!'

He murmured something under his breath, squared his shoulders, and marched into the drawing-room. The door slammed shut.

'Went whiter than a virgin's tits,' Potter sniggered.

I shepherded him into the library. Grant and Barron were discussing the ins and outs of art forgery. Kelly was listening attentively.

'If you have access to a valuable painting then invariably a copyist will hear about it and make the approach.'

'It couldn't be sold openly, surely?'

'Good God no. A private collector would buy it. Of course, you'd only get a fraction of its true worth.'

I slid beside Kelly, whispered, 'How does it feel to know your boy friend's an art thief?'

'Relieved in a way.' It came out as a sigh.

'Relieved?'

'It puts him in the clear as far as the horsenap is concerned. If he masterminded the snatch then it's hardly likely he'd demand a painting he knew to be a fake.'

True enough, I thought. I reckoned he'd taken the painting as a form of insurance. If he fell short 'will-wise' then whatever he made out of the sale would tide him over during the year to come. He liked the good life and didn't want to sacrifice any of it. The Stubbs would give him plenty of buying power while he had another crack at earning the old man's fifteen thousand.

'I read abaht it in the *Globe*, see . . .' Potter's ramblings interrupted my train of thought. 'Lennie's gonna be needed, I says. Drakey's gonna want an 'elpin' 'and.'

Grant looked briefly across at him. 'But you ran out on us. You showed us you panic far too easily.'

'That were Stroudy, weren't it. Diff'rent now 'e's popped 'is clogs, ain't it.'

'I'm sorry, Potter,' Grant shook his head.

He mouthed an obscenity and began picking at an acne spot.

'Where do we go from here?' I asked.

Grant kneaded his forehead. 'I apply for a warrant and we make a thorough search of Chinhurst.'

'But that will take—'

'Time? I know. There's no guarantee that the horse is there and if we crash in without that necessary piece of paper—'

'Far too risky,' Barron agreed.

'So we do nothing?'

'For the moment we sit tight.'

I let out a sigh of exasperation. I was suddenly weary of the whole stinking business. 'I've a lunch date with Vicky,' I said, 'so if my presence isn't required . . .'

'You're seeing Mrs Annesley?'

'I had arranged—'

'Good, good.' Grant glanced at Barron, then smiled at me. 'Have a few hours away from all this. You've been through a lot, Simon.'

'Yes, relax a little, old love,' Barron agreed, gazing into the mirror, fastidiously adjusting the knot in his tie.

I looked at Kelly. 'This is too easy. Am I being got rid of?'

'I thought you wanted to go.'

'I do.'

'Then go.' She gave me a brief disinterested smile.

'You'll be taking Len with you, of course.' Grant dropped that one as I palmed the door-knob.

'Len? What on earth for?'

'Security, Simon. We can't let him wander off, not now. Until this is all over, I'm afraid you're stuck with him.'

'Bloody hell!'

'He could stay here but there'll be a lot of confidences exchanged. We can't afford to censor words. I'm sorry.'

Potter grinned.

'Bloody hell!' I said again.

Grant asked where we would be lunching and then he added, 'Give me a few minutes alone with the boy. I'll make damned sure he behaves himself.'

I thought about arguing the toss but Grant's inflexible expression told me not to bother. It was a case of go with Potter or don't go at all. I left them and made my way outside. Raised voices filtered from the drawing-room. I could only catch the occasional word, an odd phrase or two, but what I heard made me glad I wasn't heir to a fortune.

Little wispy drifts of fog rolled into my face as I crossed the tarmac to the M.G. It was closing in rapidly. Come darkness, travelling was going to be hairy. I leathered the condensation from the windscreen, lit a cigarette and slid behind the wheel.

'That Kelly's gone a bit cool, ain't she?' Potter hulked himself into the passenger seat. 'Thought you two fancied one annuver—'avin' it away wiv Fallerway, is she?'

'Why don't you ask her?' I growled.

'Don't fink she likes me some'ow.'

'So tell me something new.'

'I ain't bovvered. I don't give a monkey's whether she likes me or not . . .' He raked a hand through his lank hair and stretched lazily. 'Don't 'spect she gives a monkey's whether I give a monkey's either.'

I took a calming breath. 'Is it impossible for you to hold an intelligent conversation, Lennie?'

'Huh?'

'Never mind. Just be nice to Vicky—O.K.?'

'Grant 'ad a word wiv me abaht that.'

'And you listened?'

'Oh, I did Drakey,' he said smugly, 'every bleedin' word.'

The restaurant was almost empty. Two or three fog-dampened couples sat huddled at window tables peering out at the crawling ooze of traffic. A poker-faced waiter glared disapprovingly at Potter's appearance and relieved us of our coats. I lent the boy a comb and packed him off to the washroom. By the time Vicky arrived he had almost managed to look human.

'Partners we are, miss,' he explained, digging into the first course. 'Sorta Biggles and Ginger, ain't that right, Drakey?'

I leered at him.

She looked amused. 'I remember meeting you at Chinhurst,' she said. 'You were very convincing.'

'Inside man, weren't I.'

'Really?'

'Checkin' up on Fallerway, see.' He smacked his lips, wiped a dribble of soup from his chin. 'Reportin' back t'Drakey 'ere. Dead risky it were.'

'Is that right, Simon?' she asked, intrigued.

'More or less.'

'Gonna 'elp 'em find the General, ain't I.'

'That mouth will be the death of you,' I growled.

He chuckled, said to Vicky, 'Takes care of me, dun 'e.'

'And me.' I felt her cool fingers on my hand. 'Simon's the kind of man a girl can depend on.'

'That's fast becoming a cliché,' I grinned.

Her eyes, veiled by long dark lashes, held mine for a brief responsive moment. She was asking for an answer to this morning's question. I suppose I should have had one correctly phrased and ready for instant delivery—the kind of stalling tactics that come easily to most guys. Truth was I didn't want to quit the case or say no to the girl I loved. Luckily I didn't have to say either. The arrival of the second course and a question from the waiter, temporarily postponed my decision.

'Mr Simon Drake?'

'Yes?'

'Telephone for you, sir.'

I looked at my porterhouse steak and cursed.

'The Captain knows we're 'ere,' Potter reminded me, attacking his meat with relish.

I told Vicky to start without me, and asked the waiter to lead on. The phone was in a recess by the lobby.

'Hold the line, Simon,' Grant requested as I grunted a hullo.

I broke open a fresh pack of cigarettes and waited. The fog was getting thicker. I could see people, collars upturned, handkerchiefs pressed to mouths, scurrying along the pavement. Headlit cars made slow progression along the High Street. I turned tobacco into ash, and thought about my steak getting cold.

'Something's come up, Simon,' Grant said at last. 'Can you come straight back to The Cedars?'

'We're right in the middle of lunch—why, what's happened?'

'Some new evidence. I can't say any more.'

'Is it immediate?'

'I'm afraid it is.'

I breathed heavily into the mouthpiece. 'O.K., we're on our way.'

'Potter's with you?'

'Of course.'

'Hurry, please.' He severed the connection.

I made my way back to the table. My own thoughts insulated me from Potter's moans as I broke the news.

'But I ain't finished . . .'

'I haven't even started—now get your coat.'

'You're going back to The Cedars?' Vicky's eyes were wide and questioning.

'I'm sorry,' I said inadequately. 'I really am.'

'I understand.' She suddenly fell silent, stroking the stem of her glass.

I gave her a brief people-are-watching-us kiss, and told her I'd phone her later. There was something in the way she looked at me, something intangible, yet something I could feel and knew I ought to question. I didn't have time. Potter was making noises in my ear and nudging me to pay the waiter. I left more than enough to cover the bill and we headed for the exit.

The M.G. was a nebulous blur parked on the corner of a cul-de-sac. I dug into my pockets for the keys as we hurried towards it. Potter was saying something about the build-up of traffic, but I wasn't listening. Uneasy questions were nibbling at the fringes of my consciousness. *New evidence?* I kept churning the words over. What new evidence? It must be important, bloody important, for Grant to phone. Something he couldn't handle himself. Something that needed me and needed me fast. I turned the key in the lock, snapped open the car door.

'Hold it, Simon,' the voice came from behind me.

I swung round and through a swirl of fog saw Grant emerging from a basement.

'What the hell . . . ?'

He looked at Potter. 'Did it go O.K.?'

'Ace, Captain,' the boy smirked.

'Join Mr Barron.' He tilted his head towards twin cones of light on the opposite side of the road. I saw them dim then brighten as the battery turned over the motor.

'Now look, Howard,' I grabbed the sleeve of his raglan. 'You phoned me from—'

'That call box,' he indicated an illuminated shape in the distance. 'I'm sorry for the deception, Simon, but Potter and your lunchtime appointment with Mrs Annesley provided the ideal set-up.'

'Set-up? What the bloody hell are you talking about?'

Barron's yellow Vauxhall cruised slowly past us and parked, its engine idling.

'Follow,' Grant instructed, opening the M.G.'s passenger door and worming his way into the upholstery. 'I'll explain on the way.'

'You'll explain now!' I could barely drag my words out.

'Get in, Simon.'

'I want a bloody explanation!'

Wild, crazy images were bouncing blindly across my brain. I was having trouble connecting any of this with actuality. I felt like a spectator sport and I didn't like the feeling. For some illogical reason I wanted to hit Grant. I wanted to drag him from the seat and beat hell and a few straight answers out of him. I clenched and unclenched my fists and breathed deeply.

'Get in,' he said again, more firmly this time.

Like a good boy I did as I was told. Perhaps the voice of authority had prevailed or perhaps subconsciously I knew what he was going to say.

'Poor Simon,' he glanced uneasily at me, 'she really has made a fool out of you, hasn't she.'

Chapter Thirteen

ONLY INSTINCT kept my hands on the wheel as I did a violent U-turn and tucked the M.G.'s nose in behind the Vauxhall. Barron checked his rear-view mirror and the car moved slowly off, its headlights raking the road ahead.

'Chinhurst, Simon,' Grant said quietly.

I slipped the lever into bottom and followed. Suddenly I had no compulsion to finish what I'd been paid to start.

'The phone call served a dual purpose,' he explained. 'It gave Potter a few minutes alone with Vicky Annesley and it got both you and the boy out of the restaurant.'

'What did he tell her?' I asked coldly.

'That we have a search warrant and come nightfall we were going to tear the stables apart.'

I ran my tongue over dry lips. It was all beginning to fall cruelly into place—the reason for Potter tagging along, the private 'I'll make sure he behaves himself' patter, was all too vividly apparent. The voices returned to my skull, one by one, in sequence, like a tape machine on play-back.

Grant leaned forward. 'We have to make McQuillan show his hand,' he said. 'Truth is we haven't enough evidence for a warrant. This way he'll be forced to move the horse and we'll be ready and waiting.'

'Clever,' I said dryly. 'And you expect Vicky to make all this possible?'

'I'll bet my pension she's on the phone to him right now.'

'You're bloody crazy.'

'I know how you feel about the girl, Simon. I'm sorry.'

I hardly heard him. My mind was wandering, recalling her

unashamed femininity, the touch of her warm flawlessly smooth skin. Skin that could soothe yet tantalize, caress with the softest touch imaginable, yet excite and explode during the passions of lovemaking. Real love. There was nothing phoney about Vicky's love. No call-girl tactics, no fiction. I remembered the way she'd fallen asleep in my arms, that first responsive kiss of the morning. Grant was wrong . . . Christ, he was so bloody wrong.

'How long has she been under suspicion?' I muttered.

'I've had doubts about her for some time,' he folded his arms, sighed with feeling. 'The blood-boost business tended to obscure her guilt—it was easy to confuse the two issues. I suppose my doubts turned into real suspicion the moment she dropped Wesley for you. The timing was too coincidental to be true.'

'Assumptions, goddamn misguided assumptions! Why the hell didn't you tell me how you felt?'

'You're in love with her, aren't you?'

'What?'

'Love, Simon. I said you're in love with the girl.'

'So maybe I am. Does that give you the right—'

'Every right. Do you think you could have worked dispassionately or objectively if I'd confided in you? If I'd told you we'd had her under surveillance? What would your reactions have been if you'd known that when she wasn't with you then more often than not she was at McQuillan's?'

I felt my stomach lurch sickeningly. A spasm ran through my fingers as they tightened on the wheel. I looked across at him, unable to believe he had spoken those words.

'I had to tell Kelly of my suspicions,' he admitted soberly. 'She was getting too fond of you and I couldn't allow that to happen. Her indifference towards you and her attachment to Falloway was my doing. She was acting under instructions.'

'Jesus bloody Christ,' the words curdled as they rolled off my tongue. 'Kelly might have come between Vicky and me, huh? It suited your perverse reasoning to have a lovesick stooge keeping Mrs Annesley occupied while you ferreted around for your so-called evidence.'

'Not *so-called*, Simon. We have all the pieces.'

'Like her visiting McQuillan's?' I found myself groping for excuses. 'She keeps her horses there, doesn't she? It's suppositional crap and you know it.'

He slowly shook his head.

I forced out a derisive laugh and fumbled for a cigarette. Both helped ease my nerves. Barron's Vauxhall was stopping at a red light. I nursed the M.G. to a halt. I could see vague shadows of people hurrying across the road. Boy friends, wives, lovers—I envied them. At least they appeared to have a direction, a future. All I appeared to have was a disorientated past.

We moved off. Grant said, 'Vicky's brother is a student at Wroxford College, I believe?'

'So?'

'The anti-bloodsporters came from Wroxford College.'

I gaped at him. 'Something else you conveniently forgot to tell me?'

'The rest we stumbled on by chance—or rather Barron did. I only learned of it yesterday. I did a deal with the *Globe*. Our blood-boost information—'

'Have you got something to tell me or not!' I growled impatiently.

He waved a finger to indicate that Barron was turning off the main highway. I dropped down a gear and went with the Vauxhall, hugging its red tail lights. Finally, after checking his wristwatch, he launched into the denouement.

'Barron wanted a follow-up to the horsenap story. For the last week he's been ploughing through past issues of the *Globe*, tabulating background material on the Falloways. He went back eleven years—to Alison Falloway's accident, in fact. Do you remember any of the details?'

'She was thrown from a horse,' I murmured, wondering where the hell this was leading us.

'Yes, but not just any horse. A rather special one, Simon, and one that could provide a deep-rooted motive for this whole affair.'

I frowned, breathed smoke.

He settled well down in his seat and proceeded to take me back to that tragic night of eleven years ago. 'Julian Ratcliffe was a comparatively inexperienced trainer then. He was struggling for clients with good class horses and he used to seek out the big names in owners and throw dinner parties to impress them. Clement and Alison Falloway attended such a party.' There was an irritating glimmer of humour in his eyes as he went on, 'Alison was rather reckless in those days. She had a reputation for drinking too much and saying a lot of bizarre things—nobody ever took her seriously. She did precisely that the night of the party.'

'Precisely what?'

'She suddenly announced she was going for a moonlight ride. As I said before, nobody took her seriously.'

I looked at him. 'I can't see the relevancy—'

'She *did* go for that ride. She took a horse from the stable and went up on the moors. It was dark, she was in an intoxicated state, and the horse collided with a car. The poor animal had to be destroyed . . .' He sighed, looked down at his legs. 'And Alison Falloway of course is still paying for her foolishness.'

My palms had gone clammy. Somehow I had a premonition of what was coming.

'The horse was an extremely promising two-year-old. A gift from a Mr Sam Tyler to his daughter on her eighteenth birthday. You remember the name from the dossier?'

'Vicky's maiden name,' I said tightly.

'Money and revenge rolled into one. Eighteen is an impressionable age, Simon. She's nurtured a grudge for eleven long years.'

'An eye for an eye?' I shook my head emphatically. 'If that's taken to its conclusion . . .'

206

'The General will die?' He quirked an eyebrow.

'She wouldn't kill a horse. I know Vicky—she loves horses —she wouldn't have any part . . .' I stopped as I heard myself almost pleading.

'How do you explain the wreath?'

That jarred my senses. 'A gag?' I temporized. 'Little brother's sick humour, perhaps?'

'Perhaps,' he grunted expressively. 'Don't worry, if I thought the horse was dead I wouldn't be here. McQuillan's no fool, he's in it for the money. There's no profit in a carcass.'

The fog-bound outline of the Lodge loomed ahead of us. I saw the Vauxhall extinguish its lights and crawl the last distance to the entrance gates. I touched the brakes, killed the electrics, and coasted the M.G. alongside.

'The motel!' I shouted the words as my thoughts gave a sudden twist. 'Vicky was with me when that bottle was thrown. How the hell do you explain that?'

'I can't,' he said. He jerked open the door.

'Now hold on just a minute—'

'Hello, old love,' Barron looked in at me, his lips drawing back in an amused leer. 'Has Captain Grant been putting you in the picture?'

I ignored him, said to Grant, 'You can't just brush off something like that. She was very nearly burned to bloody death . . .'

A figure emerged from the cover of some bushes and signalled to Grant.

'I have to contact my men,' his tone was final. 'We'll talk about it later.'

I swore impotently as he strode briskly off.

'Sorry about your girl friend, Simon.' Barron didn't sound at all sorry as I climbed out to join him.

'Yeah,' I muttered, shivering slightly.

'Lovely but lethal, eh?'

'Your aphorisms don't amuse me, Nick.'

'Still tender, old son? Bound to be, bound to be,' he pushed his hands deep into his pockets. 'Well let's hope McQuillan doesn't keep us waiting too long.'

I looked towards the Lodge. The big house lay veiled in obscurity and silence. A solitary lamp in the yard glowed moistly, illuminating the swirling fog and very little else.

'Still think she's tipped him off?' I smiled thinly.

'Not a doubt in my mind.' He sounded conceitedly sure of himself.

'Because of something that happened eleven years ago?'

'That and the money. Don't tear your heart out, Simon, she's not worth the pain.'

'You're crazy! You're both bloody crazy. Digging up something that's buried in the past—something she's probably long forgotten—'

'Hardly, old love.'

'What?'

'She remembers it every time she pushes open her gate.'

I looked at him blankly.

'She bought her bungalow in the Quantock Hills two years ago. Externally it looks the same as the previous owners left it —except for the nameplate.'

'*Serendipity?*'

'Mm,' he repeated the word slowly, emphasizing all the syllables. 'Nice word. Comes from a fairy-tale, you know. It means an unforeseen piece of good fortune,' he sighed theatrically, adding: 'It was *misfortune* in Vicky's case. You see, it was the name of the horse that was killed.'

The corroborative nail was driven well home. I suppose it drained the last tenuous traces of hope from my body. I felt deceived and embittered. I slammed my fist hard against the M.G.'s paintwork, gritting my teeth to keep a hold of my febrile emotions.

'Keep your voices down . . .' Grant reappeared and beckoned me towards the gates. 'Activity in the yard, Simon. We need you and your car, fast!'

Barron protested bitterly as he was ordered to join Potter

in the Vauxhall. I released the M.G.'s handbrake, and with
Grant's help manhandled the car around to face the entrance
gates.

'McQuillan's using the travelling box,' he said breathlessly.
'The ramp's being lowered.'

Faintly, barely piercing the blanket of fog came the crunch
of gravel under shoes, the muted clatter of hooves. It was all
beginning to happen—just as Grant had predicted it would.

'We're going to block him as he makes his exit,' he explained. 'Hit your headlights when I wave him down. That
ought to make sure he damn well stops.'

I sat back and stared out at nothing, a finger poised over the
light switch. Several minutes passed.

I could hear the distant throb of an engine, the slight clatter
of a clutch as an ageing transmission was eased into gear. Two
yellow beams began cutting a hole in the fog. Security men
spread themselves across the opening. The wattage increased
as the seconds elapsed, and suddenly the box lurched out of the
milky opacity.

Grant stepped forward, waving his arms.

I threw the switch.

What happened in the ensuing moments, happened in such
close order as to be nothing more than an indistinguishable
blur.

The big vehicle bulled forward, its engine roaring with increased revs as it sent security men scattering. The arc from my
headlights illuminated the cab. I could see McQuillan squinting into the glare. His good hand shielded his eyes while his
hook wrenched at a steering spoke, levering the wheel around,
fighting to clear my obstruction.

'He's getting through!' Grant's voice was hoarse, lost in a
shriek of tyres as the box slithered broadside. I heard glass
shatter as a massive overrider scuffed along my wing and
annihilated a sidelight.

'After him!' Grant signalled his men to their cars.

As they fumbled with doors, battled with ignition circuits,

McQuillan gained precious seconds. The box zigzagged away and melted into nature's own smokescreen.

'Much damage?' Grant limped towards me holding his side.

I shrugged, hardly grasping his question. I was dazed by the speed of it all. The damage seemed trivial somehow, totally irrelevant.

'Can you follow?' he panted.

'In this weather?'

'We have to try.'

'No way.'

'But, Simon . . .'

I did a hasty three-point turn. 'Vicky must know where he's taking the horse. She's going to tell me, Howard—that I promise you.'

'No, wait!'

'No time,' I jabbed the throttle impatiently.

'There's something I've got to tell you!'

'There's nothing I want to listen to.'

I let in the clutch and drew slowly away. I could see Grant via the mirror, shouting, waving me back, his silhouette diminishing with every yard. I switched him off, watched him fade like the dot on a television screen. I had a lot on my mind.

Serendipity. The nameplate framed itself in my headlight beams as I arrived at the house. I parked, pushed open the gate, and dragged my feet a little on the walk to the door. I felt about as bad as any guy can feel. This morning I'd had a relationship. A clear-cut, unquestioned, uncomplicated relationship. And now . . . ? I stabbed a finger on the bell-push. The peel of chimes did nothing to alleviate the maelstrom of doubts.

A negative response. I rang again, and then a third. Nothing. Somebody was in, I could hear music. I took a credit card from my wallet, pressed hard against the door to cause a gap, and slid the piece of plastic between the lock tongue and its housing. I thought I'd find a safety chain, but I didn't. The door opened sweetly.

I traced the music to the bathroom. Vicky was taking a shower. I could see her feet below the curtain. Bare, brown, beautiful feet. Beautiful yet beguiling. The radio rested on a cork-topped stool. I bent and snicked it off.

'Simon . . . ?' She parted the curtains, modesty sending a hand to cover the neat downy triangle that caressed her thighs.

I folded my arms and looked at her.

'Has something happened?' She smiled unsurely.

I kept on looking.

'Simon?'

'Uh-huh?'

'Something's wrong. Why are you staring at me like that?'

'They set you up.'

'What?'

'Grant and Potter, they set you up.'

'I—I don't understand?' She began stroking tendrils of wet hair from her eyes.

'No? I thought you were pretty good at playing double games.'

'Simon, please—'

'They have a name for me, don't they . . . ?' In the condensation on the mirror I etched the words: *fall-guy*. 'I have to hand it to you, Vicky,' I said, 'you took me for one helluva ride. I would have stayed the distance too if it hadn't been for Grant. I wanted to hit him when I heard. Hit my own boss! Christ, you really wound me up, baby.'

She had nothing to say to that, well nothing verbal, that is. She had plenty to say in those big blue eyes, in the nervous little movements of her fingers, in the way her breasts lifted and fell with her breathing, anxiously, betrayingly.

'Why, Vicky?' I asked bitterly.

She tried me with a look of injured innocence.

'First Wesley Falloway and then me. Both of us conned by a pretty face. It took a phoney search-warrant line and a little

berk like Potter to deliver it before Sam Tyler's daughter coul{ }
be seen for what she really is.'

'No! No!'

'Yes, baby, yes. It's too late for lies.'

'Oh God . . .' She shivered.

'Get dressed.' I threw her a towel.

'It's not like you think—I didn't—' She tried to wrap he{ }
arms around my neck but they fell away as I backed off.

'Save it,' I said. 'Once bitten . . .'

'All right!' Her mouth hardened. 'What version do yo{ }
want? The yes Simon I really love you version? The I hate{ }
deceiving you version? The first lie came easy and then they go{ }
progressively harder and harder until I hated myself and th{ }
whole hideous mess. Is that what you want to hear?'

'Try the truth.' My fingers tightened around her wrists.

'Oh, the truth? Well, how about it was laughs all the way{ }
I lied to you and I enjoyed the lies. How would your male eg{ }
feel if I told you I only tolerated you in bed because I had to{ }
I made a fool out of you, Simon. Satisfied now?'

'Are you proud of your achievement?'

'Maybe I am.'

'Well, don't be. I was easy pickings.'

She began to laugh, quietly at first, then with mountin{ }
hysteria. 'You believe me,' she gurgled. 'You believe I enjoye{ }
all the lies—It's easier for you to accept me as a bitch—'

'Cut that out!'

'I'm a bitch, right? Bitch! Bitch!' she screamed.

I slapped her hard across the face. The screaming dissolve{ }
into sobbing as she hung limply over the washbasin. Tear{ }
welled in her eyes as she turned to look at me.

'The lying did get progressively harder,' she said brokenl{ }
'I wanted . . . I tried to tell you the morning we went to Chin{ }
hurst. In the car, do you remember? I said that people aren'{ }
always what they pretend to be, that pretence and realism—
oh, Simon, what I didn't count on was falling in love wit{ }
you . . .'

I looked beyond the glassy film that covered her eyes. I was looking for something I could believe in, something more than just words.

'I love you, don't you understand? *I love you.*'

I wanted to tell her that this whole ugly scene was eating out my guts and that I loved and wanted her more than I'd ever wanted anything in my life. I was on the verge of taking her in my arms and excavating that corny, but all too veritable line, about nothing else mattering so long as we had each other. But somehow my tongue got tangled round the words and I settled for a weak, 'Take it easy, baby—take it easy . . .'

She was still sobbing and shivering as I wrapped the towel around her slim shoulders. I found her pants, slacks and jumper hanging behind the door. I pushed them into her hands and told her to get dressed. Then I went through to the lounge and poured a couple of stiff drinks.

'I want to do a lot of talking, Simon.' Her voice sounded shaky but controlled as she padded towards me. 'Have you ever felt so hopelessly lost that you can't remember how it all began, or even why it all began?'

'Eleven years is a lot of mileage,' I said.

'You know about Serendipity.' She sighed, swallowed hard. 'Barron dug it all up. Has it been festering all this time?'

'I suppose it must have been, although I wasn't conscious of it. Eddie deliberately reopened the wound when he needed my help.'

'Wesley?'

'Yes. Eddie knew we were close and he wanted details of General O'Hara's movements. A stunt, he said. Hijack the horse, keep it hidden for twenty-four hours and then give it back. Publicity for the college it was supposed to be, nothing more.'

'And you agreed.'

'I didn't see the harm. Eddie kept going on and on about how this would be a way of getting back at Mrs Falloway. He never talked of anything else. He made me relive Serendipity's death over and over again. In the end I found myself wanting to help him.'

I lit two cigarettes and pushed one between her lips. She drew on it deeply. I watched her nails bite deep into her palms as she told how easy it had been to extract our hideaway location from Wesley. 'During the drive to Looe he almost volunteered the information,' she murmured, sitting tensely on the edge of the sofa. 'I simply turned the conversation towards the General, and Wesley's vainglory did the rest. How the Security Division had switched horses—how important his role had been at the farewell party—he was so pompous about it all.'

I grunted at the aptness of the description. 'So you contrived a row and came home?'

'And like a fool I told Eddie about Animals Unlimited.' She looked at me steadily and went on: 'When I found out that Neil McQuillan was supplying the trailer, then everything crystallized. I knew he wouldn't have any part of a student prank. I knew it had to be money and plenty of it. I had it out with Eddie. Do you know what he said?'

'Tell me.'

'That he'd rather I'd been kept out of it. That an attempt to bribe the box driver had failed and that my friendship with Wesley had only been used as a last resort. God, I could have killed him . . .'

I watched as she stroked the knuckles of a hand over her wet eyes, as she rolled her glass nervously between her palms. I listened as she told how McQuillan, Eddie, and my good friend with the Zapata moustache had snatched the General. How the horse had been kept on the sick list at Chinhurst, and how she had warned the trainer of my plan to look inside the box.

'I phoned him while you were waiting for me to get changed,' she admitted, looking at the floor. 'I was torn between loyalties, Simon. Eddie is my brother and I couldn't . . . not wittingly . . . Oh, God, how do you put feelings into words . . .'

I took a swallow of my drink. The liquid felt cold against my tight throat. I said, 'And was it this loyalty for Eddie which kept us together? Was it easier to say yes and keep close, than to say no and lose contact?'

'You don't believe that?' Her eyes widened.

'I don't want to believe it.'

'My one hope was that you'd give up the case. I wanted to break free of the vortex which threatened to engulf us both. I thought the fire—'

'Might scare me off?'

She nodded listlessly.

'That's been puzzling me,' I said. 'Who threw the bottle and why?'

'Neil thought you were getting too close and he panicked. He concocted his stupid petrol bomb and went looking for you at The Cedars. You were coming out of the gates as he arrived.'

'So he followed me to the motel thinking I was alone.'

'That's the way he tells it. It's logical I suppose, although I still can't help wondering whether he meant to kill us both.'

'Nice company you keep.'

She shuddered.

'Did McQuillan send the wreath?'

'Wreath?' She repeated the word as if she hardly knew its meaning.

I took her through the 'in loving memory' bit, plus a brief summary of the travelling-box sortie. Her lips quivered as she said, 'I—I didn't know about the wreath. They won't harm the horse, Simon. Eddie promised . . .'

'Where's he been taken?'

She moved her hands in a helpless gesture.

'*Where is he, Vicky?*'

'He'll be released tonight.'

'I doubt it. The Stubbs is as phoney as one of Falloway's miles.'

She hesitated, her voice tremulous as she said, 'Mason and

215

Sons at Wroxford. I don't know the address. It's some sort of warehouse, I think.'

I crosssed to the telephone, reached for a directory. I thumbed through the pages, Marx, Maskell, *Mason.* I ran my finger down the list, skidded my nail to a halt as I found the relevant entry. The small print set my heart pounding in my ribcage. I lifted the receiver and dialled The Cedars number.

Vicky looked at me expectantly.

'There's only one Mason & Sons listed,' I said, 'and that's—' I let the words die as the ringing tone stopped on the second ring.

Bexson's voice breathed, *'Falloway residence.'*

'Drake,' I said. 'Is Howard Grant there?'

'No, sir, he left soon after you and hasn't returned.'

I groaned. Still chasing shadows in the fog. Christ! I told Bexson to get a pencil and dictated the name and address from the directory. I heard Vicky give a little gasp of horror as I added, 'Tell him it's a slaughter-house and tell him to hurry.'

I dropped the receiver back in its cradle, turned and found Vicky at my side. She was a fusion of conflicting emotions.

'Eddie's got a shotgun,' she was saying. 'Promise me you won't hurt him—promise me you'll be careful—I couldn't bear . . .' Tears squeezed from tightly shut eyelids as she trailed off.

I took her in my arms, nestled her close, brushing my mouth across her cheek and finding her damp, sweet-smelling hair. I felt her soft breath on my face as she whispered, 'Is there anything left for us, Simon?'

I searched my vocabulary for a reassuring answer, but nothing came. I could only manage a brief 'Stay here', as I headed for the door.

'You're coming back?' she asked hopefully.

The past didn't matter any more. The truth had eased the hurt, the nagging bitterness. I knew what I wanted and it was right here. I had no intention of ending my days on an abattoir floor. She was too damned right—I was coming back.

Chapter Fourteen

I STOOD looking at Mason & Sons' sombre building, my mind peeling away more than a dozen years of my life. I was fifteen again, listening as my father made a two-hour visit to his place of employment sound like a coach excursion to the Tate Gallery. In furtherance of my education, very instructional, he'd said. He was a buyer then, the place of employment was a sausage factory, and the visit had included a tour of the abattoir.

I remembered the way I'd felt as I'd entered the slaughter-hall. Time hadn't changed me very much. My stomach echoed that same kind of feeling right now.

The fog rolled in, swathing me in its clammy dampness. A sign on the double gates announced the building was closed for alterations and warned that trespassers would be prosecuted. I couldn't imagine anyone of sane mind wanting to trespass unless they had good reason, the way McQuillan had good reason.

He also had a key. The gates were heavily padlocked and hadn't been tampered with. I put the M.G. into reverse and backed up until I heard them rattle. Using the car boot as a ledge I scaled the metal structure and dropped silently inside the yard.

I circled to the side of the building. I could see the travelling box now. The ramp was down, and it had been cleverly sandwiched amongst a host of Mason vehicles. I checked it out. The cab was empty and the radiator was still warm.

I stood for a moment, narrowing my eyes, panning the brickwork. A thin strip of light infiltrated the fog as it leaked from beneath a metal door. An array of animal pens stood nearby. It didn't take intellect to figure where the door would lead me. My feet dragged across a diseased patch of grass as they made their stealthy approach.

I listened. I don't know what I expected to hear—probably nothing seeing the door looked pretty soundproof. Anyway, nothing was exactly what I heard. I smothered a flicker of apprehension and held my breath. I pulled gingerly at the catch, and to my surprise, it gave.

I found myself in a dimly lit corridor, a narrow passage of concrete construction with rusty iron bars running up to the ceiling. The memories were coming back, plucking at the raw edges of my nerves. I felt my nostrils recoil at the sickly odour of a thousand dead animals, tens of thousands, which had trodden this path before. I walked slowly on, past a door on my right and into the stunning pen.

My mind was partly absent, drifting between keeping my head low, my balance on the angled floor, and my lopsided view of the captive-bolt pistol which hung in front of me. Voices floated over the top of the pen. I marshalled my thoughts, listened. It was McQuillan—muffled, indistinct, but unmistakbly McQuillan. I backed out of the death-box and retraced my steps to the door I'd passed.

'Make sure that horse is properly tethered!' I could hear him quite clearly now. He was barking instructions, the resonance of his voice carrying sinister overtones as it wafted through the deserted building. 'Points of entry,' he said shortly. 'Show me them, Carlos. All of them.'

Seconds elapsed. The conversation grew weaker, footsteps dwindled. I don't know what I had in mind as I reached for the door handle. I certainly didn't intend to tackle them alone and unarmed. I might be headstrong but I wasn't a fool. I figured I'd play it by ear, keep myself in purdah as it were, until Grant and his men arrived.

The door groaned on its hinges as I inched it open. Standing before me, framed in the gap, was General O'Hara. The big horse turned, ears pricked. His nostrils flared red as he blew out a fine mist of moisture and whinnied uncertainly. I heard his hooves clatter and slip slightly on the tiled floor as he backed away.

'Quiet, you big bastard,' I hissed, moving tentatively inside, taking stock of the surroundings.

My eyes flitted over the macabre fitments; the chain elevators, bleeding rails, and conveyor belts; then lingered momentarily on the large dehairing machine. The plant was more or less centrally placed and offered perfect concealment. With bated breath I moved cautiously towards it.

'Freeze, brother!'

I froze, mid-stride. The words had a familiar ring. I remembered the command, the harsh inflection in the voice. They belonged to a stocking mask and a sawn-off shotgun.

'Turn around—easy!'

I turned, faced a pair of fashionable boots standing wide and high up on a platform. The platform ran along one side of the room. Some kind of cutting balcony, I suspected, although its more orthodox usage was hardly my prime concern. Brother Eddie was. I lifted my eyes to the weapon which rested in the crook of his elbow. He grinned down at me, slowly but decisively bending his arm so that the twin barrels drew level with my brow.

'My sister's got a big mouth,' he said. 'And you, Drake— you've got a defective fear gland. You must have blown your mind walking in here like this.'

A gold crucifix hung on a thin chain around his neck. I watched it sway across the blond hairs of his chest as his feet took a firmer footing.

'I've come for the horse, Eddie,' I grated.

'So take him, man,' he gestured with his free hand. 'There stands the unrivalled General O'Hara. Three million quids' worth of living, breathing horseflesh. Untie the halter, give a couple of clicks of your tongue, and I dare say he'll follow you out.'

I glanced at the horse. He was nodding his head feverishly, scraping a hoof along the tiled floor.

'I think he heard me.' Eddie laughed his derision.

I glared at him, said nothing.

'What's stopping you, Drake? Is your fear gland functioning now? Are you thinking there's a trigger mechanism between your walking out of here and a funeral oration?'

'Maybe I'm biding my time.'

'Waiting for reinforcements?'

'Maybe.'

'Maybe? Only bloody maybe! That's rather a negative hook to hang your hopes on, man,' he chuckled, stroking his fingers lovingly over the bluish barrels. 'Well let them come! Let your Captain Grant try and outsmart us. Let's see how good he is at digging lead shot from your sponge of a brain.'

'You're going a little haywire, Eddie.' I gave him my acidy smile. 'A crazy situation for crazy people with crazy motives, uh?'

'Shut your mouth!' His knuckles went bone-white on the triggers.

'You don't know much about shotguns, do you, Eddie? Do you plan to pull both triggers? Can you handle the recoil?'

'I said shut—'

'From that height and angle the spread will pepper both me and the General. Try selling a horse with half his backside blown open.'

'You clever bastard!' He sprang from the platform.

I anticipated the reaction and sidestepped. I didn't step far enough. Eddie came fast—fast and accurately. I felt the polished butt graze over my skull just before it buried itself deep into my lip.

I heard myself cry out as I went floundering away, cannoning into the General's quarters, rolling and writhing with pain. My mouth was bleeding inside, I could taste the gummy sweetness ebbing over my tongue. I spat and choked, coughing blood-streaked mucous in all directions.

'*Clever bastard! Clever, clever, bastard!*' The words reverberated in the tunnels of my mind as my blurred vision received a picture of Eddie dancing gleefully in front of me.

I shut my eyes tight. The pain eased a little as the seconds ticked away. I could hear voices. I lifted my lids, waiting for the filmy opalescence to clear. The perforated black tube of a silencer, hovering between my eyebrows, smothered any thoughts of avengement I might have been contemplating.

'How did he get here?' McQuillan spoke to Eddie, but his eyes clung to me.

'I suppose Vicky—'

'Of course it was Vicky!'

'Drake must have wheedled—'

'He didn't have to wheedle anything! It's bloody obvious that your cow of a sister has changed sides.'

'Now listen, Mac—'

'No, you listen, Eddie! The T.S.D. were waiting for me as I came out of those gates. She deliberately fed me the wrong information. She's sold us down the river, can't you see that?'

This was digested in silence. Zapata was standing nearby taking intermittent swigs at a gin bottle. He decided to gnaw at his thumb. 'Little shit of a tart!' he said with feeling.

I could hear the wheels turning as McQuillan's chimpanzee features crinkled up thoughtfully. I didn't underestimate the intelligence behind those small diagnostic eyes. This was no tea party. This chimp had a full quota of brains and was making good use of them.

'Does Grant know you're here?' The silencer jabbed at my forehead.

'Maybe,' Eddie mocked, 'maybe, eh, Drake?'

'Wrap it!' McQuillan growled, repeating the question.

Pain pulsed in my lip as I spoke. 'Sweat on it,' I said.

Zapata didn't like the tone of my voice. He stepped forward, the gin bottle clenched in his hand. His lips formed as if he was about to utter some sort of threat but McQuillan's hook guided him away. From the stench of his breath he hadn't cleaned his teeth for a week, and from the glazed unpredictable look in his eyes he was floating in a limbo world all his own. It was something more than just liquor. It was a look that told me his reasoning power was being governed by Speed or Acid or whatever the current vogue was in drugs.

'Is Drake carrying a gun?' McQuillan asked crisply.

Eddie shook his head. 'He can't be or he would have had it in his hand when he came in.'

'Check,' he said.

'It's a waste of time.'

'Check,' he said more forcefully. 'You underestimated your damn sister, don't underestimate Drake.'

Eddie made moody noises as he laid the shotgun on the conveyor belt and began rummaging through my clothing.

'A slaughter-house,' I said thickly, licking the blood from my lips. 'The perfect setting for twisted minds. You certainly dreamed up a beauty, McQuillan.'

'Nobody dreamed it up.' His eyes rippled over Zapata. 'Carlos fixed it for us. These premises are owned by his father. Their temporary closure offered us a hideout and some breathing space.'

'Until I walked in, uh?'

His eyes narrowed instantly. 'You're a minor embarrassment, nothing more. It's the people who will follow in your wake that I'm concerned about.'

'Assuming they know he's here,' Eddie pointed out.

'They'll know,' he affirmed. 'Drake isn't a fool, he's left a message with someone.'

'They'll be going round in foggy circles.'

'That's as maybe, but sooner or later they'll get here.'

'It's nice to see you sweat,' I goaded him.

'Don't get smart, Drake!' His gun hand twitched.

'The way Stroud got smart?'

'Stroud was a fool.'

'So you stuck him with a pitchfork.'

'He deserved a little pain. It was he and Falloway who put you on my back.'

'Their scheme was conflicting with yours, uh? So you severed the partnership.'

'Because of the blood-boost?' He laughed raggedly. 'I knew nothing about the damn blood-boost until it was too late. No, I killed Stroud because he stumbled upon the General. Mouth-money he wanted. He tried to bleed me dry.'

'Didn't he fall for the sick-horse caper? You missed your vocation, McQuillan. You might be a lousy trainer, but as a make-up artist you're quite a pro.'

'That was my doing,' Eddie bragged. 'Thick Vaseline around the nostrils, linseed oil on—'

'He's stalling for time!' McQuillan barked. 'Have you finished searching—'

His gun wavered fractionally as he turned to hustle the boy. I saw my chance. Eddie was half bending, half crouching, running his fingers down my thighs. I grabbed him in a head chancery and pivoted. The timing was perfect. McQuillan's legs splayed out as they tangled with Eddie's scrambling feet. Unbalanced, he tilted towards me. I slammed my elbow hard into his cheek-bone, dislodging the automatic as his hand jerked involuntarily open. He went high-kicking away, thrashing at the air with his hook, trying to defy the law of gravity as he grabbed at a whole lot of nothing. It was as if he was caught by a bow-wave. His back hit the conveyor with a resounding crack, and he slid heavily on to his backside.

I retrieved the gun. I didn't feel the need to drag out any stock stay-where-you-are phrases. Eddie, squirming under my arm and the silencer massaging his temple, said it all for me.

'What happens now, Drake?' McQuillan's hatred glowed in the depths of his eyes.

'I ask a few questions,' I said.

He smiled lazily.

'Who sent the wreath, and why?'

'Eddie sent it—the reason for which is a little obscure.'

'Try me.'

'I think he planned to shoot the horse. When our continental buyer confirmed the Stubbs was a fake, Eddie felt bilked—we all did. I'm afraid the boy's rather highly strung. The wreath was a stupid inelegant gesture, that's all.'

'You had more subtle ideas.'

'Of course. Our bargaining power would have died along with the horse, if Eddie had had his way. While we had an intact General we had a good chance of squeezing the old girl for more.'

'Much, much more.' Zapata's blood-shot eyes viewed me with jeering resentment. His cataleptic brain was overriding his common sense. He took a defiant step forward, testing me.

I tightened the head-hold.

'Cool it, Carlos, f'Chrissake!' Eddie's breathing hissed like a perforated beer can.

'I'm not gonna listen to this bullshit! I think he's a gutless bastard and I'm gonna—'

'C-Cool it, man! Please, Carlos. Cool it, huh?' Little beads of sweat stippled my hand as Eddie's face started to quiver.

'Stand still!' McQuillan ordered.

He stopped as the command percolated.

McQuillan was getting ideas too. There was a look of anticipation in his eyes as they strayed to the shotgun on the conveyor belt. Only a fool or a desperate man would try to reach it. I put temptation out of his way. I dragged Eddie to the wall, stabbed the gun butt on a switch marked 'conveyor', and watched McQuillan's lips curl as the apparatus hummed into life. I stopped the belt as the shotgun receded from view.

'Tell me about Vicky,' I said shortly.

'Such as what?' McQuillan growled.

'How much she knew, how deeply she was involved—the works.'

'You don't need me to tell you that, Drake. I'm sure the lady has already denied any knowledge of the conspiracy.'

'And is that true?'

'Do you want reassuring?'

'Answer the question!'

He smiled with sour amusement.

'You drew her into your net by evoking dormant memories. Once in, she was forced to conform because rebellion would have exposed Eddie.'

'Sounds good,' he mocked. 'Poor, innocent little Vicky. Trapped by brotherly love.'

'You admit it?'

'I admit nothing! In your own words, Drake—sweat on it!'

'Yeah, *sweat on it, man*!'

I was so incensed with McQuillan's sarcasm that I was only half aware of the bottle held high in Zapata's hand. I caught a glint of green glass as the missile took me across the forehead. I coiled, sinking to my knees, vaguely, dizzily aware of the bottle shattering somwhere behind me.

'Christ, the horse!' McQuillan's voice.

'Sod the horse—get the gun!'

Shifting bodies. Scrambling feet. Hooves skelping the tiles. A hideous tormented whinnying was tearing at my ears, twisting in the convulsions of my brain. The slap-slap-slap of a halter being wrenched to breaking point. The screams of an animal in pain. The noise was deafening.

I slumped forward, fighting back the vertigo that threatened to render me insensate. Through clouded vision I could see the General. Muscles rippled violently in his hind quarters as he battered his forelegs against the wall in front of him.

'He's going bloody berserk!' Eddie shrieked. 'The gin—it's all over his face!'

'I'll cover Drake,' McQuillan pushed Zapata towards the horse. 'Try and calm him before he snaps that halter.'

'Go screw yourself!' His mouth fell open as he backed away.

'Calm him, you idiot!'

'And get kicked to bloody death?'

'The alcohol's in his eyes—are you scared of a blind horse?'

He refused to be baited. 'Balls!' he said.

'Whoa! Whoa!' Eddie grabbed frantically at the head-collar, his boots scuffing the floor as the animal's seesawing neck tossed him to and fro.

I felt McQuillan's hook pierce through the collar of my jacket, felt myself being dragged bodily over the tiles. I was in no fit state to resist. My sentience was in tatters. Only a thin thread of obstinacy stopped me from blacking out.

'We dispose of Drake quickly and cleanly,' McQuillan was saying. 'No bullet holes, no corpse to litter the floor—with luck the Security Division won't even find him.'

Zapata looked down at me, a grin spreading over his gaunt, pock-marked face. 'We use the pig line,' he chuckled. 'Send him through the scalding tank, the dehairing machine—'

'We haven't time for entertainment,' McQuillan countered. 'The cattle line will serve our needs nicely.'

I couldn't see Eddie. I supposed he was still wrestling with the horse. The whinnying was being drowned by the rattle of chains. McQuillan had hold of my right foot. He gave a short bark of laughter as something hard and cold wrapped itself round my ankle.

'You're shackled with a leg chain,' he grated. 'At the push of a button you will be elevated like a carcass by the dressing hoist. From there you will pass—' He paused, smiled slowly. 'I won't give away the gruesome details. First-hand experience is so much better, don't you agree?'

I moved in an attempt to utter an obscenity but could only manage a weak groan as Zapata stood heavily on my shoulders, pinning them to the floor.

McQuillan motioned towards the control box. 'You saddled your horse the moment you stepped in here,' he said, lancing a finger at a button. 'Now let's see just how good you are at riding it.'

The machinery whirred into motion. I felt the chain bite hard into my ankle as I was dragged slowly along on my back. Zapata's feet slipped from my shoulders. My right leg began to rise up. I took the weight on my arms, balancing, lifting, trying to ease the ligament-wrenching power which attempted to tear my limb from its socket.

Up. Up. Up. Sprawling hands, contracting fingertips, precious inches. Fear plaited my guts as the hoist rattled on. My last vestige of countering the pain had evaporated. I swung involuntarily out, climbing higher and higher. I wedged my teeth together as the crude metal links gouged into soft flesh, bruised into bone. Blood began surging in my ears. A film of sweat threaded down my neck and into my eyes. Hatred, torment and futility streaked into the gyratory course of my thoughts.

'I hope you stay the distance,' McQuillan shouted amusedly as I drifted away. 'Although you may find an icy reception awaits you in the winners' enclosure.'

The laughter bubbled then ebbed as the machinery carried me forward. I was dangling some fifteen feet from the floor, moving on an overhead runway. I tried to keep my muscles limp, my body as static as possible. Any slight deviation, any fractional unevenness in the rails and that leg shackle responded with the tenacity of a cheese-wire.

The pressure was building behind my eyes like a dam about to burst through my skull. Giddiness washed over me. I was getting an inverted view of offal bins, the brief glint of an electric saw. My body lurched as the track dipped sickeningly. I was going down. Some kind of tunnel. Cooling air began fanning my cheeks, frisking my clothing. I welcomed it, but only provisionally. I began to feel cold. Very cold. The temperature was dropping dramatically. My brain worked pitifully for some method, some means . . .

The electric drive ceased. Momentum took over and I went skidding down an incline towards the refrigeration chamber. Once inside I'd never get out. Unless . . . unless . . . I glimpsed a meat hook anchored behind some wall piping. An idea brushed lightly across my consciousness. This was it. A god-given gift. I couldn't afford to blow it.

I waited, poised. My progression continued. As the hook crept within reach I stretched, clawed, barking my knuckles along the wall. I gripped it convulsively. The metal felt raw-cold as it stuck to my trembling fingers. I didn't care about ice burns. I didn't care about anything. I'd unhitched that big beautiful meat hook and I knew just how I was going to use it.

Further damage to my fettered ankle was inevitable. I used my free leg as an agitator, working up a pendulous rhythm, hitting the wall with my foot and swinging backwards and upwards to the overhead runways.

I lunged for a rail. I felt the shock-waves shudder through my right arm as the tip of the hook caught, then slipped. More power, I cursed. More bloody power. Every ounce of strength had to go into the rebound. It did. I wanted to scream aloud as pain tore into my ankle. I lunged again and this time the flailing hook held fast.

I hung suspended, rather like a hammock, gulping air in an effort to ease my strenuous breathing. By arching my body and worming the hook along, I was able to get my left hand to the rail. The hook was beginning to butcher my fingers. I discarded it. With both hands on the overhead runway I had sufficient purchase to use my free leg as a buttress and haul myself up and on to my belly. I lay sprawled out, letting recuperative moments pass as I recovered my faculties.

The whole of my right leg had started to throb. It felt bad, but not half as bad as the intense torment of the shackle. I could feel the chain hanging loose across my foot. No bodyweight to hold it in position now. A mere waggle from my ankle and the link rattled blissfully away.

I began to shiver with cold. It was a long drop to the floor and one I didn't relish. I lowered my legs over the side, gripped the rail tightly and let myself hang. I groped my way along, working arm over arm to where the gradient lessened. I positioned my legs so as to take most of the impact on my left foot, mentally braced myself, and released.

No floor ever felt so hard. I landed awkwardly and stumbled.

I sat where I had fallen, massaging my biceps with cramped fingers. A peeling back of my right sock revealed folds of torn skin and a sizable bluish swelling. I winced as I managed to stand.

Limping back along the tunnel sent a ream of thoughts ricochetting through my mind. I found myself wanting to kill, telling myself I had every justification to kill. I wrestled with these emotions, trying to counterbalance them with the fact that I wasn't a mad dog, that I still had some kind of choke on my sanity. Revenge was sweet but transient. Resorting to their methods showed a lust for savagery and very little else.

It was all too easy to invent donnish idioms of philosophy. It didn't help the overriding factor that I was dealing with real people with real intentions—that ultimately because a lame man was now free it was a case of either kill or be killed.

Footsteps, hollowing, echoing.

The sound galvanized my aching legs into motion. Plant and machinery obstructed my view, but the cover offered the element of surprise. My eyes flitted to a large steel tray. I remembered seeing it as I'd passed overhead, remembered the contents of knives, handsaws, cleavers . . . I hobbled towards it, selected a knife with a twelve-inch blade and wrapped my fingers round the handle.

I flattened and waited.

Zapata saw me almost instantly. He stopped some ten feet away. It was a gradual slow-motion stop, as if he was being restrained by some invisible leash.

We just stood looking at each other. The smile of hate had congealed on his twisted mouth. He was unarmed and I guessed he was going to yell for assistance. I couldn't have been more wrong. His brain, fragmented by dope, was dictating a suicidal course. He could see the knife in my hand yet he kept right on coming. He leapt at me like a spring uncoiling.

The knife arched up from my hip and plunged into his ribs. I felt my arm jolt as his breastbone grated against steel. My full weight went behind that thrust. The handle gave an involuntary twist as the blade skewered an entry. His chest devoured the inches. Warm blood erupted over my hand.

I stepped back as he folded, my muscles contracting against an upsurge of sickness. He didn't cry out, a slight whimper was all that escaped his lips. He fell on his face and was still. I watched the blossoming redness as it swam from his shirt, lacquering the gullies.

'Carlos!'

The word acted like high-voltage. It shocked me into alertness, made me forget the horror of the past seconds and my own bodily fatigue. I limped away, keeping low, eyes scanning for McQuillan.

'Eddie's checking the exit,' he was grunting impatiently. 'Come and give me a hand with this horse!'

I could see his hook curled around the General's head-collar, his gun hand resting by his side. The animal was still in a pitiable state. He was shaking his neck and occupying the trainer's full attention. McQuillan cursed as he was momentarily unbalanced.

I saw my chance and scooted across the open expanse of floor. I wasn't fast enough. My ankle gave way as I reached the gambrelling table. I almost fell across it. McQuillan homed on the noise in an instant. I heard a muted *phttt-phttt* as he loosed off two bullets in rapid succession. The first tore a piece of worsted from the sleeve of my jacket, whilst the second sent a chip of tile whining into the air. I crawled for cover, my outstretched fingertips clutching, scrabbling, dragging myself towards the comparative safety of the scalding tank. Pain was lancing through my ankle and I was having difficulty controlling my movements. I strained to pull air into my lungs and the exertion set my lip bleeding again. I felt the slime of blood on my fingers as I wiped a hand across my mouth.

'What have you done with Carlos, Drake!'

I lifted my head, summoned awareness. Through a gap in the equipment I could see McQuillan. Smoke curled lazily from the silencer as he edged his way towards me.

'Mac! Mac!' Eddie's breath rasped in his throat as he burst through the door brandishing the shotgun. 'The bastards are here—they're out there in the fog! I heard the gate rattle—they're coming in—we've got to get out!'

'Security Division?'

'We're going to be caught like rats in a trap!'

'We're going to be caught—nothing!'

'What?'

He gestured with his hook. 'That horse buys us a free ticket out of here. If Grant so much as—'

'We knacker the General. End his military duty—right?'

'Right.'

Eddie chuckled with soft relish, a chuckle which petered out as McQuillan pointed out my location.

'I'll get the sod,' he moved forward.

McQuillan restrained him. 'We haven't time! I'll cover Drake while you cover the door. We don't shoot our way out. We bargain—got it?'

Eddie nodded.

They both took up positions on opposing walls. McQuillan stood next to the horse, his eyes and the automatic wavering between the animal and me. Eddie leaned against the conveyor, gripping the shotgun expectantly. The barrels were getting restless, so were those pale rebellious eyes. I could see all the danger signals. The way he kept dragging a sleeve across his glistening brow, the way his fingers were beginning to twitch on the triggers. He wasn't going to wait to bargain. He was so wound-up he was going to blast away at the first thing that moved.

McQuillan looked towards the scalding tank. 'No heroics, Drake,' he breathed, stroking the silencer gently along the General's neck.

I saw Eddie stiffen as footsteps echoed in the outer passage. Both he and McQuillan had an angled view of the door. They wouldn't be able to see Grant, and he wouldn't be able to see them until at least one step was taken inside. Only I had a full frontal outlook. Somehow I had to stop that fatal step being taken.

'Come on, come on,' I heard Eddie mutter.

McQuillan told him to shut up.

The passage seemed endless. The torment of time stretched, clung on with parasitical foreboding. Breathing hung like a spell. My brain was scavenging for ideas, probing for some way . . .

The footsteps stopped. Eddie braced himself. The hinges gave a rending creak and there framed in the doorway, pushing strands of golden hair from her eyes . . .

'No, baby, no!'

'Sim—'

'*No!*' The word tore flesh from my throat.

Vicky took that fatal step, arms outstretched, reaching, reaching . . .

The flash of flame. Noise crashed in on my ears. The whole building seemed to fall apart as the blast took her in the side. The curved litheness of her body jerked inexorably from me, reeling, shrinking, absorbing the full force of those cartridges. Her eyes flickered briefly to her brother and then she crumpled.

Eddie watched, stricken. The shotgun slipped from his fingers. He was a quivering mass of penitence. In a choked, shaking voice he kept saying, 'I've killed my sister. Jesus God, I've killed my fucking sister . . .'

I was oblivious to his cries or my own safety as I dragged myself towards Vicky. My thoughts were in shreds, consumed by a tidal wave of grief and impotence. She felt limp and frail as I knelt beside her, lifting her gently, cradling her head in my arms.

'Baby, baby, baby,' I kissed her neck, stroked her hair, tasted the saline of her tears.

'I had to come,' she said almost inaudibly.

'You fool, you damned silly little fool.'

A vivid circle of blood was steadily expanding around her midriff. She was having difficulty in breathing. I felt the smoothness of her lips on my cheek as she whispered raggedly, 'You're with me, darling.'

'The kind of man a girl can depend on?'

'That's fast becoming a cliché,' she mocked softly.

I hugged her close, the heat of our bodies welding together. I had this inept feeling that if I held on for long enough I could replenish the life that was ebbing away, that somehow I could prevent the inevitable. But slowly, irrevocably, I could feel her slipping from me.

I tried to manage a reassuring smile. I uttered optimistic words. Useless, comforting words—while all the time I was crying inwardly, silently, brokenly.

Her slim fingers clenched at my hand as she listened. She looked at me through those big blue eyes, hanging on to every syllable. They were the eyes of a day-dreaming child. We were trying to live our lives in the framework of seconds.

'I—If only we'd been two other people, Simon.'

'If only,' I said.

I felt her grip on my hand subside, heard a gentle intake of breath. Her head fell flaccidly forward, and she was gone.

Through swimming eyes I could see McQuillan. I watched as he broke the shotgun, ejected the spent cases, and slipped two fresh cartridges into the chambers.

'I—I didn't know,' Eddie gasped sobbingly, arms wrapped around his face. 'Oh, Jesus . . . Jesus . . .'

'Pull yourself together, for God's sake!' McQuillan thrust the shotgun at him. 'Here—it's loaded. Now let's finish Drake and get out of this place.'

Eddie snarled something and pushed him away.

'So you want to stay? You want to be caught? The Security Division will hand you over to the police and they'll grill you medium rare, Eddie boy. Is that what you want? *I said is that what you want!*'

Eddie wasn't listening. He was kneeling by Vicky, mumbling incoherently, hands clasped prayerlike in front of him.

233

'So the boy's cracked up, eh, Drake?' He mulled that over, adding, 'You'll have to take his place. I'm going to need help with this horse. Untie that halter!'

He slipped the automatic into his pocket, favouring the shotgun. He jabbed the barrels into my stomach, coaxing me to the wall. I looked at those small eyes sunk deep in their sockets. Cruel, confident eyes. I wanted to tear them out. I was devoid of all reason, wrapped in a cocoon of hate.

'Untie that halter!'

The horse was tethered to a hydrant point. As I worked on the knotted rope I found my eyes fixed to the nozzle of a high-pressure hose. It took a tenth of a second for me to seize on the possibilities, for me to realize just how close my fingers were to the water-pressure wheel.

'Try hurrying yourself, Drake!'

'It's tight,' I growled, turning my back on him, palming the nozzle.

'Give it to—' His hook went to drag me away.

In a triple movement I spun the wheel, opened the valve, and pushed the surging jet of water into his eyes. The force sent him floundering. He teetered like a dislodged skittle, his mouth gaping for breath as the stinging spray swirled over his face.

I flung myself at him. The shotgun went spinning away. He let out an animal scream as the heel of my hand smashed into his nose. *Hit! Hit! Keep on hitting!* Tearing at bone and cartilage. Pulping him into the ground. Each blow easing the hurt, soothing the bitterness that bubbled and seethed at the back of my mind.

He was fighting for his life and he knew it. His hook slashed, scythed. I could feel that lethal metal limb snagging down my backbone, rending through the cloth of my jacket. I kept right on hitting, brutally, insanely. His face was a red mask of blood, but he was far from unconscious. His good hand was groping for my throat. I retched slightly as his fingers dug in. I could see the tendons ridging his forearm like

234

cordage as his thumb pressed ever more firmly into my wind-pipe.

The floor was awash. Water was spilling everywhere. I tried to stand, to ease the grip on my throat, but I couldn't maintain leverage on those slippery tiles. I wasn't helped by the hook which had furrowed its way into the belt of my trousers. It held me rigid, the spiked end snicking into the flesh of my buttocks as McQuillan fought for survival.

I felt I couldn't batter his face any more. There was nothing left to batter. He had the constitution of an ox. There was no relaxing of the throat hold, no sign of that coupling easing its sinister embrace. I could have unclipped my belt, released my-self that way, but I didn't relish the consequences of such a move. Instead, I gripped at his good wrist with my right hand and worked my left around to the small of my back. The claw was undoubtedly his strongest point, but the forearm it entrapped . . . ?

'NAAAAA!'

The frenzied ejaculation told my probing fingers they had found his vulnerable spot. I'd dragged up his sleeve to expose the stainless steel sheath and managed to prise loose the ligature. I scored my nails into the puffy ridge of skin and gristle, aggravating the tender zone where the years had chaffed metal against flesh.

'NAAAAAA!' The hook snaked and squirmed to free itself. Now I was free.

I broke the throat hold and hauled him to his feet. His good hand flew to the automatic in his pocket, but my fist was al-ready arching through the air. I aimed for his jaw but the viscidity of blood sent my knuckles askew, and the blow took him across the cheek.

It was enough to capsize him. He went tottering backwards, his feet searching for grip on the waterlogged floor. His back hit the static water tank and he overbalanced into it. There was a tremendous upsurge, a momentary thrashing about, and then calm.

I bowed my head, clasping hands on knees, trying to release the tension from my trembling muscles, waiting for my strength to slowly ooze back. *McQuillan was dead, McQuillan was dead.* I kept saying the words over and over. The bastard was dead. Drowned and dead.

Faintly, above the sound of my own voice. I could hear this tap-tapping. The rasp of metal on metal. Through sore, tired eyes I looked towards the static tank. My scalp began to tingle as I listened hard. Christ, he was moving. The water was beginning to ripple. Unbelievably, the hook had emerged. It was curling itself around the outer lip of the tank, raking for support . . .

In the corner of my vision I could see a pair of stunning tongs. The instrument churned up old memories. I'd seen them used for pig slaughtering. I still had enough rationality left to remember how they worked. They offered hope, a fresh influx of strength.

I limped towards the wall-mounted transformer. I was coldly aware that the face-plate had been damaged by the shotgun blast. A corner of the unit was missing and pellets of lead shot had punctured the casing. My expectations weren't very high as I fumbled the plug into the mains.

The pilot light glowed. At least part of the circuitry was functioning. I turned the dial to maximum voltage and lifted the tongs from the wall. My hands were slow and ponderous as I gripped the insulated handles—an action immediately rectified as guttural groaning and splashing water energized my sluggish reflexes.

McQuillan was standing in the tank. He was swaying slightly, trying to get a leg to the ground. Our eyes locked. His battered face was a compound of crazed paranoia. The groaning rose in pitch until it exploded in a crescendo of delirium. He began swinging his hook wildly, his bleeding lips uttering disjointed sentences about tearing out my throat if I came any closer. It was almost a game. The wheeling hook—the tongs. Probability versus possibility. A madcap game of death.

I closed on him, baiting him, goading him. I held the tongs sword-like in front of me. I waited, judged his swing, and caught the hook mid-arc.

The tongs clamped hard. The electrodes bit in. A blinding orange flash and a cascade of sparks set the water shimmering. I held on, gritting my teeth, squeezing on the handles. I felt the vibrations shudder through my fingers as his body smashed against the tank. He shook in a brutal spasm of electrocution, his lips stretched so tight I thought his mouth would bisect at the corners. But slowly, very slowly, he crumpled. He submerged, gurgled, and lay still.

I stood for a moment watching an air-pocket bubble its way to the surface. I stood long enough to satisfy myself that this time was the last time. That Neil McQuillan was undeniably a dead man.

Eddie was still sobbing. He was oblivious to me and to the events of the past few minutes. I left him to it. My concern wasn't for him, but for the shattered, trembling specimen of a racehorse that people had been willing to die for.

The animal sensed no danger as I limped towards him. That strange telepathic communication which existed between man and beast told us both it was over. He looked at me with those big molten eyes, rubbing his muzzle against my hair. I spoke soft, comforting words. I stroked his neck, fondled his ears, ran a soothing hand down . . .

I stared at my fingers. White fingers. A sticky white substance was clinging to my *bloody fingers*!

The star!

I rubbed frantically at the large triangular mark between his eyes. It was streaking, smudging into a hideous disproportional shape. I could smell gin. The alcohol had loosened the dye. This wasn't General O'Hara at all, this was . . .

'Boy Blue, Simon.' Grant's voice touched a nerve in my mind. It seemed a billion light-years away. 'I tried to tell you at Chinhurst, but you were in such a damned hurry—'

I was suddenly aware of security men all around me. One of them was helping Eddie to his feet, nursing him outside. I felt Grant lay a consoling hand on my shoulder.

'You look all in,' he said. 'Get yourself cleaned up and I'll—'

'H—How long . . .' I struggled to squeeze my words out. 'How long have I been chasing a double?'

'We'll talk about it later—away from here.'

'We'll talk about it now!'

He sighed, shifted uneasily.

'How long!'

'Since Animals Unlimited.'

My emotions were running amok. Anger, bafflement, betrayal. I felt like an all-time loser, and I didn't care for the feeling.

He went on, 'You brought General O'Hara from Gaylawn Stables and I took him back. There was no switch—just a find-the-lady routine. I guessed the horsenappers would be watching our movements so I pulled the double bluff.'

'Smart,' I scoffed.

'The swop that never was. It fooled you, and of course it fooled them.'

'And I got my scalp stitched up protecting Boy Blue.'

'That was unfortunate.'

'That's a classic understatement.'

'Some consolation can be drawn from your display of protection. If McQuillan had any doubts about the animal's authenticity then your actions must surely have quashed them.'

Did he think that made me feel any better? It didn't soften the blow, it worsened it. 'So I was the patsy who kept the wheels so convincingly greased?'

'Telling you would have achieved nothing,' he said with calm preciseness. 'I did contemplate it at one stage, but then your affection for Vicky—'

'Produced a huge vote of no bloody confidence, uh?'

'I felt it would be better—'

'Thanks for nothing.' I fumbled for my crumpled pack of cigarettes, pushed one between bruised lips.

Grant snapped a lighter into flame. 'Nobody knew, Simon, not even Alison Falloway. She wasn't told until after the ransom demand—and only then because we couldn't let her pay for a horse that was tucked safely away at the Newmarket Stud.' He paused, went on reflectively, 'She took it very well. She willingly donated the painting and we put up fifty thousand. She was only too aware that if the horsenappers weren't caught this time, then General O'Hara would never be safe.'

'She certainly put on a good act,' my voice was trembling. 'Her melodramatic behaviour over the wreath—that was all for me, uh?'

'That was mostly for Barron's benefit.'

I stared at him dumbly, choked.

'Our job was to protect a superlative racehorse. To safeguard the future progeny that such an animal had to offer British racing.' He looked at Boy Blue and sniffed. 'Horse-wise, playing it my way, the most we had to lose was a thousand pounds.'

'I had *that* to lose!' I thrust unsteady fingers towards Vicky. 'Or doesn't that count in your game of now-you-see-it, now-you-don't? Well you found the lady all right, and I hope it weighs heavily on your bloody conscience!'

Grant, as always, remained heartlessly indifferent to tragedy. He dredged up a few contrite words, then signalled for Vicky's body to be covered with a blanket.

The silken wisps of blonde hair were smothered from view.

A faceless shape.

A statistic.

I suddenly felt sickened by the sight of my tattered jacket, my soiled trousers, the blood and dye on my hands. I was a mess. A disgusting mess which hurt when it walked. Internal bruising, mostly. The kind cured by time. I felt like an author who'd spent years writing a potential best-seller, and then lost the typescript. I felt like a jockey who'd ridden the race of his life only to feel his saddle slip twenty yards from the post. I'd had one hell of a raw deal and I felt bitterly cheated.

Kelly was waiting by the door. Tears glistened in her eyes as I dragged myself towards her.

'Oh, Simon . . . what can I say . . . ?' Her throat was as constricted as mine.

'There's nothing to say,' I said.

Perhaps I said the words a little brutally. It wasn't her fault and maybe in different circumstances . . . In another age . . .

I offered her the best smile I could manage and limped slowly out into the fog.

Nancy Lindsay

SLAUGHTER HORSE

20p

The leading jockeys applaud another gripping Simon Drake thriller –

"A crisply-written high-tension thriller. Loved it." PAT EDDERY
"Terrific action-packed reading that's never off the bit." TONY IVES
"Another winner from the Maguire stable." FRANK MORBY

And the critics agree –

"Avid thriller readers who thought that today's authors had forgotten how to write crisp, taut books with a twist in every chapter will enjoy themselves immensely when they read Slaughter Horse*. . . Once again Drake is up to his neck in corruption, violence and murder. . . the new book is slicker and more rivetting than its predecessor."*
SURREY HERALD

"This is the author's second thriller featuring Simon Drake, and it consolidates the creation of a new fictional character of real dimension. Like the first Simon Drake adventure Shot Silk*, this story is again set against the background of horse-racing, and the pace is as fast as any Derby winner. If you like the action unflagging and your heroes tough, then you'll like Simon Drake."* LANCASHIRE EVENING TELEGRAPH